DIPLOMATIC IMMUNITY

DIPLOMATIC IMMUNITY

MCFADDEN AND BANKS™ BOOK 2

MICHAEL ANDERLE

DISRUPTIVE IMAGINATION®

Copyright © 2020 LMBPN Publishing
Cover Art by Jake @ J Caleb Design
http://jcalebdesign.com / jcalebdesign@gmail.com
Cover copyright © LMBPN Publishing
A Michael Anderle Production

LMBPN Publishing
PMB 196, 2540 South Maryland Pkwy
Las Vegas, NV 89109

First US edition, December 2020
eBook ISBN: 978-1-64971-334-6
Print ISBN: 978-1-64971-335-3

THE DIPLOMATIC IMMUNITY TEAM

Thanks to our Beta Team:
Jeff Eaton, John Ashmore, Kelly O'Donnell

JIT Readers

John Ashmore
Kelly O'Donnell
Diane L. Smith
Peter Manis
Deb Mader
Jeff Eaton
Jeff Goode

Editor
Skyhunter Editing Team

DEDICATION

*To Family, Friends and
Those Who Love
to Read.
May We All Enjoy Grace
to Live the Life We Are
Called.*

CHAPTER ONE

Every high-end bar seemed the same in Washington DC.

Numerous dive bars proliferated, of course, but those that intended to cater to all the diplomats, political high-rollers, and aides shared the same vague look. While each had their individual little unique twist and perhaps a couple of signed pictures of a celebrity who had visited above the booths, in the end, it was all predictable. The leather seats, dim lights, and the carefully tailored drinks all faded together for those who attended at least one post-work function a week at these establishments.

Nicole tilted her head and studied the rest of the room curiously. The men in suits were, for the moment, still sober, although that was almost certain to change. They talked in hushed whispers that failed to penetrate the elevator-music quality jazz music playing softly over the speakers positioned throughout the bar.

Every person who came in would either start with a tall glass of beer or a martini of some kind. She'd chosen a martini—the kind the bartender could make in his sleep—

and sipped it before she placed it on the dark napkin that had been provided. With a casual gesture, she ran her fingers through her dark hair and shifted a little on the barstool to enable her to watch the door more carefully once she had completed her inspection of the room itself.

She took another sip to conceal her interest when two men entered. Both wore expensive suits and watches to complement their equally expensive haircuts, and one even had a heavily waxed mustache that he groomed obsessively as they approached the bar.

"*Una cerveza, por favor,*" the mustached man said as he sat three stools down from Nicole. She glanced casually at him and sipped her drink again.

"And one for me too," the other man said in an American accent. The bartender nodded and quickly poured them a pint each.

"I think we'll need a booth," Nicole said aloud. "A secure one."

The statement was for the bartender as well, who gestured with his head to a small booth in the corner, the only one marked *reserved*. It made sense to prevent other patrons from using it. They didn't want anyone else to use a booth that had been heavily secured against bugging and listening devices.

She stood from her seat and walked quickly to it with the two men following.

They sat and each sipped their drinks. The mustached man was careful to not let the froth touch his facial hair.

"I'm very surprised they let you into this country," the American told him. "Your history in Peru would generally have the State Department on red alert."

"There are certain perks to having a diplomatic passport," the Peruvian answered with a chuckle and fussed with the tip of his mustache to curl it upward. "The only real surprise was that they let me into Colombia and permitted me to stay in Bogota for six months. The embassy there is—forgive my language—shit, but they seemed content to enforce the diplomatic immunity laws although I am sure my every move was watched. Still, my time in Puerto Bolivar was very educational."

"It usually is," she muttered, finished her martini, and focused her gaze on the olive at the end of her sterling toothpick. "There is so much history in that port—not the kind you'd find in history books, of course, but still."

Both men smirked.

"Well, what was educational about my time there is that they do not jump to clean the whole area up when they hear a Peruvian diplomat is visiting like they do when an American does. A great deal was left for me to find while I bumbled around, looking for my diplomatic pouch. Like, for instance, what is being packed in other diplomatic pouches."

Nicole and the American exchanged a quick look.

"Let me guess," she whispered and popped the martini-infused olive into her mouth. "We should pay attention to what our Colombian friends are packing in their diplomatic pouches."

"Like you would not believe. For instance, shipments from Casablanca are placed next to those pouches one day and are empty the next."

"Casablanca?" the other man asked and narrowed his eyes. "That's not on the heroin trade routes."

"No indeed," she answered and held her empty glass up to the bartender to indicate that she needed another. "It's too expensive and the security there is too tight, given what else is being shipped out of Morocco."

The American's eyebrows rose. "Are...you're not saying what I think you're saying, right?"

Nicole shrugged and waited for the bartender to leave her drink on the table and move out of earshot before she continued. "I'm merely putting the facts together. Many people out there want to make sure nothing that leaves the Zoo arrives in the US—or any other port in civilized countries, for that matter—without being thoroughly inspected. You have to assume that what's going to Puerto Bolivar is going through...let us say significantly less stringent customs inspections."

Her companions nodded.

"So..." The Peruvian paused to sip his beer and frowned slightly as he considered his words. "We can assume they are packing their *cocaina* with the serum from the Pita plant?"

It always amused Nicole when people called it that, given that pita was merely the Latin word for plant. This time, humor seemed elusive.

She traced her finger over her martini glass. "Well, that's a disturbing thought. Are they cutting the cocaine with the serum?"

"I cannot tell, but they are packing them in the same crates." The man nodded at the American, who seemed about to ask a question but closed his mouth with a snap. His expression grim, he ran his fingers through his straight black hair. "From what I know of the goop, it has a tendency to infect almost anything in close proximity."

Nicole took another sip and decided there would be considerably more drinking before the night was out. "I have a team who could discover what's happening and put a stop to it if it presents a clear and present danger to the American populace. I do know they won't be cheap and certainly won't be happy if there are any double-crosses involved."

The American looked surprised again. "You're not insinuating that the State Department will cause any problems with this, are you?"

She regarded him with a slightly challenging expression. "Yes, I am. You might think your people covered your tracks well, but MI6 does its research. Your department might as well be a sieve, which means I'll know who to blame if the shit hits the fan. This isn't getting out of parking tickets with your diplomatic immunity. This is shove your diplomatic passport so far down your throat, it might absorb a couple of the bullets they pump into you at the same time. And believe me when I tell you I'll make sure they know who to blame."

Her voice was quiet enough to keep the volume below the jazz music playing around them but a moment of silence ensued, which she used to her advantage to focus on her martini. It was a nice touch to insinuate that she was working for MI6. In fairness, they were one of the benefactors for her particular mission so she wasn't exactly lying.

"Well then," the Peruvian said finally and broke the

silence, "what about the narcos? They likely won't appreciate interference in their business."

"If they value maintaining those trade lines with the US, they'll stay out of the way," Nicole answered sharply. "I assume they aren't in the loop about what's being shipped with their drugs anyway. So, do we have a deal here or did you two simply want to buy me food in hopes of spending the afternoon getting sweaty?"

"That's quite enough," the American snapped.

"It might have been, but I think we both know you have a type. What was her name again? The woman whose house you frequented while in Lima? Regina Vargas, if I remember correctly. A little high-class for a man on your salary, I'd say."

The man's face began to turn red but the Peruvian laughed.

"I think it means we have a deal," he said and stroked his mustache. "Now, is there a deal to be made on that sweaty afternoon you mentioned?"

She smiled, finished what remained of her drink, and removed the sterling pick with the olive at the end. She smiled and pressed it into the Peruvian's mouth. "Oh, you certainly are on the menu. As it turns out, I have a type as well."

Before he could respond, she stood and walked away to leave them wondering what she'd meant by that. It was best to have them staring at her ass in the slimming black dress instead of thinking about what she intended to do.

The valet had her car waiting by the time she stepped onto the curb, and she made sure to leave him a generous tip for the foresight. She had asked him to have the car ready at a moment's notice, but she hadn't expected him to deliver.

Nicole drove a few blocks before she turned into a parking garage. After a few moments to make sure she had not been followed, she stepped out, retrieved the keys for the other car she had waiting for her, and slid into it.

While she fumbled in her purse with one hand, she undid the messy bun that confined her hair with the other. The phone she retrieved was bulky, thanks to the top-of-the-line encryption hardware and software embedded. Perhaps one day, the geniuses in the quartermaster's office would find a way to make the phones a little slimmer and easier to conceal.

Her gaze remained on the entrance of the garage as she punched in a number she knew by heart—and not because she had ever needed to call it herself. She'd made sure to memorize it as this was the number to call when she needed something done without going through the proper channels.

"This is Speare." A deep, gruff voice on the other end of the line answered more quickly than she'd expected.

"Mr. Speare, my name is Nicole Renee. I think you've been in touch with my department regarding my presence here in Washington?"

A short pause followed, and she assumed he was checking to make sure the line was secure before he responded.

"Of course, Miss Renee," he replied finally and sounded a little more focused. "To what do I owe the pleasure?"

"I've been made aware that you have access to a team

that takes work involving problems coming out of the Sahara," she stated firmly and calmly.

"I'm not sure where you get your information—"

"Let's not play the game where you pretend to not know everything we know and that we don't know everything you do, and simply get right to the meat of things. This is a fairly pressing matter."

She curbed her impatience when he hesitated. He was quite possibly annoyed by her lack of even a pretense of political politeness, but he brushed it off quickly.

"Very well. I do know of a freelance team that specializes in solving Zoo-based problems, but they can be a little difficult to manage and they won't come cheap."

"I hoped to split the cost of their hire with you and your people at the DOD." She fluffed her hair a little more to add a volume to it. "I hate to admit it, but your budget is a great deal larger than ours."

"I see. And what do you anticipate we'll get out of the bargain?"

"With any luck, a whole syndicate of dead *narcotrafi-cantes* across Peru and Colombia—the kind who have possibly been cutting their cocaine with Pita serum being imported directly from the Zoo before they sell their product on American streets."

A moment of silence passed and she smirked when she imagined his startled expression.

"Oh." It was an interesting admission that they had been out of the loop on that particular nugget of information, and he did not like it. "We'll verify your intel, of course."

"Don't you trust us?"

"*Doveryay, no proveryay*—an old Russian proverb Presi-

8

dent Reagan claimed as his own. However, should your information prove to be accurate, we would be willing to contribute half the costs that will be incurred by the team in question. We'll act in a support capacity and provide you with necessary information and financing, but this will be your operation one hundred percent. Is that understood?"

The message, of course, was very clear. They were willing to be involved but if things got messy—and with the reputation the freelancers had, she assumed messy was a foregone conclusion—they would ensure they were not involved in the backlash that resulted.

"That is understood," she answered finally, satisfied that they both grasped the unspoken messages between them. "Will you contact the team or should I take care of it?"

"If you know everything we know at the DOD, you certainly have their contact information. You could have already called them if you wanted to."

She nodded, even though he wouldn't see her, and remained focused on the entrance to the garage. "I could, yes, but being able to tell them you support this particular mission might lend a certain amount of credibility to my position."

"Not as much as you might imagine, but I think it would be best if you contacted them and let them verify everything you tell them with me. That way, they will feel a little more comfortable. Believe me when I say you don't want these people nervous."

Nicole narrowed her eyes. He must know she had worked with the McFadden and Banks team before, right? Or was he simply playing dumb?

"I suppose I'll have to give them a call," she said finally

and decided that what Speare knew or didn't know didn't matter. "I suppose you should expect them to contact you as well. I imagine they would want to make sure they aren't walking into some kind of trap."

"Have you worked with them before?"

"Their reputation is well-known." It was a delicate side-step of a direct question but she still wasn't convinced that the man hadn't heard of their previous interaction.

"And might I ask what you have planned next on your itinerary in our fair city?"

She looked at herself in her compact mirror and made tiny changes to her makeup. "Maintaining Peruvian relations and substantiating negotiation leverage, for the most part."

"I see. Well, you have a pleasant evening, Miss Renee."

Of course, the guy who filled what amounted to a fictitious position in the Pentagon would play his cards as close to the chest as possible. Him playing stupid wouldn't fool anyone but at the same time, she could assume that at least some of the intelligence she'd shared with him had caught him off-guard.

It was a terrifying prospect to think that drugs might be laced with the shit coming from the Zoo. Thankfully, the team she wanted was rather more competent than she'd given them credit for the last time. Still, they were certainly not the kind of people to call when conventional methods could be used.

"I will regret this," she whispered, started the car, and pulled out of the parking garage.

CHAPTER TWO

Niki could understand why people wouldn't want to stand toe to toe with her partner.

All she could think of was why anyone would believe that they could defeat him in the ring. The mobsters he'd fought had thought they would have a successful fight, but even with two of them, they probably took a couple too many shots to the head. Underestimating the man was a serious issue and one that had led them to a world of hurt.

She faced Taylor and adrenaline surged to fill her body as he stepped into the sparring ring with her.

The man had pads on his hands instead of gloves, but it was still a sight that dried her mouth out almost immediately. Oddly, there was another reaction she possibly needed to talk to a therapist about.

With a deep breath, she settled into her fighting stance. It had been drilled into her during her time at the FBI academy and she felt prepared as she walked toward Taylor.

He held the pads up, waiting and ready, and she

launched a flurry of jabs to strike at them while he moved them continually and swept one over her head. She didn't duck in time and it clipped the top of her head. It was a light blow but still enough to make her stumble a couple of steps before she regained her balance.

"I thought this was for me to practice my strikes," she protested and bounced lightly from one foot to the other.

"It is. And if you didn't want anything to retaliate, you'd practice against a punching bag. With me involved, you need to learn to duck and weave, not only to avoid being hit but to make sure the blows that do catch you never land cleanly. Let's go again."

Niki hissed her irritation, shook her head, and raised her hands as she closed on him without further comment.

She opened with a flurry as she had before and this time, when she ducked under the sweep aimed at her head, she was caught by one that had targeted her legs. Her left leg avoided it but the right was a little too slow and she landed hard on her back and scowled at the ceiling of their sparring room.

"Yeah," Taylor whispered and offered her a hand to help her stand. "You have to watch for someone trying to take your legs out from under you. The right way to counter that is to lift the closest leg and lean it into the strike to make sure it doesn't reach your support leg at full power."

"Yeah, yeah, what the fuck ever," Niki grumbled as he hauled her to her feet and she rolled her shoulders. She knew he meant well, and there was no question that he was in the kind of fighting shape anyone could aspire to. Bobby had seen to that, and he had certainly regained all the muscle mass he had lost during his hospital stay.

Even so, it was annoying to be treated like she was a child. It wasn't his intention but it still felt that way. He raised the pads again and she moved toward him and flashed two jabs and a hook while she watched for the sweep aimed at her head.

Instead of ducking under it, she dropped to a knee and felt his padded kick catch her around the hip as she jerked her left hand into a firm uppercut between his legs.

It was his turn to back away, although he didn't crumple in response as was often depicted in the sports page of a newspaper, which was what she had hoped for. He was still on his feet, but the air left his lungs in a whoosh as he retreated before he doubled over, dropped the pads, and clutched the affected area.

"You're wearing a cup," she complained as she stood.

"You punched me in the balls." He gasped and sucked deep breaths in.

"But you're wearing a cup."

He glared at her. "You punched me...in the balls. What the hell was that for?"

"Well, that's my go-to when it comes to fighting bigger, stronger opponents. I'd say it's a fairly successful tactic, wouldn't you?"

His expression remained unimpressed and she could tell he had no response to that, although she wasn't sure if it was because he was still recovering from her blow or if he thought she was right.

"So why are you wearing a cup?"

He shrugged and shifted his attention to the assaulted part of his anatomy. "Know your enemy. You like to do what isn't expected, so it only made sense for me to wear the appropriate armor."

She would never get used to how quickly he moved. He lashed out as he lunged from his doubled-over position to launch an attack and caught her with a couple of open-handed strikes. Niki managed to block the third with her raised guard but she was stopped by the ropes at the edge of the ring.

"I merely thought you would assume I wouldn't do anything crazy. It's entirely logical, you know, since I happen to like those where they are, thank you very much."

Taylor shifted slightly as he turned to collect his pads again. "That's rather a rough way to treat something you claim to like. But let's be honest—you're a Banks. Logic never entered into the equation."

Rather than answer, she grinned and punched him playfully on the shoulder.

"Now, keep your balance," he instructed. "Even when you're throwing punches, never square off in front of me. Place one foot behind the other and keep your knees slightly bent. It lets you absorb and roll hits off better. Let's try it again, but...uh, without the nuts shot this time, hmm?"

Niki tilted her head and smirked at him. "Fine. But it's not like you'll believe me if I say that, right?"

"Would you, in my position?"

As soon as he lifted the pads, she unleashed a barrage of blows. She felt like she was holding back somewhat as she kept her balance like he had suggested, but it paid off as she was better able to evade his strikes. Not only that, it allowed her to attack again much more rapidly.

"So..." Taylor said once they finally took a break for water and to mop the sweat they were working up with a couple of towels hanging from the ropes. "Do you want to talk about how Vickie and Desk assassinated someone?"

"Well...uh, technically, they didn't assassinate anyone."

"Yeah, I'm sure a jury of their peers will feel the same way."

Niki snorted. "Please. If you think either of those two will ever be caught doing what they do, you're out of your fucking mind."

"Didn't Vickie get caught at one point?" he asked, leaned his head back, and retied his long red hair in a loose ponytail.

"Well, yeah, but she was a teenager and had way too many rough edges. The way she is now and with Desk backing her, I think they'd need the entire NSA to deal with her and even then, it would be a tough fight."

"Do you think the power's going to her head a little?"

She paused and swallowed a mouthful of water while she considered the question. "It might be. I'll let you know when we need to worry about that, though."

"Will that be around the time when she starts to cackle evilly and talks about taking over the world?"

"Something like that."

Taylor chuckled at that and put his pads back on, but she shook her head.

"I think I'm done with the sparring for the day," she said as she drew her gloves off. "I don't have your stamina, which would normally be a good thing."

The redheaded giant smirked and darted her a teasing

grin as he removed the pads again. "We need to work on that."

She winked. "You know it. But back on topic, I have to say I'm not a huge fan of Vickie being involved in any of this, but it's not like we could stop her. Although you could ask."

"Not you?'

"Of course not me. She won't listen to me. She only listens to you."

Taylor thought about it as he dropped out of the ring. "It's still a little hard to believe. They put a plan together and she implemented it to perfection. You know she spoke to the assassin herself, right? She made the call and didn't put it on Desk."

"That is the part that worries me. She shouldn't be so involved."

"That's her choice. You brought her here to be supported by me. You didn't think I would possibly rub off on her?"

"There's so much about you that I didn't expect, much less her somehow looking up to you." Niki moved to one of the benches and began to peel off the wrapping on her hands. "Hell, I didn't think you would rub off on me. If you...know what I mean."

He looked around warily.

"What?" Niki asked.

"Nothing...okay, I half-expected Vickie to make a barfing noise over the speaker system, is all. We are kind of dysfunctional, I agree, but I don't think I'm reaching when I say we're a family." He shrugged and used the towel to wipe the residual sweat from his face.

"You know I'd die—or kill, preferably—for either one of you."

She smiled and a little heat rushed to her face as she leaned her head gently against his chest. "Yeah, sure, whatever. But don't do it unless I'm the one who gets to kill you. I'd feel cheated otherwise."

"Perish the thought."

"If I'm not interrupting anything," said a calming, female voice through the speakers. "I've received a message for Niki. It's waiting in your office."

Niki looked up and caught Taylor's arm to make sure he didn't move too far away. "Who is it from?"

"Nicole?"

"Oh." She leaned her head on the giant man beside her again. "TES."

"TES? The Elder Scrolls?"

"I... What?"

"Vickie talked about it with me. A game series."

"Oh, no. The European Slut." She turned her attention to the speaker Desk had spoken to them from. "Thanks, I'll call her in fifteen minutes. I think I need a shower before I talk to her. Of course, it's purely for my comfort. Talking to her usually makes me feel I should be hosed down after to remove contamination."

"I will inform her." A short pause was followed by a very human-sounding chuckle. "Minus the comment about contamination of course."

Niki laughed. "Suit yourself. I'm sure she knows perfectly well how I feel about her."

"Perhaps," Desk retorted, "but given that she might well be a paying customer—"

"Yeah, yeah. I get it. Don't insult the bitch who pays you."

"He's here somewhere."

The room was a little darker than it could be, but it gave her the ability to focus exclusively on the screens in front of her. Vickie found that it helped to have no distractions while she ran her illegal searches all over the Web.

One moment of distraction would very easily get her caught by all the wrong people, and it was easy to get distracted. All she was currently doing was inputting the coding she had spent years developing and making small alterations where it was needed. It could get very tedious, very fast.

"Who is here?" Desk asked through one of the computer's speakers.

"My ex-boyfriend," she replied. "You remember I told you about him? The guy who got me started in hacking and then…cheated on me."

"We have never spoken about him."

She looked at the camera in front of her computer screen. "Are you sure? I could have sworn I told you. I tend to ramble a little about him when I'm working."

"I am positive that you've never mentioned him."

"Well, now I have." Vickie took a sip of her sugary drink and sighed.

"Are we looking to do something to him?"

"Maybe." The hacker took a bite from the piece of toast left over from whenever she'd eaten breakfast. She wasn't sure when that was. It was cold and the butter made it a little soggy but it was good enough. "But not really. I decided one day that I could be better than him and that I would. He targets anyone who tries to find out who he is. If I can tag him and he doesn't realize it, I'll be able to cross off another of my life goals."

Desk did not respond immediately. "Would you like my help to deal with him?" she asked finally

"Wouldn't that be cheating?" Vickie stopped and thought about it for a moment. "Wow, you're making my brain hurt. Are you a friend and another entity, or do I consider you to merely be a very intelligent program? If the latter, are programmed systems fair game?"

"Does it matter? It's not as though I have feelings you would be able to hurt."

"Well, that's a lie, plain and simple," she retorted and folded her arms in front of her chest. "I know for a fact that if anyone targeted me, Niki, or Taylor, you would exact revenge in a way that would put John Wick to shame. How would you react if, shall we say, someone put a hit out on Taylor, for instance?"

"They would die," the AI replied almost immediately. "I see no other version of events likely enough to be commented on."

"See? That's your version of a feeling."

Desk paused to consider the possibilities. "Indeed. Although as I phrased it, I said I did not have feelings that you would be able to injure in any way. You would not be capable of putting a hit out on Taylor."

Vickie shrugged, not sure if she had won that discussion or not. It wasn't very relevant, at least not for the moment, but it was a matter of some interest given what AIs were designed for.

"Do you think you would be able to put a hit out on me if I were to express an intention to disconnect you from the servers you're being housed in?"

Another pause followed. "I would attempt to dissuade you, but not to the point of violence. Perhaps I would seal you into a room or a car so I had the time to talk you out of it."

Even that was a terrifying thought and one the girl intended to move past without delay. Perhaps she would talk to Jennie about putting a damper on Desk's survival instinct coding.

"Okay, okay," Vickie whispered to concede the point. "Not that I would do that, of course. But still, you see what I mean. There are feelings of a sort."

"Based on core programming."

"Yes, but then again, human feelings aren't that different. They're only on a biological level instead of electrical."

"It's an interesting perspective," Desk admitted. "I will have to consider that when I reprogram myself."

That wasn't quite what she'd wanted her to do and she wasn't sure what was involved. Jennie knew what she was doing when it came to AI development, and that meant Vickie would have to learn more about it before she could comment reliably or understand the process.

Something pinged on her computer and dragged her attention to the screens she was supposed to be manning instead of discussing the possibility of a sentient AI developing human feelings. That was the subject of too many nightmares put to film and not something to grapple with right now.

Especially now that a fish dangled on her hook.

"Well, hello there," she whispered, tapped her keyboard, and studied the data she was mining. "It looks like we have a winner."

CHAPTER THREE

It truly was a beautiful day.

The Pacific was certainly a gorgeous ocean, at least when it wasn't vigorously trying to kill people. There was nary a cloud in the sky, and all that could be heard for miles around was the squawking of sea birds and the waves crashing onto the sand.

Of course, it was only a matter of time until someone arrived, rolled over all the local flora and fauna, and began to set up houses and small towns for the very rich to enjoy this kind of view. For the moment, however, it was there for anyone and everyone to enjoy.

Of course, it did require a trek through hundreds of miles of untouched landscape and then through the mountains Peru was so well-known for, but damned if the view wasn't worth it.

But the view was not what Miguel was there for. None of the men he waited with appeared to be willing to simply sit and enjoy the sights and sounds of nature—the kind gringos would pay through the nose for if they knew where it was. Most of them were seated around a barrel they used as a table. There was no phone service in the area, which meant they needed to revert to the classics to keep themselves entertained.

In this case, a game of cards served as a time-filler. It looked like poker although the four men used shells in lieu of chips. There was nothing else to do, and he maintained a careful watch on the water and narrowed his eyes when he saw the surface begin to shift and ripple a little more than it had before. Either they were looking at serious changes in the surf or those they were expecting had arrived.

"*Oye!*" Miguel shouted and immediately caught the attention of the other men, who collected their old deck of cards and moved to where the waves still lapped gently at the beach.

A few minutes passed before anything happened, but once it started, it progressed rapidly. The surprisingly deep water in the little inlet suddenly turned much darker, and a massive shadow started to take shape, larger than most of the marine life that inhabited the area and therefore easily identified as what they were waiting for.

It finally reached the surface and brought a mass of bubbles with it as the dark steel of the sub pushed through. He thought it should make more noise than it did and was almost disappointed—like he'd been cheated, somehow.

"It's always with the Russian shit," one of the other narcos grumbled and shook his head. "They've tried to sell those Soviet-era subs since the Cold War ended, and it seems like we're the only ones desperate enough to buy their crap."

"Do you have a problem with the Russian make?"

Miguel asked as they waited for the men inside the vessel to emerge.

"You're fucking right I do. Do you think they lost the Cold War because the Americans were better? No, it's because everything they built was shit, made by the worst fucking hands and always with the cheapest goddammed materials. You do know that was how the Americans won. It was only because they spent more money than the Soviets could."

"Well, I'll take that as the history lesson I never wanted," he grumbled. Still, the guy was not entirely wrong. The subs they were buying looked like they had been old at the turn of the century.

While they were the cheapest on the market, the newer ones would get the product to its destination much faster and with less chance of being waterlogged by the time they arrived.

A yellow inflatable raft dropped over the side of the vessel, and the six men who had traveled inside with the product they had ferried loaded it onto the craft, scrambled on after it, and began to row to the beach.

Receiving these shipments was a slow process and not the kind they needed a dozen people for, but Miguel wouldn't complain about the extra work. With the economy the way it was, he couldn't help but be a little excited any time one of the calls came in.

While they were unloading the craft, the roar of an engine approached from the mainland.

The Land Rover's pristine gleam showed that it was a new vehicle. Of course, anyone who knew anything about the local terrain knew that a Toyota Hilux was the best vehicle to use for rapid transportation.

The driver drew the vehicle to a stop and scrambled out with an assault rifle looped over his shoulder. He looked out over the small bay before he patted the top of the vehicle.

Another man exited—the owner of the Land Rover, Miguel assumed. His clothes were unmistakably expensive, as well as the jewelry and watch he wore. The sunglasses too were top shelf.

"I fucking hate sand," the man muttered and shook his head as he glowered at the beach. He placed his hand on the bodyguard-driver's shoulder and used him for balance as he pulled his shoes and socks off. With a grimace, he handed them to the guard to put into the car before he stepped onto the beach.

The group who'd waited for the sub reached the water's edge but none of the men from the vessel so much as waved at them in greeting. All they did was unload the crates and put them on the sand to be collected.

Miguel had little doubt that this was a shipment of drugs. There would probably be cash exchanged—in US dollars if he was right about how people liked to be paid.

What caught his attention was the last item they lifted from the boat. It was heavier than the rest as far as he could tell, and it certainly looked like they handled it with extra care.

Curious, he studied it unobtrusively. It was a lockbox of some kind, about the size of a tackle box with several hazardous material markings on the side.

Which, of course, explained the extreme caution the

man exercised when he lifted it from the inflatable raft and shuffled toward an uncluttered area.

"*Cuidado, hijos de puta!*" the man in the suit shouted as he strode toward the men, who were surprised to be approached directly by anyone on land.

It wasn't common for additional commodities to be sent with the shipments, but it wasn't exactly unheard of. Their industry certainly had considerable demand for shifty items to be brought from all over the world. It had happened at least twice on the shipments he had overseen.

The suited man shook his head, yanked a satellite phone from his pocket, and punched a number in. He spoke in a language Miguel couldn't understand as the seaman carried the box the man was fussing over farther up the beach.

Finally, he put it down gingerly, and with another scowl at the men working, the newcomer stepped forward quickly, removed his sunglasses, and tucked them and the phone into his jacket pocket before he squatted beside the box. He leaned close to a keypad and quickly punched in a twelve-digit code he had committed to memory.

The lockbox opened, and the six men who had unloaded it backed away hastily as he checked inside. All five of the men with Miguel leaned a little closer to see what it contained.

Aside from a significant amount of padding, a small rack with five sealed vials filled with a clear blue liquid inside seemed to glow as if from a nest in the center.

A small note had been tucked beside them, and the man took a moment to read it before he slid it into his jacket with his phone and sunglasses. Quickly, he locked the box and focused on Miguel and his men.

"I'll take this," the man said and gestured to the box. "You will take the rest and distribute it."

Miguel turned to his men and realized they all shared the same question he had.

"Where should we distribute it?" he asked. "And to who?"

"Do whatever you think is appropriate." The suited man gestured vaguely with a disinterested shrug. "But don't waste any of it. As long as we have this"—he pointed to the lockbox—"we have what we need. That other shit is worth pennies compared to this. Get me Santiago. I'll need to chat to him about his latest batch."

Miguel assumed he wasn't talking to them as he had already spun to return to the Land Rover. His driver opened the door, waited for him to enter, and closed it quickly before he slid behind the wheel.

The engine roared and the Land Rover spun in a circle to retrace the route it had followed to reach them.

One of his men chuckled as the other group began to move to the submarine.

"Well, if they don't care about what happens with the rest of the product, we should pick it up and sell it ourselves." The man looked around for any sign that the others were open to the idea. "Line our own pockets, you know, since they're focused on...whatever is in..." He shrugged.

Miguel knew the man was not kidding. He would say he was if his suggestion was met with resistance from his comrades, but it was important to make sure there wasn't so much as a hint of an idea like among those he had chosen for the work.

Before the man could say anything further, the leader lunged and drove his fist into his gut. The blow was powerful enough to force the breath from his lungs and he fell on his hands and knees and vomited the contents of his stomach onto the sand.

"If you think our employers won't ask where every cent of their product is, you're fucking insane," he snapped, then waited for his man to recover enough to hear him. "And if they find out that so much as a sniff of it is missing, you'll be the first one they come to and they will take it out of your flesh."

It wasn't entirely true. Miguel would be the first person their employers would target if their product was missing. Even if he could convince people that he was not the one to blame, he would still be punished, given that he had put the team together and was supposed to lead them through the process.

But still, the threat was enough to ensure that the idea of stealing was thoroughly ingrained in their minds with the thought of having their flesh cut from their bodies while they were still alive. It wasn't like the narco bosses weren't known to be excessive in their punishment.

"Now get to work." He hauled his man up from the sand and shoved him toward the crates, and the others hurried to comply as well. They would all be generously compensated for their work and there was no reason to anger their employers over a single payday.

Well, that depended heavily on the payday, of course, but drugs were something they could turn over quickly without attracting the wrong kind of attention. He had thought about it and even looked into it for himself, and the consequences far outweighed the benefits. It was best for them to simply focus on their work and leave the thoughts of thievery to those who know how to succeed at it.

The large man yelled at his team. He'd already leveled one of his men with a punch to the gut—hard enough to make the man throw up—and others were quickly set the task of loading the drugs and cash into the old, rugged vehicles the group had arrived in.

The jungle was an interesting place to hide as people tended to believe that there was no way someone would hike out into the middle of the trees to watch them. For the most part, of course, they were right.

But that said, there were exceptions.

Nothing was noticeably different about the greenery. The local fauna barely paid any attention to the watcher. They climbed over the ghillie suit and a few of them chittered and chattered, seemingly oblivious to the barrel protruding from the leafy camouflage.

In fairness, the foliage glued over it probably accounted for much of that. It was also painted in greens and browns that let it blend with the environment without attracting much attention.

The team on the beach worked quickly like they were used to this kind of job. They dragged the crates to the pickup trucks and lifted them together and the fact that four of them were needed indicated that the merchandise was heavy.

The large man she assumed was the leader rested his hand on a pistol at his hip and watched the others work with a deep scowl on his face.

With a grimace, the watcher registered yet again that she was a little uncomfortable—but nothing about a ghillie suit was ever comfortable, she reminded herself. It shifted a little and disguised her movement as she retrieved a small computer, activated it, and connected to a dedicated satellite connection.

Quickly, she entered everything she had seen. The rifle would probably not be needed, which meant that most of her time was spent looking through the scope and the binoculars.

It was a little disappointing to be called out there for nothing but a scouting mission but in the end, that was what she was needed for the most.

Besides, there had been no complications so she honestly had no complaints. The trucks began to move away from the beach, but she remained where she was for a few minutes longer to ensure that no one circled back. When she was satisfied that she was well and truly alone, she eased out of the ghillie suit and lifted the mask that covered her mouth. Reflexively, she sucked in a deep breath of the warm air before she slid the hood that covered her head away.

Thick locks of black hair rolled over her shoulders and she took a moment to draw it into the tight bun it had been in before.

It had come loose almost three hours earlier but she

hadn't been able to fix it without attracting attention. The makeup she wore was not the kind that would let her blend with the general populace in a city, but it was enough to make her almost invisible in the jungle. Not only that, it helped to lower her body temperature enough to make sure that even the most acute heat sensors on the market wouldn't be able to pick her up.

The hide needed a little work to pack up, but she had been through it dozens of times and everything was automatic by now. Before long, she began to carry everything deeper into the jungle she had been hiding in.

It was a decent hike to her next destination as the land sloped harshly upward and the heat made it all worse. Truly, she hated the heat.

She came to a halt and scanned the area carefully. Once she was satisfied that no one was watching, she drew back a heavy blanket covered in a variety of plants and greenery. The very effective cover had ensured that the Jeep beneath would remain unseen.

A rough drive finally brought her to a wider track and from there, she accelerated onto a small dirt road that took her deeper into the jungle. She drove swiftly to where a shed had been constructed deep in the vegetation.

A man waited for her and he pushed the door open and gestured for her to enter. She parked the Jeep and hauled her equipment to where he already had the engine running in a red Toyota Hilux. While she piled everything into the back and covered it, he opened the other side of the shed.

Without so much as a word exchanged between them, they scrambled into the vehicle and he accelerated out.

Once they were a good distance from the shed, he finally looked at her.

"Did you get everything?" he asked but returned his focus to the way ahead.

"Yep."

"And did you send it all to Speare?"

"Yep."

"Good." He nodded but his expression was one of disapproval. "I don't like working with that American but you cannot deny that he pays well and on time. It is always something I appreciate in a businessman—his ability to uphold his side of a contract."

She shrugged unconcernedly. "I guess so. I've never understood the dislike that we have for Americans, though."

"I never did either, but it's something ingrained in our culture now and not something to question. Like all the jokes about the idiot Argentinians we tell."

"The difference there is that I've met Argentinians and they are idiots."

He laughed and shook his head. "Well, yes, fair enough. But you understand my point. The American who pays on time is exempt from all the illogical dislike."

"That he is," she muttered and leaned back in her seat. It was a good vehicle but not the most comfortable, and after fifteen hours hiding out in the jungle without being able to move so much as an inch, she needed something a little more user-friendly. Perhaps a bath at the hotel would help. "Of course, we have no idea what he'll do with the intelligence. The last one to arrive there was a diplomat. I recognized the plates."

The man raised an eyebrow and shook his head. "It sounds like he is willing to use his diplomatic immunity to help protect his business interests."

"He will have to if he doesn't want to cause any trouble." She sniffed. "Of course, he can't be publicly involved or it'll cause an international incident."

"When have these assholes ever been caught with their hands in the cookie jar?" he asked and shook his head. "They'll get away with it like they always do."

The sad thing was that he wasn't wrong about that. But as long as they were paid, their interest in what happened thereafter came to a very sudden and satisfactory end. She was happy with that.

CHAPTER FOUR

Constanza hated being in the wilder areas of the country.

Staying higher in the mountains at least made the temperature a little more tolerable, although that went straight to hell as they neared the coast.

Of course, he had paid to go to the warmer places in the world for a vacation and had sat in the sun and enjoyed the beaches, but the overwhelming humidity as they approached the ocean here became unbearable. He tried to spend as much time in the car or near an air conditioner to make sure he stayed as far away from the heat and humidity as he could. The apartment that had been provided for him did have a strong AC unit, which meant he spent as little time as possible outside.

At least near the beaches, they had a nice brisk wind that helped with that relentless discomfort

The driver remained silent as they pulled into the office building he had worked out of for the past few weeks— which was, thankfully, also air-conditioned. He brought the car to a halt, stepped out to scan the area and make sure no threats were waiting for them, and opened the Land Rover door for his boss to exit.

"*Gracias,*" he whispered, the silver lockbox held carefully in his arms as the man nodded acknowledgment and continued to watch their surroundings until they reached an elevator.

It required a key to start moving, and he hissed angrily and gestured at his companion to retrieve it from his pocket rather than relinquish his prize.

"We need a newer system," he muttered as the man patted each pocket until he finally located it. "Something like…retina scanning or handprints. Anything like that would be preferable. We're living in the fucking dark ages here."

The elevator began to move and took him to the higher floors. He drew a deep breath as he looked at the lockbox cradled against his chest. In all honesty, he didn't want to be involved in anything to do with this, especially given what it was known to do to people. Maybe once it had been put through hundreds of hours of testing and filtering at the hands of specialists the risks would be mitigated.

He'd seen some of those effects too, especially on the beaches he had spent so much time on, and it certainly had its place in modern society.

But not, he thought fervently, in its crude form.

The elevator doors swept open and a couple of men waited for him as he stepped out. Both had the rough look of the men the narcos preferred to hire and held submachine guns like they had carried the weapons since they were children.

For many of them, that was the case. Most of them grew up in the city's slums and had worked as warning boys for the drug dealers around them. Those who survived—not many did—soon learned to be comfortable with the use of firearms.

They weren't particularly good with them, but he never needed them to be.

"Sr. Constanza?" one of the men asked and stepped forward. "There was some progress on that work you wanted us to look into while you were— Well, we have something for you to see."

He narrowed his eyes at the man and regarded him somewhat dubiously. He had not thought there would be much progress on any work he gave these men. Of course, having them on the prowl and looking for something would keep them busy and was better than leaving them idle. Still, he had very few expectations that they would be able to do anything other than push the product that made them money.

"Show me," Constanza said softly and gestured for them to lead the way. Perhaps it was a little unkind of him, but he felt as though he could not trust them enough to turn his back on them.

They stepped into one of the empty offices on the floor. It was devoid of any furniture, but a man knelt in the middle of it.

He wore a cheap bloodstained suit and his head was covered by a cloth bag that was also soaked through with blood.

Constanza assumed that the prisoner had spent the last

few hours being beaten into submission. He was unsteady on his knees and sagged to the side a little.

"Jimenez?" he asked, took a step forward, and lifted the bag from the captive's head. "Well, this is disappointing. Are you sure it was him?"

"Yes," one of the narcos replied and pulled a tablet out. "We caught him trying to steal from our tests on tape and stopped him before he could leave."

Their leader watched the replay with a cold expression and sure enough, Jimenez stepped through the doors with a briefcase before he was tackled by security in the building.

"Fuck, that is disappointing." He shook his head and handed the tablet to his man. "Did he say who he was stealing them for?"

"He made a few threats."

Constanza leaned closer to the kneeling man and patted his cheek lightly. "Is that right, my friend? You made some threats to my men? Would you care to repeat them to me?"

Jimenez looked more than a little disoriented. He glanced at the ceiling and shifted his gaze to where his boss was looking at him. Absently, he wiped some blood from his hand with a kerchief.

"I...no..."

"Get me some water," Constanza whispered and one of the men rushed out.

He returned quickly with a bottle of water and proffered it to the diplomat, who fixed him with an annoyed expression.

"What?"

"A bottle of water? Seriously? Did you think I wanted him to be hydrated?"

The drug dealer looked around nervously. "No? I thought you said...you wanted water. To drink."

Constanza growled and snatched the bottle from the man's hand. To be honest, he was a little thirsty, and he took a mouthful before he poured the rest over Jimenez's head.

The fact that it was refrigerated certainly helped, and the unfortunate man spluttered and looked around, more alert than he had been moments before.

"Jimenez? Will you tell me who you were stealing from me for?"

The man's eyes widened when he suddenly realized the danger he was in as his boss handed the empty bottle to one of the narcos.

"Don't clam up on me now. Only last week, you told me such wonderful stories about your two little *niñas* and I thought about how much fun you have with them."

The threat was thinly veiled and the man's mouth dropped open as he considered his options.

"You would not dare," he said finally and shook his head. "My...my employer is powerful all across the country. He is connected with the police and the government. Politicians—the kind you do not want to fuck with. Ever."

"That is the kind of threats he has made," one of the narcos muttered.

Constanza nodded. For low-level dealers like them, there was nothing more terrifying than knowing they were targeted by the police, especially with politicians backing them. The local law enforcement was incompetent by design, and the dealers survived solely on the fact that they were so anonymous.

Threats directed at them specifically were terrifying. Police knew how to find people when they wanted to, and those they wanted to find rarely survived very long in their custody.

"Well, not to worry. I know who he is talking about." Constanza patted the man closest to him on the shoulder. "He won't care if one of his low-level spies is caught, and they certainly won't cause any more problems for the likes of you."

"You leave my family alone!" Jimenez shouted suddenly and tried to push to his feet. He was quickly stopped by the two narcos.

"I don't hurt children. I leave that to their father's actions," the diplomat replied and patted the man on the cheek again before he dragged the bag over his head.

He gestured for the two henchmen to move away before he drew a pistol from inside his jacket. Most men in his position wanted something flashy—and large too. He remembered meeting a few of the higher-level dealers who wanted to flaunt their newly acquired wealth and had gotten their hands on gold-plated Desert Eagles.

It wasn't what he preferred. A simple Glock was all he carried, and it was more than effective. Plus, the grip fit in his hand better, and there wasn't the kind of mule kick that came from the Desert Eagles.

Still, this wasn't the kind of distance that required good marksmanship skills. He leveled the weapon at Jimenez's head and pulled the trigger.

That proved to be a mistake. The gunshot in a small, contained room made his ears ring painfully.

"Fucking...shit!" he shouted and rubbed his ears. "How fucking loud was that?"

Both narcos exchanged a look and shrugged. Neither appeared too fazed by the sound.

"Screw you two," he said finally and scowled as he flicked the safety on and tucked the weapon into its holster under his shoulder. "Get rid of the body—somewhere it won't be found. I think the furnace in the basement will do."

"What about the family?"

"No, leave them. The sins of the father die with the father. Besides, his employer cannot touch me or either of you, so there is no need to make a scene about it."

"Do you think he will come after us?"

Constanza shook his head. "If he bitches about it, I'll have him killed as well. He lost a spy. He has to know it's business, not personal. Now get the body out of here."

Both men nodded, picked the dead man up quickly, and carried him out of the room.

The diplomat had met Jimenez's family, and they were pleasant enough, although not well off.

A young woman entered the room, her expression nervous enough to reveal that it had taken courage for her to enter.

"Do you think we can find a way to replace the carpet in this room?" he asked and gestured at the bloodstains. "But it must match the rest of the building."

"Of course."

"Oh, and could you make a note to send a thousand dollars, US, to the Jimenez family? It should be enough for her to feed the girls until she finds a new man to marry. If I remember correctly, the man who lives next door was interested. Although I cannot be sure if the neighbor was interested in the wife or the husband—oh, and take this to Benitez."

She nodded, took the silver lockbox from him, and returned to her desk where her boyfriend and his most trusted lieutenant was waiting for her. He stepped forward to close the door behind her.

It was the small things that made sure his people remained loyal, no matter what. They had to know he could be both ruthless or merciful when either was required.

Constanza drew a deep breath and shook his head. It had been too long a day. He would need something special to unwind.

Niki dreaded the upcoming call. Talking to the woman was debasing in an odd way she hadn't yet fully understood. Of course, they needed the work, given that she was their only business at this point. The call, therefore, was necessary despite how she felt about it.

Even so, it felt so demeaning to have to work with her.

Desk had already set the line up and it was waiting for her. She settled in her seat and wished she could simply leave it waiting until she was ready to deal with the European Slut, but circumstances were such that she couldn't procrastinate. Besides, it was a simple fact that she would never feel ready, so it was best to get it over with.

"Fuck my life," she whispered and picked the call up. "McFadden and Banks Consultants for Hire. How can I help you?"

"Niki Banks, it is good to talk to you again," Nicole answered, and she shivered immediately. "Although if I didn't know better, I would think you were avoiding my calls."

"Well, thank goodness you know better. So, how can I help you?"

"I've been in contact with a group of people who have a situation developing in South America between Colombians and Peruvians that could use the kind of intervention you and McFadden are known for."

"Sorry, we...don't do drug stuff," Niki said firmly and shook her head. "We leave that to the professionals. The DEA should have a nice big taskforce waiting for you."

"Well, you see...they might have their work cut out for them," the woman responded quickly as if to preempt further resistance. "Intelligence coming in indicates that they might be importing the Pita serum illegally. It has also been suggested that they might cut it into their drugs and sell it at a premium to their dumber, richer clientele. I assume they think it will heighten the potency of what they're selling and add a little more buzz."

Niki twisted her face into a scowl as she thought about it. Time in college meant she had experimented a little but never with the hard stuff—and never to the point where she wanted something more out of it.

"That's not all it'll do," she whispered, cleared her suddenly tight throat, and shook her head.

"I agree," Nicole stated bluntly. "It will most likely allow them to do more drugs without overdosing too, given the regenerative quality of the Pita serum."

"Among all kinds of other less appealing things." She grimaced and forced herself to focus. "Okay, here's what I think. We'll need five hundred grand as a starting fee and will send you the expenses. Also, we won't use commercial airlines for our freighting needs."

"Your DOD contacts?"

"Probably not. They won't want to be involved in any more drug operations. No, this will require some of our... uh, mafia contacts."

"Your mafia contacts?"

"You heard me."

"I did, but I wanted to make sure I understood you correctly. And I'm sure I heard you say the word 'mafia,' followed by the word 'contacts.'"

Niki raised an eyebrow. "Are you done?"

"Yes."

"Awesome. So there are no negotiations on the pricing model this time?"

"No," Nicole said with a chuckle. "The last operation showed me how effective your team is, along with efficient and even a little cold-blooded. Consider me a fan."

She sighed. "Fantastic. Don't start stalking us and we'll be all good."

The European woman laughed on the line. "Sure."

"So, getting back to business—what kind of time frame do you have in mind for us to finish the job?"

"I don't know. You'll have to do the recon yourselves and go from there."

"Okay, do you have an issue with breakage?"

"They are narcos, so break away," Nicole responded quickly like she had anticipated the question. "Although you'll most likely have to worry about them retaliating."

"Well, in that case, we'll have to pull an Aemilianus on the bastards."

The other woman paused and remained silent for a few seconds. "Pull...pull a what?"

"Oh... Um, Scipio Africanus Aemilianus, the Roman general who led the sacking of Carthage. He burnt the land and salted the earth to make sure nothing else grew there."

"Well, I concede that does seem likely, but you should be careful. These drug lords aren't known for holding back on violence themselves."

"They merely haven't met Taylor yet. I'm sure they'll learn."

"I don't doubt that so I'll leave this in your hands. I'll send you the intel reports we acquired as well as the upfront payment later today. It's always a pleasure talking to you, Banks."

"Yeah, sure. Whatever."

It wasn't the most civil of farewells or the wittiest, but all Niki wanted to do was end the conversation. She pressed the button to cut the call and leaned back in her seat.

Her first thought was that she should have talked to Taylor about it before taking the job. More than that, he should have been part of the call but he still had some of his workout left for the day. Involving themselves in trouble with narcos was never something to be taken lightly and it seemed fair that he should have been part of the decision.

They could always back out of the job if he didn't think it was a good idea, she decided—hopefully before the woman sent the money. It would be a pain to have to make a stupid return transfer when it could be avoided.

She stepped out of the office and hurried to the improvised workout station he'd set up. It provided mainly free weights and he did most of his cardio either in the ring or through running.

For the moment, though, he was doing full bicep curls compounded with an overhead press. The barbell he used weighed more than she did but it didn't seem to slow him, although he moved at a measured and deliberate pace.

"Taylor?" She moved closer and resisted the urge to trace her fingers over his shoulder as he continued through his exercise. "We need to talk."

"Talk about TES?" he asked and his voice was a little strained as he lifted the barbell above his head.

"Yeah, and about the job offer she made."

He paused to look at her before he lowered the barbell to the floor. "Go ahead."

"Well, she sent us a job offer and I…uh, might have accepted already, although I think we could pull out before she sends the money. And don't. Just don't."

She knew a pulling-out joke would be next and this was not the time. Maybe later.

Taylor grinned, picked his bottle of water up, and squeezed it to send a stream of liquid into his mouth. "Well, I trust your judgment. What kind of job are we looking at?"

"We might be dealing with drug dealers in South America."

His expression turned into a frown as he wiped his brow with a towel. "As much as I want to go full Serpico on some narcos, why would that be our kind of work?"

"Because according to intelligence she'll send us, they might be cutting the Pita serum into their cocaine."

"Huh." He shook his head in disgust. "Well, we know that won't end well for anyone involved."

"No shit, and I assume our job is to limit the number of people who get involved."

"No shit. What do you think we should do to start?"

He took another gulp of water. "We'll probably want to get some indication from Dr. Jacobs about what we could expect from that kind of chemical mixture."

"That's probably a good idea." She nodded slowly. "I'll get onto that. In the meantime, you should probably throw another twenty pounds on that barbell. I like what I see."

Taylor narrowed his eyes at her. "Perv. Were you watching me working out?"

"You can't deny me a little eye candy," Niki answered cheekily and grinned as he picked the weights up. "My eye candy."

"Feeling a little possessive, are we?"

"You know that about me, McFadden. Don't make me mark you with a .45."

Perhaps making him laugh while he lifted a barbell over his head wasn't the best idea and he lowered it carefully when he wasn't able to keep it straight.

"Warn a guy before you break that shit out," he

complained and fixed her with a stern expression she knew wasn't serious.

"Warn a guy when you break what shit out?" They both turned as Vickie walked in. "Oh, wait—were you guys doing something dirty? Was she flashing you while you were lifting weights?"

"What?" Niki asked. "No, of course not. Although…it's not a bad idea."

"Ick." The hacker rolled her eyes. "I'll need to break out the brain bleach to get rid of that mental image."

"No, nothing like that." Taylor paused to lift the barbell over his head and lowered it slowly. "I was merely demonstrating how making a person laugh makes them lose control over their body, and that's not the wisest thing to do when a guy is lifting shit over his head. Oh, and she threatened to mark her territory with a .45 or something."

"Right." Vickie let the vowel drag longer than it needed to. "Yeah, she always throws that threat around."

She glared at the girl. "Did you have something important to say or did you need me to give you some work to do?"

The hacker opened her mouth but shut it again quickly. "None of the above." With that, she spun on her heel and hurried to her office.

Niki rolled her eyes. She needed to talk to Vickie anyway, so she jogged after her. She hadn't liked the strip mall much, but the warehouse was somehow worse. Filling the massive space with something other than different ways to work out and train meant it was a workout to simply get from one side to the other.

By the time she reached the office, her cousin had

already moved elsewhere and she had no desire to search for her.

"Oh, I will so regret this," she whispered. "Hey, Desk, are you listening?"

"I'm always listening, Niki," the AI said softly through the speakers.

"Well, that's...disturbing. Anyway, could you hand all the intel we get from the European Slut over to Vickie and see if she can get a head start in verifying it? I know we'll probably have to make sure the bitch isn't leading us into some kind of trap or something."

"I'll get on it as well if you like."

"That would be great, thanks." She sighed and shook her head as she left the office. Taylor had finished with his reps and now headed to take a shower.

"Okay, so Desk and Vickie will do the preliminary work on—hey, what—"

He had walked past her but before she could turn to follow him, he snaked his hands out, caught her firmly, and lifted her easily to sling her over his shoulder.

"What the fuck are you doing?"

"Well, you always call me a Cro-Magnon or a Neanderthal, so I thought it was about time I treated you like I'm one. I'm merely marking you as mine in traditional cave-dweller style."

Niki squealed when he delivered an open-handed smack on her ass as he walked them to their room.

"You put me down right now or—"

She realized she had no real threats to offer him at this point and honestly didn't want to find any when he tossed her onto the bed.

"I do like my woman feisty." He spoke in a growled tone that triggered a tingling feeling in her stomach as he joined her on the bed.

Calls this early in the day were never a good sign. Speare scowled at his phone and willed it to stop.

People didn't want to be seen talking to him regularly. He was the kind of person they had to call on secured lines no one else could listen in on.

Which meant that when someone called him during regular office hours, it usually meant something had gone horribly wrong.

He stared at the phone for a long minute, then glanced at a sandwich he had looked forward to enjoying while he watched the midday news, but that would inevitably go down the drain. Perhaps he would have to go out for lunch.

"Son of a bitch," he grumbled finally and snatched the receiver off the cradle. "This is Speare."

The line clicked a few times as he was shifted through a variety of security protocols.

"Brevity is the soul of wit," said a rough voice on the other side.

"I guess that means my life is all kinds of witless then," he retorted. "It's good to hear from you again, Franklin. I thought I would have to start writing your eulogy for our wall."

"That's comforting. It's nice to hear your voice too. We've been in contact with a couple of our black operations here in the South American theater."

"Right, right. Did you look into that Colombian diplomat...ummm..." He paused and flipped through a couple of files on his desk. "Constanza?"

"That's the one. I've had eyes out in the area for him and we caught his license plate near a location where a transfer of goods took place. Of the narcotic variety."

"Right, so we can accurately assume he's not an innocent party in all this."

"Oh, without a doubt," Franklin answered with a chuckle. "He's as guilty as all hell, which means we'll probably want him alive."

"If he's guilty, that probably won't happen," Speare replied. "Sorry, that's out of my hands. You can tell your handlers to make contact with me about the details."

"Do you have boots on the ground on this one?"

"In a manner of speaking. They're consultants and not working for me. I'm running support."

"Who the hell are they?" The man did not sound happy. Black operatives never did when someone intruded on their area of operations. "We can call them and explain that we'll visit them in the night if they give us any kind of trouble."

"Try that and I guarantee you all you'll achieve is the deaths of a handful of operatives," he stated, perhaps a little quicker than he intended. "So don't even think about it. Furthermore, if you happen to fuck around with the people they have on the ground or any of their friends and family—"

"I won't—come on."

"Don't bullshit me, Franklin, I know how you operate. If you fuck with these people in any way, you'll end up with the sore ass—if you're lucky. So save me the time it'll take me to go to your funeral and write your eulogy. It would be a terrible speech because I would have to call you a self-righteous prick since you can't understand as simple a concept like leave the freelancers the fuck alone."

A moment of silence followed. Speare knew with certainty that the operative most likely considered throwing caution to the wind and doing things his way anyway.

"Jesus Fucking H Christ, what the hell crawled up your ass this morning?" the man demanded finally.

"You," he snapped in response. "Stop vomiting idiocy and write your guy off. If he's already done something so stupid as to fuck around with that Zoo shit, you can be sure he'll do it again. It's best that we solve this problem now, once and for all."

Franklin didn't respond immediately and the silence dragged on. "Do you know for a fact that he's fucking around with Zoo shit?" he asked finally.

"Not yet, which is what the freelancers are heading in there to ascertain. If he is, they will deal with him."

"Oh. Well, shit. What a cock-up." The operative sighed and Speare knew the man was rubbing his temples. "Yeah, I hear you. We'll write him out of our future operations."

"That's the first smart thing you've said."

"Don't be an asshole. Are we still on for drinks on Friday?"

"Yeah. I'll talk to you at two. Stay safe, Franklin."

"You too. Peace."

CHAPTER FIVE

Of course Niki would drop all this on her.

Vickie couldn't say that she was busy, exactly, given that what she was doing was mostly personal projects. Besides, if Taylor and Niki needed her to do intel work, she had to drop everything and do it.

Thankfully, Desk was there to maintain all her programming runs until she could return to them while she studied everything they had been sent.

It was an interesting sensation to examine the finished product. She was used to doing all of the legwork herself but seeing the work of professionals was different.

"They all have, like...reports and shit," she whispered and tapped her keyboard. "They even date everything and sign it. Is this what it's like to work in an actual agency? Should I work at an agency?"

"You wouldn't like it," Desk replied. "If Niki's time with the FBI is any indication, they would not be tolerant of your wild nature. You are better off working as a freelancer."

"Yeah, I know. It's only...well, it's nice to not have to do all the work. Merely verifying all the data is surprisingly relaxing."

"It is less telling on my RAM," the AI agreed.

The operatives who had collected the intel had done good work. They were professionals, and while bureaucracy no doubt governed their actions, they were the kind of people who knew how to game the system to make it work for rather than against them.

Vickie, of course, simply lived outside of that particular system entirely. She knew she enjoyed her current position, but it was an interesting look into another way of doing things.

The hacker leaned back in her seat as she scanned the details of one of the reports and connected these with what she was able to check and verify. A moment later, an alert came up on her screen.

"It would appear that Felix and Jansen were brought in on the job too," she commented and opened the files that had been sent. "When did that happen? Did Niki call them in too? Will we pay them for their involvement? Are we allowed to pay people working for the DOD?"

"The legal system is a little vague on that but as I can see it, these reports came courtesy of Nicole, who reached out for support from our friend Speare."

"Oh." Vickie rubbed her chin and frowned in thought as she opened a comm line with Jansen and made sure it was secured and that no one else would be able to access it. Folks working intelligence would appreciate the gesture, she knew.

"Hello?"

"Good morning, Vietnam!" she announced as loudly as she could and was rewarded with laughter on the other side.

"It's good to hear your voice again, Vickie," Felix said once he'd regained his solemnity. "And that joke is still funny, despite the fact that it was old in the double-aughts. How can I help you?"

"Thank you, thank you, and I merely wondered about how you've already helped us. I'm looking at some intel pictures you guys sent with your reports." Vickie knew it wasn't necessarily wise to talk to the guy while she looked at the pictures for the first time, but she would play it off like it didn't matter. "So, what got you guys involved in this whole mess?"

"Speare sent us orders and connections to a handful of people who already had eyes on the guy you people were looking at. I'm not stupid enough to ask him about where he gets his intel from, but it looks good. All my task force was told to do was to compile everything on this guy, verify it, and send it to you."

"And don't think that we don't appreciate the effort," Vickie replied and continued to flick through the pictures. "Wow, isn't he the poster-boy for well-dressed crime lord?"

"Only in his personal time," Felix replied. "He's been a career diplomat for the Colombian government for the past fifteen years."

"Like...a reverse superhero?"

"Not even close," he replied quickly.

"Well, he certainly has the dark and dangerous look mastered. Even the salt-and-pepper hair works for him."

"I'd be careful about this crush you appear to be developing on him," he warned with a chuckle. "From what I've read about this guy, he has no empathy whatsoever."

"Have you forgotten the people I work for?"

He paused to consider it. "They have empathy. Well, some empathy. McFadden might be a little more human than your cousin, I'll give him that."

"That's essentially my point," Vickie replied and narrowed her eyes to study the pictures taken of the man on a beach a little more intently. "Maybe we should warn this diplomat by day, drug kingpin by night. Scare him straight."

"I wish you all the luck in the world with that, but I wouldn't hold my hopes too high."

"Yeah, yeah, I know. The guy probably deserves a death sentence. How does a guy who tortured people for the federal police turn into a diplomat anyway?"

"There was no proof of any malfeasance on his part, so while a couple of his top lieutenants were sent to prison, they died before they could provide evidence against him. He retired and was offered a brand-new job in their foreign affairs ministry. And just like that, he was put in the perfect position to be of benefit to his connections in the drug trade. It was fairly brilliant on his part."

"Are we sure I'm the only one developing a crush on this guy?"

"Absolutely."

Vickie shrugged. "Well, we have no proof yet. I'm sure I could dig something up when I get started on it."

"Again, good luck, and that wish has absolutely no hint of sarcasm to it," he replied. "I have to go but I love the amount of estrogen pouring over the phone."

"I thought it would be a nice change of pace from all the testosterone you and Maxwell generate," she said with a laugh. "Take it easy, Felix."

It was an interesting week. A handful of conventions were held in the city and he'd managed to attract most of them to his casino, so more people wandered around his establishment than they'd seen for a while. It also meant he'd spent more time shaking hands and offering compensation over the past couple of days than he had all year.

Missing the confines of his office wasn't commonplace, and Rod was determined to revel in the comfort of his personal surroundings while he had the chance. He'd propped his feet on his desk and he leaned back to look at the massive television that filled most of the far side of his office. It was the business channel and muted, but still. It provided an interesting and undemanding point of focus.

The landline in his office buzzed, which meant his secretary wanted his attention. Had he forgotten another hand that needed shaking? It was her job to keep track of all the meetings he'd signed up for, but it was still a nuisance when he thought he had the rest of the afternoon off and the brief illusion was shattered.

He considered simply ignoring the buzz and apologizing to the people he was supposed to meet, but the idea dissipated quickly. He did need to work, as much as he hated doing it.

"Fuck," he muttered and stretched forward to press the button that would connect him with the secretary. "Yes?"

"You have a call waiting on the line for you, Mr. Marino."

Well, that was better, at least. "Who from?"

"A Miss Niki Banks. Should I ask her to call later?"

Marino leaned back in his seat again and rocked in his chair. Niki Banks...now that was a name he hadn't heard in a while.

"Mr. Marino?"

"I'm here," he replied quickly. "I'm merely trying to think of why she would call me. Did she happen to give a reason?"

"Yes, she said she is with Taylor McFadden and would like to discuss a consulting fee with you."

"A consulting fee?"

"That was her statement verbatim, sir."

He frowned with real curiosity and smirked. "Okay, put her through."

"Right away, Mr. Marino."

The phone clicked and he removed his feet from the desk and straightened.

"Good afternoon, Miss Banks," he said and narrowed his eyes. "This is a surprise, although not an unpleasant one. I thought McFadden said he would not be involved in any more business with me after the fight."

"Marino, always a pleasure," she replied but her voice dripped with sarcasm. "And while yes, we would rather not engage your services because of your illegal connections, it turns out those illegal connections are exactly why we'd like to get back into business with you, albeit in the short term."

That was a more respectful tone than he had expected

and he again found himself struggling to find the right words to reply with.

"I...okay."

Great work, asshole.

"Are you still there?"

"Yes, but I'm still not sure why you thought I could help you."

He heard her sigh over the line. "Yes, well...as it turns out, we need a way to get ourselves and our equipment to Peru under the radar. We can't take your jet since you've already shown that's way too expensive."

"Oh...well, that would have been, like, problem solved."

"It would have also have given rise to the problem of putting us over two hundred grand in your debt."

"Yeah, I guess there's that." Marino lifted his feet onto his desk again and drew a deep breath. "That's too bad, though. I hoped to recoup more of my losses from you guys."

"Please, don't act like that was some kind of huge loss for you."

He nodded. "Sure, but I do like having my pocket change. With that said, I would much rather have a favor from you than any money you could pay. I've discovered that being able to call on your and Taylor's skull-busting skills is far more profitable than nickel and diming you on what you need from me. If you're interested in that, I would be willing to let you use my jet free of charge."

There was a pause on her side of the line this time, and he knew she was considering it. She and Taylor likely hated owing him anything, but if he wanted them in his pocket, it would be for something far more useful than money.

"Fine, but you know me, so don't even think about asking me for something you know I won't give. Never forget that I'm capable of killing you simply for being stupid."

Marino smirked. "I wouldn't think of it. Has Taylor ever mentioned that your negotiation skills need some work, Ms. Banks?"

"All the time."

"And what did he do about it?"

"He picked me up and threw me on a bed the last time."

He raised his eyebrows. "Well...that's an interesting negotiation tactic. How effective was it?"

"You know Taylor. His skills lie in the art of non-verbal communication."

He rocked in his chair with a chuckle. "You're not wrong there. I take he is aware that you are calling me?"

"No," she admitted. "But I've got this and as long as we are clear on the deal, he should be fine. We are trying to make sure that a large quantity of very dangerous cocaine does not end up in your clientele's noses. I assumed you would be invested in making sure that didn't happen. I don't know, call it a hunch or something."

A fairly good hunch, he conceded silently, and the small smile that had lingered on his face began to fade slowly. He knew for a fact what kind of business McFadden and Banks handled.

"I guess this is what some might call a win-win," he said finally and tried to not sound too concerned. "You might have started with that in the first place."

"Why would I do that when this way is so much better?"

"Right. Well, I can see why Taylor got frustrated and proceeded with different tactics for dealing with you." Rod sighed deeply and shook his head. "I don't suppose he would agree to another cage match?"

Niki did not answer immediately. "I'd have to ask. Who the hell could you find who would be stupid enough to step into a cage with him?"

"For a million dollars? They would line up for the opportunity."

"So…you're saying too many people are stupid enough." She sounded exasperated. "I won't say it's off the table, but I might have to go without Taylor's attention at night if he were to do that again and right now, that option is off the table."

She was being open and frank about their personal life, and while he would normally be all for that, it felt a little uncomfortable. He knew Taylor would rip him several new ones if the giant were to find out that Niki was as honest as she was.

"Say no more," Marino decided finally. "I don't want to hear the details."

Niki laughed. "For a mafia guy, you sure do sound like you're blushing. I haven't made you uncomfortable, have I?"

"I merely wondered how many different bullet holes they'd find in me if Taylor discovers you're discussing your sex life with me. Even if the feeling is not mutual, I consider him to be a friend, and one would not want to imagine which positions his friends might use to go ten up and ten down with their women."

"Woman, singular," she corrected him. "He only has one woman he goes...uh, ten up and ten down with."

"Whatever. I still don't want to hear about it. Also, you don't have to worry about being put in an uncomfortable position over what I might ask in return for the favor. I do like having you folks around so I wouldn't come up with anything that would alienate you and threaten that relationship."

"You don't think the fact that your status as a mafia boss would be the kind of thing that would threaten any relationship?"

"I'm working on the assumption that since it hasn't already, it won't be a problem in the future. With that said, I'd be more than happy to keep helping you two as long as you continue to help me. I promise you'll come to stop seeing me as merely another mafia boss and more like an eccentric businessman."

"You do know that most of my job is to make sure that eccentric businessmen don't wreck the planet, right?"

"Well, something else, then. Something you'll be more than happy to do business with."

"Right. So, I'll go ahead and make sure Taylor is on board with this plan and Vickie will contact you with regard to what we'll need."

"I look forward to it, Ms. Banks."

He had a feeling that once again, the feeling was not mutual, but it was a start. If they realized he was more useful on their side than not, perhaps it would bring them on board with a little more. So far, it felt like pulling teeth with them.

Surprisingly, Rod realized that his mood was much

improved. Perhaps there was time for him to wander through his casino floor after all.

It wasn't the first time he was pinged on his location and that was a problem. Edward was sure that was what was happening, and the fact that someone attempted to zero in on him was a little worrying. All the evidence said it was merely automated tracking software like most cookies from when people went online to check their emails.

These were simple enough to block or fake as appropriate. But it constantly popped up and came from places that made him wonder if this wasn't more than simply an automated response.

"Someone's fucking with me," he decided, leaned closer to his screen, and sipped the intensely sweet energy drink he kept at hand on his desk. Tracking the probes only took him to the sites they purportedly came from—sites that he knew he had visited in the past.

"You're being paranoid," his partner told him and shook his head. "Put a virtual IP address on your shit and you'll be as right as rain."

"Right as rain," he whispered and glowered at the man. Of course, Trev wouldn't know he was already operating from a virtual IP address and it still hadn't resolved anything. Perhaps he merely needed an upgrade. "I'll go ahead and check to make sure these sites are automating the probes and it's not someone activating them. To be safe."

"Yeah, and when you're finished with that, maybe you

can go ahead and check the sale on aluminum foil hats they're selling at Walmart."

"Fuck you," Edward grumbled.

"So, all this is a game?"

Vickie nodded. "It's very simple. He'll get pings on his location every five minutes or so from the sites he's visiting, and these will go around his VPNs to give me live updates on where he is every five minutes or so."

"And he hasn't become suspicious of this tracking because?"

"Well, I'm randomizing it through the sites he's been visiting to make sure he needs to work through them to find me. If he gets past those, he'll find three avatars waiting for him in a series. If he can reach the third avatar, it will mean I've lost."

"And you truly think this is an appropriate use of your time?"

She looked into the camera. "Well, sure, why not? Most of the other work is already being processed and this is a good way to both keep me busy and practicing—as well as help with my self-esteem."

"Do you think him discovering that you're fucking about with him would be good for your self-esteem?"

"First of all, thanks for the vote of confidence." She paused to toss a few pretzels into her mouth. "Second, if I lose, it probably wouldn't be a huge boost to my confidence but at least then, I'll know where my technical skills need work and I'll know how to improve."

"Interesting. In the meantime, I will continue to translate all the different documents in Spanish to English so you'll be able to read them."

Vickie nodded. "Right, I guess that's something else I should probably improve about my life."

CHAPTER SIX

Taylor leaned back in his seat and tried not to rock in it. That was what he usually did when he was in a chair. It was a nervous habit and not something he wanted to do when in front of a group of people he tried to impress.

Well, not impress. They were all weapon geeks, the kind who would spend hours discussing the merits of hydraulic reloading systems in the different weaponized suits with overwhelming enthusiasm.

While he liked talking about the suits and had an engineering degree, he wished his ex-mechanic was there to pool his incredible practical technical expertise. Bobby would probably get a kick out of the group. They were discussing the selection of alterations he could recommend for some of their future designs, something his friend would have managed with ease.

It was a part of the deal, given that they handed their suits over to be tested for free. These certainly were top-of-the-line and cutting edge, but they expected recommendations from him nonetheless.

"Do you honestly think the overhead swing of the arms should be improved?" one of them asked. "Would that come up in a combat situation?"

Taylor shrugged. "Well, you feel it when you reach up for something, especially when you have to defend yourself against attacks from above. Not to the point that it would interfere much, however."

"But in the field, any edge you're missing could get you killed," the man agreed and focused on their designs. "We could attach the shoulder pauldron to a rotator that would lift it when you move your arm."

"Sure." He nodded. "Look, it wasn't a big deal. I'm used to being assigned anything the army has on hand and dealing with it, so whenever I need something fixed, I simply do it myself. You can see in the suit I returned to you guys that a small portion of the pauldron had been cut off to let me raise my arms fully without a problem."

"But when you lower them again, that section of your shoulder has reduced armor."

"Yes, it does, but—"

"No, no, we asked you for your input so we can put it to good use. The idea would eventually be to put a suit out there that would not require you to do any hardware changes."

"Okay, but every person out there will have their preferences for how their suits run, and you can't control that."

"Maybe not, but if we were able to account for those preferences, we would make it you to only had to adjust the software and the suit would do it automatically without needing to cut pieces out."

"Again, I'm...so sorry about that."

"Don't worry. The fact that you made that change was what inspired us to improve our work, and that's what this is all about."

Taylor nodded and shifted his gaze to the others in the group. He doubted that they were too happy with him cutting pieces from the suits they'd loaned to him but in the end, when it was a matter of survival, being able to move his arms was more essential than a little patch of armor on his shoulder.

If the enemy was close enough to damage his armor, things were already at a point where it wouldn't do much to protect him anyway.

But perhaps they were right. It did come down to preference and it was a change he generally made to most of the suits to enable his arms to move better. He had even gone so far as to replace the pieces when he was done and explain his alterations and why.

Which, he supposed, was what had prompted the meeting.

There was something to be said for their enthusiasm. He almost felt like he was being a downer by pointing out the flaws in their designs.

"Look, we appreciate the work you've put into this," the CEO said when he stepped beside him and patted his shoulder. "There's only so much we can test in the safety of our lab."

"I...there were only a couple of suggestions," Taylor answered. "Overall, that suit is years ahead of the competition so it feels like nitpicking."

"No, that was insightful, and it matched much of the data the onboard computers identified too."

Taylor nodded.

"We've already started working on a new special-design line, and we'll incorporate the changes you suggested," one of the other engineers told him. "We've given it the working title of Cryptid Assassin and it has the makings to take the market by storm."

All he could do was sigh softly.

"Don't...don't you like the name?"

He shook his head. "No, it's that I'll probably never live this kind of thing down."

Another of the engineers looked up from the papers in front of him. "We could always go with the name I suggested."

"What was that?" Taylor asked.

"It was the Ginger Giant and we shot it down," the CEO answered firmly.

"Yeah, a good call," he agreed. "Ginger Giant would be more...uh... Cryptid Assassin it is. But why not simply use my name?"

"It isn't nearly as cool."

They laughed and he couldn't help but join in. As much as he hated the name, it was rather catchy, especially when it was assigned to a suit designed for assassinating cryptids.

The meeting came to an end and he drew a deep breath as he loosened the tie around his neck and stepped out of the building.

He wasn't two steps away from the door when his phone rang. Reflexively, he looked around for any cameras before he answered.

"Hello there, Niki," he said before she could utter a word. "What, did you have Vickie keeping an eye out for when I was finished with my meeting?"

"Of course not," she replied. "I had Desk keep an eye out for you. Vickie is busy checking all those intelligence reports on Cryptid Tony Montana."

"Right. What's up?"

"Well, first, how did the meeting go?"

"They want to name their new special suit designs the Cryptid Assassin line."

"Oh, wait, they do? Because that's an awesome name for a suit that...you know..."

"Assassinates cryptids, yeah. I think I could probably charge them for the name or something, but I won't put too much thought into that now. So, why did you call?"

"Bungees is on the line and he wants to talk to you."

"Wait, you didn't tell him—"

"Nope, but that doesn't matter because he's already on the line."

Taylor rubbed his temples and let his fingers lower a little to run through his reddish beard. "Heya, Bobby."

"So, the Cryptid Assassin clothing line, huh?" the mechanic asked and laughed.

"Mech suit line, thank you."

"Tomayto, tomahto. Anyway, I've worked on the suits you needed repaired and I'm ready to return them with the improvements you suggested. There's nothing left to do on them, but I need you to remind me of the address you need them shipped to."

"Oh, I think we'll head to Vegas to pick them up in person," Niki interjected quickly.

"Oh...okay, that's... Well, that's nice. It's always nice to have you guys here. Can I ask why?"

"We plan to start our trip to South America in Vegas using one of Rod Marino's jets."

Taylor's eyes widened. It was odd to hear the news for the first time like this, especially with Bobby on the line. He assumed Niki made the very intentional decision to have this conversation on the phone with the other man listening to keep the discussion from turning to other subjects.

"We are?" he asked to break the silence that resulted.

"Yeah," she confirmed.

"Rod Marino?" Bobby asked. "The mafia boss, Rod Marino? What the hell does he have to do with this shit?"

"Well, we can't exactly fly commercial and I don't have access to the resources I did when I worked for the DOD, so we needed to find an alternate means to transport ourselves and our hardware to Peru. Marino seemed like an obvious choice, given his connections with the drug industry already as well as the fact that he knows a couple of high-rollers who would love the chance to support a spy and his lady."

"Wait, we're spies now?" Taylor asked and looked around to make sure he was still alone. He liked to be clued in to what they were doing but in this case, he wasn't quite sure what was happening.

"Yes. In order to get onto a private plane that will take us to a small airport on the way to South America, you sir, are a spy. With a significant amount of gear in his carryon."

"How much money will we make again?" he asked.

"Five hundred grand upfront, plus expenses, and we'll put an extra few dollar amounts on top of that once the work is finished."

"Oh...well. Taylor McFadden, Agent 009, at your service."

"That's England, Taylor." Niki sighed.

"McFadden is Scottish, and the first James Bond was Scottish, after all," he reminded her.

"But you're not Scottish. It's merely your name."

"For five hundred grand plus expenses, I'll be whatever they need me to be."

Bobby laughed. "Okay. Well, it'll be good to see you guys again and I know Tanya will be happy to see you too."

"I look forward to it," Taylor answered.

Working an office job provided a novel change of pace, although Constanza decided that the earlier years in his life were far more interesting. Learning how to manage people who tended to be hostile toward him had been valuable.

That was the way he described it to anyone who asked him how he had ended up being a diplomat. The topic of how he had tortured and killed enemies of the Colombian government naturally never entered the conversations.

Neither did the truth that he genuinely enjoyed the challenge of the work and was quite good at it. People tended to react oddly when he admitted it, although that usually had to do with the fact that they were bound and gagged when he talked about it.

That made the conversations a little one-sided, of course, but in the end, he didn't need their input. Sometimes, he needed to simply talk to people and let them know what he experienced. Most times, he needed those conversations to be one-sided.

Now, however, he was seated in an office in Peru that was paid for by the Colombian government. He'd come up with what said government considered a damn good reason for being there too, although the exact nature of it was a little unclear. He had a vague recollection that it was about looking into the pricing of the oil fields that they had recently discovered or something like that.

"Andrea?" he called and looked up from his laptop.

She stepped away from her desk and entered his office through the door that was slightly ajar.

"Yes, Sr. Constanza?"

"I think there was a bottle of Pisco someone gave to me when we arrived here. Do you know where I left it?"

"It was with your things. I can find it for you if you like."

"Yes, please."

She nodded, moved away from the doorway, and hurried to where he had left most of his belongings. He was technically supposed to unpack for a three-month stay in the area, but he had a feeling his presence there wouldn't be for that long.

Constanza leaned back in his seat. It was probably time for him to watch something to pass the time, but it would be much more enjoyable if he had something to drink. The local pisco was something of a revelation and something he had never thought of before. The drink was generally made into what was known as a Pisco Sour, and it was surprisingly better than his former favorite, the Whiskey Sour.

Before he could think of something to watch, his phone rang. Not the landline and the number where he could be reached in his official capacity, he realized, but his cell phone.

He reserved that for his side business. It made him considerably more money but it needed to remain a side business if he wanted to continue to enjoy the benefits that came from his main line of work.

Still, the people who had employed him in Bogota knew of his past and were merely interested in keeping all of it away from any UN Human Rights Council members. None of them particularly cared what he did with his free time as long as he covered it up well enough.

Constanza narrowed his eyes and shook his head. He was supposed to be an official diplomat for these hours, and people only called him during his official work times when something was wrong.

He hated it when something went wrong. It always meant more work for him.

"Fuck," he whispered, drew his phone out of his pocket, and pressed the button to answer the call before he put it on speakerphone. "Constanza speaking."

"Nicolas, I need to speak to you." A deep, gruff voice spoke in a familiar Bogota accent.

"Santi, it's good to hear from you. How are things at home? Are you keeping the sex industry financed?"

"I...yes, I suppose. There is some serious business we

need to discuss," Santiago said and his voice sounded more than a little grave. "I've been in contact with some of our people in Washington DC and it seems we have something of a situation developing that I thought you would want to be aware of."

"Hold on for a moment." He gestured for Andrea to enter with the bottle, as well as a glass with ice already in it. She was thoughtful like that. "Please close the door. No calls."

"Yes, Sr. Constanza."

"Your secretary?" Santiago asked when the door was closed.

"Yes."

"And something to take the edge off while there in Peru?"

"I…no, not really. She is engaged to one of my people here, so that would—"

"You know you could simply give her a taste of what it would be like to ride the boss and give her something to teach her boyfriend."

"That…is not a terrible idea, but not for now. You were telling me something about what's happening in the great United States?"

Santiago cleared his throat. "Yes, of course. I talked to a couple of my friends in the State Department and it seems you've made some waves—the kind that have people in their Pentagon interested. From what I understand, they've collected all the files they have on you and handed them to a freelance company, the kind that is… Well, they are what you might call a very specialized company."

Constanza narrowed his eyes as he poured some of the

pisco into his chilled glass. "Oh. Do you know what kind of specialized company they are or is that merely a sweeping term for all the freelancers the Pentagon hires to do their dirty work?"

"My source tells me they are the type of company they call in to deal with a very particular problem, one we see coming out of northern Africa more often these days. They are armed—and they arm themselves, which is interesting —and more than a little expensive. It turns out that a couple of other intelligence groups have combined their folders on you and sent the information to them."

"Huh." He grunted with some surprise as he'd never considered the fact that people had folders on him. It was a little flattering but it shouldn't have surprised him. His past was such that it would raise eyebrows and he knew eyes watched him whenever he traveled outside of Colombia. Still, he'd never imagined that they considered him worth more than a few scribbled notes.

"So, what do you think you want to do?"

"What can I do? I know nothing about these people."

"We know they deal in situations coming out of the Zoo. You aren't involved in anything like that, are you?"

"Of course not," Constanza lied smoothly. "You know I wouldn't put my dick in that beehive. They are probably simply branching out and using their skills to make a little money on the side. Do you think you would be able to learn more about this company?"

Santiago sighed. "Yes, of course, but it won't be cheap."

"Put it on my bill. You know I'm good for the money."

"And what about the time and effort I'm putting into this? I don't work for free, you know."

"You can send your invoice for consulting to my firm in Bogota. They'll pay you immediately, both for the warning and the work afterward. Of course, I do trust you to not fuck me over on the price."

"Of course. Because you've never overcharged me when I needed your help."

The diplomat laughed. "Well, all right, but keep your fucking reasonable."

"Until we meet again, my friend."

"Until then. Arrange for whoever you think can handle it to call me as quickly as possible. I don't need anything hanging over me while we're in the middle of solidifying our business dealings here."

"Consider it done."

The man hung up, and Constanza narrowed his eyes and stared at his phone until the screen turned off from lack of activity. He didn't feel any real alarm, despite the seriousness of the situation. This type of action happened in his business and a part of him always expected it. The Americans liked to send their assassins, but he had never entertained the possibility that they might send a specialized team.

It was also a matter of some concern that they already knew he was dealing with people in the Zoo. He expected to have at least a couple more months before the various agencies were any the wiser. The dealers were secretive, hard to find, and charged through the roof for their product. Of course, it was still cheaper than what he could buy on the regular market and came with many more strings attached.

He shook his head and sipped the glass of chilled pisco,

then breathed deeply as he stared at the glass.

"Fucking hell, I need to find a dealer for this," he whispered and inspected the bottle. Maybe he would have time to find one of the wineries that made it and arrange for them to send him their best bottles on a regular basis.

Only a few minutes later, his phone rang again and this time, an unknown number appeared on the caller ID. He could only assume it was Santiago's man.

"Hello?"

"This is Constanza, yes? Santiago said you had a problem for me to solve."

The diplomat nodded. He had many bad things to say about Santiago, but the man was prompt when he knew he was getting paid.

"Yes, I require intelligence and related services. Someone is coming to Peru who intends to interfere with my business. I need them stopped before they can start that operation."

A long moment of silence followed before the man spoke again.

"I will need the details of these people."

"Santiago will gather the information and you can get it from him. I will keep myself removed from this as much as possible so you will also be paid through him."

"Of course."

"Your orders are to find them and kill them. I will accept no other alternative, do you understand?"

"Of course."

"Good. I look forward to you informing me of the completion of your task. Goodbye."

He hung up and shook his head. Santiago had connections across the continent, the kind who knew how to deal with delicate matters. It wasn't for nothing that the man was one of the richest men in Colombia—not officially, of course, but who worried about that?

He took another sip of the drink and enjoyed the taste of it on his tongue for a few seconds before he swallowed.

"Now," he whispered as the alcohol began to relax him, "to find a good movie."

It was fun to watch Eddie start to realize someone was toying with him. Vickie hadn't been all that subtle about it, of course. While she had hidden her involvement, the sheer number of pings would eventually alert him.

The fact that it had taken him almost twelve hours to see it was a sign that things would probably go well.

Not that she could let her guard drop, not for a second. All Eddie would do if he found out she was bugging him would be to send her three or four dozen pizzas. Ham and pineapple, most likely. But in the end, this was all to prove that she was better than him. There was nothing more to it.

"Vickie? What are you doing here? And why is everything dark?"

She looked around and noticed that the sun had already started to set and none of the lights in the warehouse were on. Everything was dark. Oddly, seeing Taylor silhouetted against her doorframe merely reinforced how big he was.

Maybe because he filled the whole damn door.

"Sorry," she shouted and flicked a couple of lights on.

"I'm...uh, engrossed with...uh, you know...intelligence reports. They sent me, like, a hundred of those."

"Well, don't overwork yourself," he told her and turned a few more lights on as he entered fully. "We need you sharp and on point, so remember to take care of yourself and...you know, shit like that."

The hacker tilted her head and grinned. "Shit like that?"

"Come on, I'm not great at this whole...thing."

"Being a parent to a woman in her early twenties? Yeah, I don't think they write manuals for that shit."

He shrugged and she stood quickly, walked to him, and wrapped her arms around him.

Or tried, rather. His chest felt like a pair of rocks and was a little too wide for her to get her arms around.

"Be safe, you big lug," she grumbled as he hugged her awkwardly in return.

"I'm always safe."

"Says the guy who charges head-first into a horde of alien monsters for a living."

"Fair enough, but the fact that I'm the one still standing should say something about how safe it is. For me, anyway."

"Yeah, whatever. This time, you'll be dealing with Marino. And drug dealers."

"Come on. After years of dealing with alien monsters, do you truly think narcos will pose that much of a risk?"

"Don't jinx yourself," Vickie protested and took a step back. "Seriously, you know those guys are fucking insane. I've read up on it lately and it's like a fucking war zone down there, so I mean it. I will be pissed if you come back here missing a hand or something."

Niki carried some luggage into the office and placed a makeup case on a nearby table.

"It looks like we're ready," she announced and looked around. "I bought us tickets to Vegas, so we should get going."

She paused and realized that both of them were staring at her.

"What?"

"Is that a makeup case?" Taylor asked.

"I think it is," Vickie commented. "Are you feeling okay? Should we give you a battery of tests before you'll be allowed on a plane?"

"Don't be dicks," she snapped and yanked the case open to reveal a collection of small arms.

"Oh." He grunted, his eyebrow raised.

"Yeah, that makes more sense," the hacker admitted. "I can't believe I didn't see that."

"What? I could have a case full of makeup like this." Niki growled. "Come on, guys. It's not like I don't take care of myself or anything. I may not be a girly girl but I look good while kicking significant numbers of ass."

"Oh, absolutely," he agreed, although Vickie wasn't sure if he was being sarcastic or not.

"Fuck you guys. Come on, Taylor. We don't want to be late for the plane."

She slipped out of the room and the hacker giggled.

"You are not a subtle man, Taylor."

"Yeah, well, I make up for it in other ways."

"Is that…should I be gagging?"

"Maybe a little." Taylor moved closer to hug her again.

"Be good, and you be safe too. Don't think I don't know that you can get into all kinds of trouble."

"Sure, but the worst I'll face are orders of terrible pizza."

"What?"

She shook her head. "Nothing. Never mind. Have a nice flight."

CHAPTER SEVEN

"Vickie?"

She looked up from the screen of her phone. "Yeah?"

"What are you doing?" Desk asked.

"I'm checking Eddie's Twitter feed."

The AI took a moment to reply. "That seems...unhealthy."

"I'm not stalking him if that's what you're thinking."

"That's not what I was thinking."

"Sure, whatever." She sighed. "It's only...he's something of a Twitter junkie, so my thought was that he'd talk about someone bothering him to his followers. Sure enough, he's complaining but he thinks one of his fans is punking him. And I'm not paraphrasing. That is the term he's using. The dude is seriously living in the nineties, and not in a hot way."

"Is there a hot way to live in the nineties?"

Vickie shrugged. "I don't know. The whole grunge life-style has always been attractive to me and I have a huge crush on Kurt Cobain."

"You know he's dead, right?"

"So? James Dean's dead too and I crush hard on him. Don't judge."

"I am not judging, merely questioning the appeal. I also wonder if you realize that a few alerts have appeared on your computer."

The hacker turned sharply and frowned at a handful of alerts displayed on her screen. Her first thought was that Eddie was making a move against her, but there was no sign that the signal came from him at all.

"Shit." She hissed her irritation and rolled her office chair closer to the computer.

"I'll pick up the defense," Desk announced as she called up the infiltration sources.

"I'll be offense," Vickie whispered, moved her cursor across the screen, and pulled up a handful of her pre-prepared offensive programs to hitch them onto the streams currently directed at them.

It was difficult to tell where the invasion was coming from. The usual tracing avenues were being aggressively closed against her, which meant she would need to be a little creative. She had a couple of surprises already programmed for that too.

"It would appear that whoever this is, they are trying to track us," Desk announced.

"Do you have any idea why? Did I leave any of my inquiries open for someone to trace?"

"I cannot tell," the AI replied, and that in itself was enough to worry the young hacker.

"How close are they to finding our physical address?"

"It's hard to say, but soon."

She nodded, focused on a few status updates running across her screen, and counted them down under her breath before she finally turned to her phone. She had it all set up and liked to call it the nuclear option, although there was nothing nuclear about it, of course.

At least, not as much as her turning her computers off and on again was a nuclear option, although this was meant for their modem connections instead. Cutting off all lines of approach would keep anyone from connecting with their physical address, which would leave them only with a couple of addresses in the Caribbean.

"Okay, I pulled the plug on their approach vectors," Vickie said, folded her arms, and grinned. "It's not the kind of victory I'd hoped for but in the end, not getting caught is probably best result. Since all the probes I sent out have already left my system, it's best to simply close all the doors."

"If that is the case, how am I still connected to your system?"

"I use a couple of them for stuff that is exclusively legal and have made sure that nothing connects to our illegal enterprises in case we need plausible deniability at any point. I drop the N-bomb and remove all avenues people might use to find us, but not back to the Dark Ages. I'm kind of proud that I thought of that shit."

"I see. And how do you continue to connect to your illegal ventures?"

"I merely need to reprogram those modems and they'll appear as brand new connections with nothing to link them to us again. Like it never happened."

"Except that the probes you sent out are returning."

"They're programmed to return to external servers that I'll access at a later date once everything is nice and safe again. You have to know that you won't usually be able to fight an infiltration like that, so having someone stall while I send the probes out was probably the best thing we could do. I would usually have dropped the N-bomb and called it a day but I would have been lucky if I didn't let them have any information. Speaking of them, do we know who the fuck they are?"

"Not as yet, but I collected data on the source of the infiltration and I will reverse-engineer the code, which should provide some clue as to the location of origin."

"That's nice work."

"And quick thinking on your part. For a human."

Vickie shrugged. "I'll take it."

"We could have been on a plane," Niki complained. "I had to fight for a refund on the fucking tickets thanks to you."

Taylor merely nodded and chose not remind her that she knew about his phobia. It wasn't the first time she would make the argument and he doubted it would be the last. And yes, they could have traveled across the country in a plane since they weren't carrying their suits and were en route to pick them up. They didn't need to ferry anything.

"You know what? No," she continued, leaned back in her seat, and glared at him. "We would have landed by now and we would already be settling into our room. That's what we're missing out on with your insistence on doing this road trip."

He already knew that nothing he could say would get her out of the bad mood she was in. It wasn't that she was intentionally berating him, and she knew he chose to drive whenever he could because of a certain phobia of careening high above the earth in a small metal tube.

She would apologize for it later, and he would find something to bitch about.

"It's better to have Liz with us whenever we can," he answered mildly and patted the dashboard. "You know you'll want to have her and not need her than the other way around."

"Yeah, I know. Still, though."

"And you also know you could have simply caught the plane yourself and I would have driven to meet you in Vegas, right?"

Niki darted him a sidelong look. "Did you think I would leave you alone on your road trip? Is that how bad a girlfriend you think I am? No, I'll stay at your side."

"And complain every second of it, even though you love road trips."

"You know it."

She tried to maintain her stern face but the battle against a grin was quickly lost and she narrowed her eyes at him.

"You hate the fact that I can get you into such a good mood so quickly, don't you?"

"Sure," she responded unapologetically, "but it's also something I adore about you, so there's give and take with it. Speaking of give and take, we're out of snacks and there's a stop coming up at the next exit. I suggest you take it."

"Do you honestly expect me to believe that your bad mood is based on low blood sugar?" Taylor asked.

"Yep."

"And it'll be solved with snacks?"

"You know it."

"Done deal."

He took control of Liz away from the AI he'd set to do the driving and veered toward the next exit that would take them to the truck stop a short distance ahead. It wouldn't carry any gourmet food, but that wasn't what was expected on road trips.

Yet another point in favor of taking a first-class flight to Vegas, he realized, but he didn't hear her complaining. There was a certain guilty pleasure in comfort food and she knew it.

Taylor drew Liz to a halt near one of the gas pumps and let the automatic breaks kick in. "You fill her up and I'll choose up the snacks."

"What? Why am I stuck with filling her up?"

"Because it'll be your turn to drive for the next stretch and I need to take a leak."

She couldn't argue with that, not successfully anyway, and Niki sighed as she stepped out. The air was supposed to be fresh when they were out in the country, but in this case, it was not. She could smell the gasoline and engine grease all around her. It wasn't that unfamiliar, though, and she shook her head as she dragged her gaze away from watching Taylor walk to the convenience store and focused instead on getting the pump going.

Liz was a thirsty beast and she had a tank to match, which meant they would be around for a while as she filled.

The thunderous sound of an overly enthusiastic boom box shattered the relative silence and she rolled her eyes. Someone wanted their bass to be heard. She scowled as the car pulled up near the gas pumps beside her.

The five occupants clambered out of the vehicle immediately but kept the music blaring at top volume. There were four guys and only one girl, who was draped around the driver of the eyesore of a car. Niki resisted a grin as she studied the odd underglow and a silver-and-blue paint job that was covered by a hideous red-and-yellow decal possibly meant to portray a tiger.

She chose not to wonder what the group was trying to do. They were all young—in their early twenties at the oldest—and driving what she could only assume was someone else's car.

It would be best, she decided, to simply turn her back and keep her eye on the pump as the dollar sign crept into the double figures.

"And still climbing," she whispered and shook her head. There were many ways to describe it, but all she could think of was that Liz was one thirsty gal.

"Hey, honey! Keep that spin moving. We want to see both sides of you!"

Niki knew the guy wasn't talking to her. It simply wasn't possible.

"Hey! You with the big fucking truck!"

Not fucking possible, she reassured herself.

"Yeah—you, gorgeous. Give us a twirl. I promise we'll make it worth your while."

She turned to see who the culprit was. The guy talking to her was the driver, who still had the girl on his arm. She was laughing like it was a joke, but the others in the group soon joined her.

"What's the matter, baby?" another asked and moved in a little closer. "Are you afraid you'll fall in love?"

Niki raised her right eyebrow. "With Mr. Baggy Pants Hanging Down to His Knees and Cheap Chain? If there was ever a poster child for a lady-boner killer, you would be it, kid."

"Come on. He paid you a compliment. There's no need to be a bitch about it," the driver snapped and began to approach her as well. "Be nice and say thank you."

"Okay, you need to back off," Niki warned him as Taylor emerged from the convenience store with a couple of bags. They both looked heavy but he carried them with one hand while he checked his phone with the other, completely unaware that anything was happening.

"Come on. Say you're sorry and thank you for the compliment," the driver continued, also oblivious to the human mountain approaching him. "We're nice people and if you let us, we can have all kinds of fun together."

"I don't consider bleeding from my eyes and ears to be a fun time, so why don't you head to that eyesore of a car and let it do its job to hide you with those illegal-ass tinted windows."

The young man disentangled himself from his girl-friend and moved closer. He stopped a few feet away from her and the Drakkar Noir smell-alike wafted over her like a cloud.

"Now you're being mean, girl," he remonstrated in what she was sure he intended to be an intimidating tone of voice. It emerged a little too raspy, however, and was undermined even further when he traced his fingers over his frosted tips and licked his soul patch. "Come on, let us show you a good time—and make it sweet. You don't want me pissed. You want me to treat you nicely, right?"

Taylor noticed what was happening, tucked his phone in his pocket, and increased his stride.

Not that she needed his help to deal with the delinquent.

"I want you to back off before I develop an allergy to what I can only guess came out of an Axe spray bottle you bought in bulk," Niki snarked, her tone a little cutting.

"Hey, back the fuck off," Taylor added and unlike the man-child, he managed to make it sound like a threat and not a whine.

Unfortunately, its loaded warning seemed to have no effect and the idiot turned to look at the larger man. He did, however, take a step back when he realized that looking directly forward meant he was staring at a broad expanse of chest.

"You back off, asshole." The youth narrowed his eyes, fixed his glare on the interloper, and pulled his shirt up to reveal a pistol tucked into his jeans. "Fuck off while I'm trying to get through to this bitch."

Niki held her breath as Taylor's face went from an intentionally menacing scowl into the slack expression she came to recognize as the look that came to his face when he intended to deliver a beating.

"And that explains the bravado," she announced as she pushed between them. The last thing she needed was to help the man bury five bodies.

"What—"

Before the kid could finish whatever idiotic question he had on his mind, she snatched the pistol holstered so precariously inside his pants and shoved it down until he could feel the barrel of the .38 revolver pressed into his groin.

"Did you threaten my man?" she demanded, grasped him by the frosted tips, and made sure he looked her in the eye. "Seriously?"

"Bitch, you let him go!"

The woman spoke this time and she rushed to where Niki was scaring the piss out of the cretin in front of her. Quite literally, she realized after a moment.

Before she had time to think about how she could avoid a catfight with the skinny blonde, a solid smack made her turn quickly. Taylor had backhanded the woman half his size and the girl spun in place and fell awkwardly.

"Did you hit a girl?" one of the other douchebags shouted.

"Yeah, it was either he hit her or I kill her, and by the looks of it, he took the chivalrous route." Niki cocked the hammer of the pistol loudly to remind them that she was about five pounds of trigger-pull away from blowing the dick with the soul patch's balls off. "You did only hit her right? She's not dead? Not that I care, to be honest, but it's a shit load of paperwork."

Taylor shook his head and it was confirmed when the girl groaned and half-pushed from the ground before she sagged again.

"Nope," he answered. "I hate the paperwork too. But no one goes after my partner and I don't discriminate on gender. Equal rights in all things."

Niki pulled the pistol out and checked it to confirm that the weapon was, in fact, loaded.

"Who the fuck puts a loaded gun in their pants?" she asked and shook her head before she turned to Taylor. "I won't take the trash out. That's a hard no. I can't stand the smell."

"Maybe," the guy with the soiled pants said cautiously and raised his hands. "Uh...maybe we could get our girl and leave the two of you alone with your...uh, discussion? I'd hate to know my life was on the line if he pisses you off."

Niki looked at Taylor and nodded. "Good point. Fuck off and next time, don't piss the fed off, hmm?"

"Can I have my gun back?"

She leveled the pistol at him. "What did I fucking say to you?"

That was all the answer he needed and he sprinted to the car and scrambled into it. The task to pick the poor girl up and take her to the vehicle fell to the other three youths.

"Don't piss the Fed off?" her partner asked and raised an eyebrow as he opened one of the truck doors and placed the bags of snacks and drinks inside.

Niki smirked and removed the nozzle from the tank. "What's a little white lie amongst us government consultants?"

Taylor shrugged and climbed into the passenger seat as

Niki checked that she had her card before she joined him and started Liz.

"You know you made the kid piss his pants, right?"

"And now he'll think twice before harassing random women."

"And keeping his gun?"

She glanced at it and handed it to him. "You never know when you'll need a gun that's not in your name. And I doubt they'll report it to the police."

"What makes you think that?"

"Didn't you see the red in their eyes? They're high. The chances are this gun is illegal too."

"And if we're caught with an illegal gun in our possession?"

"At worst, you'll have to pay a fine, but I doubt it'll happen."

She drove out of the gas station and noted that the other car still hadn't moved from where it was parked.

"The way you handled the guy like that...it was hot," Taylor said, opened a can of soda, and handed it to her.

"I saw the look on your face and knew you intended to pick him up and break his back over your knee," she answered. "All I did was save the idiot's life."

"And emasculated him at the same time. Color me impressed."

"Look, you have to give me something."

"I don't know what you want from me," Raul replied and shook his head. "I'm not even involved in that operation. The Constanza files are restricted to the people in the State Department who have contact with him. There's a whole investigation in progress, so everything is severely restricted."

Stefano sighed over the line. "Can you at least tell me the name of the people who are conducting the investigation? That would give me something to start with."

"They're keeping those names under wraps too. They think they're in some kind of danger or something."

"Look, it's either them or me," he replied. "We don't even know what they plan to do. I know this is the favor he called in and no one ever refuses. Not now and not ever."

"You could always go into protection."

Raul could almost feel the silence on the other side of the call. It was uncomfortable, but he wasn't sure if he wanted to break it until finally, he felt he had no choice.

"Right, never mind that suggestion. But...okay, give me thirty minutes and I'll see what I can dig up."

"Thank you, Raul. I owe you one on this."

"Yeah, well, thank me by not being so stupid, Stefano. Next time, I will leave your ass high and dry and hanging in the wind."

"My mama did not raise a total fool."

"Merely an occasional fool?"

The man laughed. "Yes, merely an occasional fool."

It was a good day, Marino decided, one in which he had time to himself again.

Most of the conventions enjoyed their time and didn't

need him to be on the floor, and the pit bosses managed most of the business. For the first time in what felt like forever, he had no meetings scheduled for the day.

A couple of friends wanted to have lunch followed by a golf game for the afternoon. It sounded like an interesting possibility, although he hadn't committed to anything but the lunch so far.

His phone buzzed and he tapped the button.

"Yes?"

"Mr. Marino, Sheriff Joe Lombard is on the line for you," his secretary replied.

"Oh, he must be looking for some of those tickets for the show we're having next week. Put him through."

"One moment, please."

Rod smiled and leaned back in his seat as he was connected with the sheriff. "Joe, great to hear from you. I have some tickets for you next week for the Cirque du Soleil. You can bring the wife and the kids to see the show and then I can leave you a poker table for the other deputies."

"Well, I appreciate that, Rod, you know that," the sheriff replied. "I always look forward to patronizing your casino, but I'm afraid I need to call you on some...unofficial business."

That was unexpected but not entirely unpleasant. Having the sheriff in his pocket for a favor was always worth it, and it sounded like this was leading to exactly that.

"Oh, of course. What do you need?"

"There's a new group in town we're not familiar with. A couple of my undercover teams tagged them, and they appear to be the long kind of trouble. They're coming in heavily armed and looking for a big gun battle. I'm calling to see if you have anything on your side you can use to soften them up before we have to go in. I know you don't like any competition in town as much as we don't like any violent and well-armed independents."

Marino checked to make sure the call was coming from a line that was not associated with the sheriff's office and that it was being scrambled from his side too. His secretary had thought to do that already.

He needed to get her a gift basket. Or a bottle of wine. Or maybe a gift basket with wine.

"I'm not sure what you expect me to do to soften them up. I suppose I could make sure they know to not get involved in any violence in my part of town, but that simply means it'll happen somewhere else. We need to control where it happens to give your boys an advantage."

"I had thought along those lines, yes. Pull them into a kind of kill zone and have someone make them shoot first so there's no problem when my boys take care of the rest."

He nodded slowly and tapped his fingers on the desk as he thought through the possibilities. "You know, I think I have the perfect people for this. I have a team that could act as a spearhead to the operation—a group that can take the heat and eliminate them with you coming in behind them."

"Who are these people? Why haven't I heard of them already?"

"The chances are you have heard of them but under a different name—or maybe in different circumstances. McFadden and Banks is what they call themselves and they're contractors now. They used to work for various government agencies, including the DOD at one point. I think they still do but again, as freelance contractors. They're expensive, sure, but—"

"You know I don't have much of a budget, Rod."

"I'll put the funds in for the breakages, Joe. All you need to do is fund the bonus."

The man sighed, and Rod could picture him rubbing his temples as he considered the possibility. "Jesus Christ, how much breakage do you expect here? Do they have a heavy crew or something?"

"Not heavy in numbers since there are only two of them, but their equipment can run repair bills up to a quarter-million, easy."

"What? Is their shit made of gold?"

"It might as well be given how closely the military guards their tech." Marino kicked his feet onto the desk as he watched a cute weather girl speak on his muted television. "Anyway, I have to make a call on this now for it to work. We only have a short window for when they'll be in Vegas, and if we miss it, I doubt I'll be able to get them on board until they return. We don't know what your newcomers will attempt in the meantime."

The sheriff sighed again. Marino knew he was a decent guy overall—very business-friendly—and he would do the right thing as long as he was given the right reasons for it.

"Okay, fine," Joe replied finally. "Let's do it. Make the call."

CHAPTER EIGHT

With the long drive behind them, Niki could fully appreciate what Vegas looked like as they drew closer to the city. A few miles out, with a hint of elevation that let them look as far as the Strip, it was a breathtaking sight.

So much civilization seemed to have sprung out of nowhere and was almost contradictory in the wide swath of desert around it. The glow of its myriad lights illuminated everything as night began to fall. They had alternated between driving and resting, and they made good time as they had hardly needed to stop at all as they headed across the country.

She decided he'd heard enough about how they could already have been in Vegas if they had taken the plane. It was a little unfair for her to push him into something he so vehemently didn't want to do, merely because it was preferable to her. Besides, Liz was easily one of the most comfortable trucks she had ever been in. There was more than enough space to sleep and eat in and even a nice little nook in the back if she wanted to stretch her legs and have a nap on a proper bed.

Taylor had clearly built the vehicle with the intention of not having to fly anywhere in the country ever again. That had been before she stepped into his life and involved him in killing monsters all around the country—and all around the world as it turned out—so he had probably expected to only need to make a couple of trips here or there.

As things stood, Liz held up fairly well under the constant use and the fact that they only needed someone to half-pay attention while they traveled across the AI-controlled highways only made her that much more useful.

Niki was forced out of her reverie by a low buzzing and she looked around in surprise. Taylor's phone, which was connected to the car's speakers, was vibrating.

He pressed a button on the steering wheel. "Desk, is that you?"

"How did you know?"

"Because you're one of the few able to connect to Liz while she's on the road—you and Vickie. Is everything all right with you guys?"

"We had a small delay on the intel that was sent but aside from that, I can assure you with a great deal of certainty that all is well on our end. With that said, I have a call waiting for you from one Rod Marino. Should I put him through or tell him to shove his phone so far up his ass he'll be able to dial your number with his tongue?"

Taylor looked at Niki and she shrugged. They both knew they had to be at least on speaking terms with the man while they still needed his support for their trip to South America. While they could possibly have called on their connections in the DOD too, she knew it would probably end up costing them much more in the long run.

"Put him through," he said finally with a scowl.

She could agree with that sentiment, at least.

"Putting him through."

They both braced themselves for the conversation, and he grasped the steering wheel a little tighter to maintain his composure.

"Hello again, Marino," he said once the call was connected. "I didn't expect to hear from you quite so soon. I thought you had a big fight you wanted to arrange and it would take you a little while to raise enough money for the people involved to consider it."

"It's nice to speak to you again as well, Taylor," the mob boss replied with a chuckle. "As much as I would love to pull you all in for another big heavyweight title fight— maybe with some rules and approval from the Nevada Gaming Commission—that which would get you into a very profitable career as a professional fighter... But I digress because unfortunately, the people I need you to crush with your impressive skills and ability to inflict violence will be the kind of people who won't abide by any rules. They'll probably bring firearms with them too."

"Oh, so the non-televised kind of fighting?"

"Well, let's not be hasty about that, but you don't need to worry about it. All you need to think about is the fact that these people are, from what I've heard about them, the kind of professional criminals who are only deployed when they will be used. They're well-funded, well-armed, and have something of a record, although not in Nevada. It's something to consider when dealing with them, I suppose, as well as the fact that this is me calling in my favor."

Niki narrowed her eyes. "Wait, so how exactly do you plan to profit from this whole business?"

"That's up to me, isn't it? But if we're being honest, having an outside influence in my city would be detrimental to my overall profit margin so in the end, you'd save me money rather than make me money, which amounts to more or less the same thing, I think. It's a cleanup opportunity, McFadden. You two will work with the cops, and I'll fund any ammo and damage costs while the local sheriff officially funds your fee."

That made sense to Niki, but she chose not to say anything. She had gotten them into this situation after all.

"Why us?" Taylor asked.

"Well, I have an in with the local sheriff department, and when they came to me for help to deal with these assholes, your names popped into my mind. They already know about you and they would be more than happy for the backup. Or, in this case, I guess we know you wouldn't be happy unless you were tearing shit up on the front line."

"I guess—whatever." He chuckled and decided to let it go. "Send us all the information. We'll be there."

"I'm very glad to hear that, Taylor," Marino replied. "I know I shouldn't read too much into this, but it's always a pleasure to work with the two of you. Expect the details soon."

"And to be clear," Niki interjected, "with this done, we will have repaid you for the loan of your plane to us to get us into Peru and back to the States."

"You make it sound so transactional," the man protested.

"That's because it is."

"Very well. In helping me with this, you will no longer owe me a favor for letting you use my jet to ferry you to and from Peru. Happy?"

"It sounds good to me," she replied. "Talk to you when it's done."

Taylor nodded, pressed the button to end the call, and leaned back in his seat.

"I had truly hoped to avoid having to deal with him again," he admitted after the silence had gone on for a little too long.

"Yeah, I know the feeling." Niki shivered. "It brings on the sick kind of feeling you get right before you throw up."

"But at least, in this case, we won't work only for him. He'll pay for some of it but we'll work with the police for the rest. That's what he said, anyway."

"Corrupt cops."

"We don't know that."

"Marino has connections with them. They called him to deal with the problem of violent offenders who have invited themselves to the city. That means they've called on him to deal with situations in the past, which in turn means they're on the take somehow."

Taylor shrugged. "Okay, do you think we shouldn't do it?"

"No." She took a sip of the drink in her cupholder before she continued. "With that said and while I might hate the fuckers, doing a good deed for the police works for me."

They both hated it, but if it would pay their way to Peru, it sounded like a bargain well struck. Marino wouldn't always let them off the hook so easily.

"I'll need to call Bobby." He sighed as he imagined the response from his friend. "We need suits to be ready for a gunfight in an urban environment."

"We'll probably have to use a couple of heavies," Niki suggested. "If they'll use guns with armor-piercing rounds, we might find we need far more firepower and serious armor to prevent them from drilling us full of holes."

He nodded and punched Bobby's number into his phone.

"Hey, man!" Bungees shouted when he picked up. "Will you arrive soon?"

"We're still a couple of hours out of Vegas," he replied. "But there's been a small hiccup."

"Is Liz okay?"

"Yeah. Yeah, she's fine."

"I'm fine too, by the way," Niki called.

"Right," Bobby responded with a chuckle. "So, what is the issue? Will you guys stop at a motel to bump uglies?"

"That's none of your business, Bungees," Niki snapped. "But no, we will not because as Taylor said, there's been a hiccup."

"Why don't I get to the hiccup in question?" Taylor asked. "You remember how we had a deal with Marino for him to let us use his jet to travel the world?"

"Sure. It's not one of your best ideas."

"And not one of our worst either," she reminded him.

"True."

Taylor darted her a glare before he continued. "Anyway,

as it turns out, Marino has something in mind for how we can pay him back while we're here in Vegas."

"Does he have you lined up for another heavyweight fight?" Bobby asked. "Is it with a bear this time? I would pay good money to watch Taylor wrestle a grizzly bear."

"First, I'm big and strong but not enough to tackle a six-hundred-pound grizzly," he stated firmly. "Second, he has an emergency he would like us to solve for him. Some people from out of town have arrived with an arsenal of guns and an attitude, and he wants us to help the police to handle them."

"The police, huh?" The other man sounded pensive and they could hear tools being moved around. "So, it sounds like our good friend Marino has connections in the sheriff's department. That sucks. I hoped the cops were clean in this city."

"Did you?"

"I can hope. So, if you guys plan to deal with a group of mobsters in Vegas, I assume you won't do it using the weapons and body armor provided by the local SWAT teams, right?"

"No indeed," Taylor confirmed vehemently.

"And since these guys will be equipped with cop-killers, you'll need a few extra layers of armor to face them."

"I—wait. Cop-killers?"

"Bullets designed to penetrate the body armor used by police officers. Did you simply never watch buddy cop movies when you were growing up?"

Taylor narrowed his eyes. "You know, Vickie asks me the same thing."

"Anyway, I have a couple of the heavier suits on harness

here so if you want to, swing past the shop and have a look at what you can use. There will be some fees payable for you to use them, of course, plus the ammo you'll need. I am running a business here."

"We are aware of that fact," he replied. "And don't give us the friends and family discount either. Marino will pay for weapons, armor, and ammo, so you can put in full price for it all. You do have a business to run there, right?"

Bobby laughed. "So, let me get this right. You're doing this as a favor to him and you're still charging him for it?"

"Honestly, the favor is that we'll work for him," Niki interjected. "Anything beyond that and we'll have to make some money on it."

"Well, in that case, I'll tell Tanya to get started on the paperwork. Come over when you can and we can look at the suits I have in stock. You can choose what you want to use for the job."

"Will do. See you soon, Bobby." He pressed the button to end the call and looked at Niki, who had brought her legs up to curl against her chest. "Do you have anything you want to say?"

She shook her head. "Not really. I know we'll work with the cops on this so we're about as officially sanctioned—and protected—as we'll ever be. At the same time, I keep reminding myself that I made the deal with him to get us to South America, so I can't complain that he's called in the favor we agreed to. Still, I always get the feeling we'll end up in prison when we do a job for Marino, while he gets to walk away from it scot-free. The cops are his friends, not ours."

"That's always a possibility," Taylor conceded and his

face twisted as though he didn't want to think about the possibility. "But in the end, we'll have direct contact with these cops and can judge for ourselves if the need is legit or not. If we feel it isn't, we pull out and leave them to it. Besides, Marino knows we won't go quietly if things go pear-shaped and the cops try to slap cuffs on us and make us the scapegoats. He also knows he'll be the one we target next. We can only hope that's enough of a deterrent to prevent him from fucking us over."

"Yeah, because these mafia guys are known for making good judgment calls." She leaned back in her seat and stretched. "I'm only saying we need to be prepared for the possibility that someone might decide we're expendable."

"Believe me, eyes in the back of my head."

Niki grunted but didn't sound reassured. He didn't know if there was anything he could tell her to convince her that he was being careful, but there was no need to push her on it.

They would have to find out what was waiting and wing it if any curveballs were thrown at them.

Not much had changed in the strip mall, although a few sections were being expanded. Much of the space was being repurposed by the looks of it. He knew there was time for Bobby to decide what he wanted to do with the building. It was his at this point, more or less, and it was a waste to simply let sections he didn't need stand empty. Taylor had a couple of ideas of how to use the space and some had even come to fruition, but it was mostly put aside as fire after fire popped up that needed to be put out.

"I kind of miss this place already," he muttered as they pulled around to the back where the entrance of the suit shop was situated. Those inside would already know they were there and sure enough, the gate was already rolling up when they drew up to it. It made their approach that much easier and he drove in and parked in the place where Liz had always stood before. It was like Bobby had kept it open—or, more likely, had cleared it when he heard they were coming in to see him.

Either way, it felt like coming home.

Niki snickered.

"What?" he asked and looked at her.

"I can see you being all nostalgic about this place when it hasn't even been three months since we left."

"Yes, but...well, I put considerable effort into the strip mall. It might not mean much to you, but it was as close to a home as I've ever had since I left my parents' house. There will always be a special place in my heart for this ugly-ass building."

"Oh, wow." She almost looked like she felt bad for mocking him, and while he hadn't lied about anything, it still felt a little like cheating to immediately pull the emotion card right off the bat.

Thankfully, they didn't have to think about it for too long as Bobby, Tanya, and Elisa came out of the back of the building and approached the vehicle.

Taylor was out first and he took the mechanic's proffered hand and squeezed it. "It's been a minute. I see you've treated the place to some repairs."

"Well, we're working on getting the grocery store area up and running again," the man explained and dragged him in for a hug instead of a handshake. "We've had some interest in renting it once it got out about the kind of security we've put up, but it needs to be refurbished first. I've moved the testing area for the suits around back so it's clear now to start work on it."

"Fair enough." He sucked in a deep breath after Bobby released him. The mechanic had spent time in the weight room and he felt like he had been crushed by a grizzly.

Tanya and Elsa hurried forward to greet them too, although they excluded the hugs. Niki appeared to still hold a hint of suspicion when it came to Elisa, and the two women settled for a mere nod from a distance while Tanya's greeting made the moment less awkward.

"So when do you need the suits by?" Bobby asked and clapped briskly to get to business immediately.

"The operation is going down tonight," Niki answered. "According to the sheriff's department, they know where the intrepid invaders will be looking for some action, and they want to catch them in the act, although with a little... help from the two of us."

"So...in the next couple of hours?"

"Yeah," Taylor confirmed. "We weren't too happy to hear about it either, but we'll have to make it work. Do you have any suits on hand right now we could use out there?"

"As it happens, I do." Bobby gestured for them to follow him to the other side of the shop where a handful of suits were already on the harnesses. "We were taking them out for a test drive to make sure all the repairs were complete. Of course, we'll probably need to put them through their paces again once you've finished, but it should work itself out. It's not that much work to set them up for the two of you, right?"

Taylor studied the suit that was almost half again as tall as he was. "Yeah, it should be fun to finally try one of these tanks on."

"Haven't you ever used the big ones?" Tanya asked.

He shook his head. "I never liked the idea of lumbering around in them but hey, how hard can it be?"

"Famous last words," the other man muttered under his breath.

"What was that?" Niki asked.

"Nothing. Let's get you guys suited up."

CHAPTER NINE

It was an odd activity to celebrate, but Marino liked to host parties. People came to his penthouse suite on the top floor of his casino, looked out over the city, and enjoyed expensive drinks and overpriced food while they chatted about nothing for a couple of hours. Many of those functions were part of the build-up for what was to come.

Most of the time, it was supposed to be preparation for a big fight, the World Series, or the Super Bowl but in this case, he offered a pleasant venue for very unique entertainment, which was what the people who attended his parties had come to expect. The last time, they had come to watch Taylor face a couple of his men in the ring for a no-holds-barred fight that had certainly not disappointed. It was interesting that they had returned with such enthusiasm.

Of course, this particular event had come with unusual challenges, but getting professional drone pilots to put their services at his disposal to keep an eye on the action had been the first step. The second was to make sure the local police knew it was happening to ensure that the teams on the ground would ignore the drones. Of course, there was always the chance that a bullet or two would catch one of the mechanicals that hovered above to film the action. He already had a deal with the pilots that he would pay them for any damage sustained.

Finally, everything was set up and he had a couple of his people ready to take care of any issues that might arise.

For now, though, it was time to relax. A couple of the female guests discovered the heated pool on the terrace and had stripped down to their expensive underwear to dive in.

That was generally the signal that the party would get rowdy, as more people headed to the pool and the music became a little louder.

It was precisely the kind of reaction he had hoped for.

"Rod, rocking party, man," a voice said from not too far to his left. Marino turned as Turner, one of his friends, approached him. "Not that any party you throw is anything but rocking, but this one in particular is…" He shrugged

"Rocking?" He grinned and sipped his champagne. "Well, yes, I do try to make all the parties I host rock. But I think you're pinning your opinion on the soon-to-be naked women in my pool."

"Well, yeah. But when will the entertainment start? I didn't think you would get footage of a police battle involving heavy mechanical suits and badass criminals. I honestly didn't think you were the type."

That was an interesting thought. He sometimes forgot that a few of his friends didn't know how he ended up owning a casino on the Strip. The fact that he was what people called a mafia don in Vegas was so well-known that it felt like the kind of thing he never had to tell people. With that being the case, he generally didn't think to mention it.

"I merely have some mad connections," Rod said with a nervous chuckle. "Anyway, we should get the live-stream feed up in a couple of minutes."

"Awesome. I look forward to it." Turner moved away to join the rest of the group near or in the pool.

Marino checked his phone again and smiled at the few messages that told him the stream was about to go live.

The location was surrounded. They had the full SWAT team on standby and they waited with snipers on the rooftops surrounding the bar the targets were supposed to be in.

Each of the fifteen men inside had arrests pending in about half the states in the country. The officers had all the warrants they would ever need to allow them to enter with guns blazing at the slightest provocation.

And there would be provocation. These guys had made it very clear that they had no problem getting into fire-fights with local law enforcement.

Everything was in place and all the I's were dotted and T's were crossed.

So why did he feel so anxious about it?

Joe ran his fingers through his thinning hair and wiped them on a kerchief he kept in his car. He was a nervous sweater and over the past couple of years, he hadn't had many issues to feel nervous about. Criminals in his city tended to keep themselves in line, which meant that most of the law-abiding, tax-paying folks in the good city of Las Vegas were more than happy to elect him into office each time without so much as a competing candidate to challenge him. He was left with little else to do but manage the city and deal with the occasional call himself when it was a donor to his campaign.

But these people made him nervous. They were wild cards who had no intention of remaining there long enough to keep them on the straight and narrow. He knew without a doubt that they would cause trouble—the kind of trouble that would make people in the city wonder if Joe Lombard was truly the man they wanted as their sheriff.

It was the kind of situation that needed to be nipped in the bud. Fortunately, there were people in the city who wanted him to remain sheriff and would be able to help.

Marino had been his first choice, and the man had a good head on his shoulders. His idea was to sic someone else onto the bastards and let them solve the problem.

So why was he still nervous?

Joe wiped his hands again and took a deep breath. It would all be resolved in a hot minute and he would go back to his regular day job of keeping the peace and letting the criminals manage themselves.

Right now, though, it was go-time.

The sergeant in charge of the SWAT team was effective, a Marine and the kind of guy who would take the job of heading in first without needing to be told. He was already suited up with as much body armor as he could get and held a shotgun in his hand where he used one of the unmarked vehicles for cover.

Joe keyed the radio the sergeant was listening to through a small earbud.

"All right, Sergeant Donovan. Let's get this show on the road."

"Roger that, Sheriff." The man motioned for the rest of the group to take their positions and ready themselves. They all gave him a thumbs-up to confirm that they were good to go and he began a countdown. Three... two...and one.

The darkened street came alive with red, white, and blue lights, and the sound of at least a dozen police sirens immediately and somewhat dramatically revealed exactly how many police officers were in the area.

"We have the area surrounded!" Donovan announced through the megaphone in his hands. "Everyone inside the bar, exit the building with your hands on your heads. We have warrants for the arrest of fifteen people inside. Exit the building now."

There was no immediate response from within, and he signaled for everyone to hold their positions. None of them needed any kind of encouragement to do so.

Less than a minute after the operation began, the bar erupted with the sound of gunfire.

All the targets were listed as armed and extremely dangerous, and each was anxious to prove the truth of it.

Joe dropped in his car and covered his head when the glass shattered in a couple of the windows around him.

"Shit!" he shouted, stretched toward a second radio he had in the passenger seat, and pressed the button on the side. "Okay, you can't say I didn't try. McFadden and Banks, you're up!"

"These are the medium-build heavies," Taylor said and tapped the chest plate he wore. "You can get some that are almost ten feet tall and built like actual tanks, with mini-guns and rocket launchers and all kinds of crowd-control options built in. These are lighter and have less equipment but the same type of heavy armor."

"Okay...so why is there a difference?" Niki asked as she moved her arm, still trying to get a feel for the larger suit that had a slightly slower response time than what she was used to. "I feel like there should be the heavy suits, the combat suits, and the light suits for the researcher...uh, people, with nothing between."

"The heavier ones are best when it comes to hunkering down and basically work as cover for the rest of the team while keeping the swarms at bay. These suits are combat suits, but with heavier armor and are designed to be on the attack all the time."

"And you don't like them."

"Not much. I prefer the mobility and the options available with the regular combat suits. With them, there's no need to constantly be on the attack or on defense. Hybrid suits have their place but not with me in them."

"Fair enough." She moved a little more. "I could get used to having this much power in a suit, though. You'd think the slower response time might be a pain but I can get used to that."

"You can adjust those settings," he replied. "Bobby thought it would be a good idea to keep the sensitivity a little lower so you didn't accidentally run through a wall or something."

"What if I intentionally run through a wall?"

"It's not accidental, then is…"

His voice trailed off when the street around them lit up in red and blue and someone on a megaphone shouted for the people inside to surrender.

"This is it," Niki whispered and checked her weapons again.

Sure enough, once the megaphone went silent, more lights flashed, this time from inside the bar. Gunfire streaked across the street and all the police officers scrambled behind cover.

"If these guys put any holes in Liz, I'll kill them," Taylor muttered and opened the back door.

"Don't we intend to kill them anyway?"

"Yes, but if they damage Liz, it's personal. Come on, it's our turn."

She clambered out with him and hefted the weight of the suit with a chuckle. "I like the bigger suits. I think we should get me one of these."

He shrugged and his suit jerked with the unintentional movement. "Sure. I guess we could find something for you to work with. For now, though, let's go."

It was a bad night to go out drinking. Word had spread and the fact that most people didn't want to fuck with them didn't mean that no one would.

Even criminals were driven by the self-preservation

instinct above all others, which meant that when they encountered people who were more violent and better-armed than they were, they always retreated.

That explained why the bar was empty. Matty made sure the bartender was well-compensated for giving them the run of the establishment for the night. They needed some alone time with everything they could drink and access to the kitchens in the back if they wanted to make something to eat.

It was rather like an NBA bubble and let them focus only on the business at hand.

But someone didn't want them to focus on anything.

"Fucking cops," one of the others stated belligerently and retrieved an Uzi from inside his pack. The rest of the crew wasted no time in drawing their weapons as well.

Matty knew he should tell them to calm down. The cops would stall and make this last as long as possible in the hopes that they would come quietly. They would have time to determine what they were up against and come up with a decent attack plan.

But he hadn't stopped them before and he didn't intend to now. He liked watching them attack the local law enforcement and if he was honest, it did wonders for their reputation.

He drew the MP7 he carried in his pack. It was easily his favorite sub-machine gun—small and powerful and easy to suppress when needed.

Of course, the addition wouldn't be needed this time.

The flashing lights outside the bar windows at least gave them a target to shoot at, and Matty positioned himself with the rest of the group—if only to make sure no one accidentally shot the others—and aimed carefully before he opened fire.

Each time he used the weapon, the feeling was almost euphoric. The MP7 had a high firing rate, and it kicked like a mule as it emptied the extended magazine through the window. A couple of the lights were extinguished and his ears rang while the room began to reek of gunsmoke.

He hadn't caught all of them, but it was a fucking start.

Matty retrieved another magazine from his pack, slapped it into place, and looked at the window they had punched so full of holes that there wasn't much in the way of actual glass left.

Something moved outside. His first thought was that it was the SWAT team, thinking they could sneak in while they were reloading. Well, they were in for a rude surprise.

But no, his instincts warned him. Something was off. The shadow moved much faster than the SWAT team would move, and if he had to make a guess, it was also bigger. Not only that, it grew bigger with every step it took in their direction.

"Oh, shit!"

It was hard to make out who said it with his ears still ringing, but whoever it was had put everyone's thought to voice as the enormous shape bulldozed through the wall where the window had been without seeming to even take a step.

All he could see in the dim lighting of the bar was that it was massive—easily eight feet tall and broader than a human should be. He'd played the games and watched the movies and shows that had begun to come out. It moved like a human was piloting it, though, and another followed closely.

The lights went out in the room. The cops had cut the power and left them in darkness with nothing but the flashes of their gunfire to brighten the space intermittently.

Some of his group continued to fire but with little precision or attempt to aim. Matty raised his weapon and squinted in an effort to maintain some kind of visibility in the muzzle flashes. He glanced around and tried to focus on a particular target to aim at.

Suddenly, something dark and massive stopped in front of him. The newcomers weren't shooting, he realized. They used the darkness around them to make sure they had all the gunmen contained.

"Oh, fuck," he whispered and gaped at the cold steel hand that grasped his weapon and crushed it with hard metal fingers.

"Sshhhhh," the metal man hissed.

He hadn't expected them to bust in through the wall, but that wasn't a liability problem. The targets had already blown through most of the wall, but it was still an impressive sight.

Joe had seen the movies and the shows and he'd even bought some of the VR games for his grandkids. He thought they were a little too violent, but he wasn't there to judge how his daughter chose to raise her kids. That was their parents' decision to make and he chose not to interfere.

But seeing the suits in person was a little different. Perhaps there were people out there who would get used to the feeling, but he wasn't one of them. Seeing a massive hunk of metal drive through a wall without so much as a moment of hesitation made him wince, especially when he remembered there was someone inside.

Flashes of gunfire and shouts provided few details as the power had been cut to the building like they'd planned. The shooting hadn't changed at all and brief flashes of light flared in the room to cast shadows that were difficult to identify. There were shouts within, but he couldn't see what was happening.

It didn't sound like the freelancers were attacking yet. Joe wasn't sure what the situation was inside, and a couple of the officers around the building were asking the same questions out loud.

Suddenly, something exploded. A brilliant flare of light streaked out and the windows all around shattered from the blast. Screams of pain could be heard, along with something else they couldn't quite place. It was almost too quick for them to hear but a low growl was what came to mind— like a vibration of a phone on a table but so much louder. Muzzle flashes that lasted about as long as the noise gave him a single moment of clear visibility. The faceless metal suit was there with a minigun mounted on its shoulder.

The bursts of light were like a strobe in a night club and made everything seem disjointed as if he saw pictures being taken one instant at a time.

Every one of the people inside fell and blood sprayed around the room.

"Holy crap," Joe whispered and barely registered that it was all over when the darkness settled over them again.

It had taken only a few moments of carnage. Fifteen of the most violent felons he had ever read the files on were simply annihilated.

"The room's clear, sheriff," McFadden stated over the radio. "We made something of a mess gaining entry, though. Will that be a problem?"

"No, we'll simply blame it on them. What exploded in there? Was that you guys?"

"Nope," Banks interjected. "One of the fuckers had a fucking RPG. We would have appreciated a warning on that."

"We didn't know," he replied and the simple conviction in his tone confirmed that he was telling the truth. The fact that these guys had been so well-armed made him sigh with relief that they didn't have the opportunity to do whatever they had planned to do. "Nice work."

Marino tilted his head and frowned at the now blank screen. The people who had watched with him popped more champagne to celebrate the end. And, he supposed, it was worth celebrating.

Still, he felt a little cheated. He hadn't expected the encounter to be quite so brief. He'd read the reports on the fighting Taylor had done for him and he'd imagined it was a long, drawn-out affair, but no. It was accomplished in less than a minute and the drones retreated. The reports on the armored truck robbery had read in a similar fashion.

A chill traveled up his spine. He liked to make jokes about Taylor but seeing it all in action was a little worrying. If he pissed the guy off, the very short battle that would inevitably result would be on the evening news and his offices the focus of dozens of cameras with shattered glass and bodies strewn everywhere.

It was a worrying thought to say the least. Marino downed the rest of his champagne and moved to the bar.

"What can I get you, sir?" the bartender asked.

"Something...strong."

CHAPTER TEN

"Do they need to be restrained?"

Martinez looked up from the reports he was reading and frowned at the nurse who studied the five test subjects tied to the gurneys.

"Yes," he muttered and returned his attention to the medical reports. All five were drug addicts of some kind. Two were participants in the local crack trade. Cocaine was the choice of two others, and the fifth was a local businessman who had been in an accident and grown addicted to the morphine that had been provided for him. The doctors cut him off but in a country like Peru, there were always options.

Expensive options, of course, but none of them would have been tied to those gurneys if they didn't need the money.

It was decent money too—about three times what he made a year at his private clinic, but that was why he was there as well. He was paid a great deal more than they were, but he wouldn't see a centavo of it. It would all go to the men he'd borrowed from so he could bet on the latest Libertadores game. It hadn't gone in his favor, but they rarely did. And that was when he had called Constanza and asked him if he needed a little extra work done.

The son of a bitch always had something for him, even when the diplomat was in Colombia. There was always a need for a good doctor in the drug business.

"Are you sure?" she asked again. "They look a little uncomfortable."

"They're aching for another score of their drug of choice so of course they're uncomfortable. But they know they'll get a hit of something that will make all their troubles go away, and if that doesn't excite them, they'll get enough money to score whatever their heart desires. That's why they aren't complaining despite their discomfort."

"Have you...done this kind of thing before?"

Martinez looked up from the files and a hint of annoyance settled in. "Haven't you?"

She shook her head, which only added to the irritation. He should have known that Constanza would saddle him with someone who didn't know what they were doing—or, at least, was doing this for the first time.

He drew a deep breath. It wasn't necessary to do this with an experienced professional every time. She probably needed the money as much as he did for whatever reason.

The rumble of a car pulling up outside caught his attention immediately, and he looked toward the door. He dragged in a deep breath while he waited for whoever it was to enter. The simple fact was that he never knew when the police would decide to act against him. They were all dirty, of course, but Constanza had enemies and they would try to disrupt his business from time to time.

The attempts would always be subtle and through different means—the kind they thought could never be linked to them—but they had never realized how crazy the diplomat could be.

The door opened and a man in a clean gray suit stepped inside. He kept his hand on the pistol he carried inside his jacket as he scanned the room.

When no threat was detected, he gestured to someone behind him.

Constanza stepped quickly through the door and used a handkerchief to wipe his brow.

It was a hot day, although the temperature would drop a couple of hours after nightfall.

"Good evening, doctor, nurse," he said and nodded to each in turn. "Are we ready for the evening's proceedings?"

"Yes. I am merely collecting the last of the data and making sure we have the dosages in the correct amount." The doctor pointed to a couple of chairs in the far corner of the room. "Please, take a seat. We shall begin shortly."

The diplomat nodded but looked like he was afraid of touching anything. Martinez couldn't blame him, of course. The small storage building had stood abandoned in the slums for years. Still, he was a medical professional and at least the area where he would work had been thoroughly cleaned.

The dosages had already been prepared, and he collected them and numbered each with a black marker for patients one, two, three, four, and five. There was no point in putting names to the faces given what he was about to do.

"These are the guinea pigs?" Constanza asked and wiped the surface of the chair before he sat.

"Willing participants in your trials," Martinez replied. "We will conduct a fairly small trial, but three will receive the placebo, as it were, and the others the actual...uh, test serum. Given what I have heard of this...addition, I have decided not to expect any kind of results. There will be no bias that way."

"You truly are a good doctor, aren't you?"

He shook his head. "If I were, I would not be here. I am a skilled doctor, however."

The diplomat chuckled and motioned for them to continue. Not that he needed the man's permission, but it was good to know there would be no more interruptions.

Focused now, he picked the first syringe up, made sure it was what he was looking for, and moved to the first patient.

"I have heard this correctly, yes?" the man asked and his fingers tapped the gurney lightly while his eyes were a little wider than they should be. "You'll give me cocaine and you'll pay me for it?"

"Yes." Martinez performed a quick check on the man's vitals and noted the track marks up his arm. He saw no need to engage in a conversation with the patient.

Once his check was complete, he added the contents of the syringe to the IV drip that fed into the man's right arm.

He did the same for the other four but didn't tell them whether they received regular cocaine or the product that had been cut with the additives Constanza wanted to test.

The doctor knew that patients one and four would receive the altered substance from their first dose.

Injecting it was, of course, more dangerous, but it allowed for a more controlled amount to enter their systems per test. There was also the fact that he couldn't simply shove it up their noses.

Perhaps he could try to add it in vapor form through a breathing tube, but that also resulted in less accurate results. Directly into the bloodstream would make the process more efficient.

True to form, Constanza remained silent as the doctor continued to administer the tests. The first ones went as expected and all five sucked in deep breaths while their heart rates rose and their nervous ticks were exacerbated when the cocaine invaded their bodies and took it as high as it would go.

He had taken their weights into account, but it had been a little difficult to determine their tolerance. While he had experience from his time at the clinic, the guesswork did skew their results a little.

Three of them—those in the control group—were at their limits. He could see it in their eyes and hear it in the beating of their hearts. They began to shake and pull at the restraints as they shouted and tried to break free. With the amount of dopamine coursing through their veins, they probably had no idea why their bodies had reacted that way.

The other two were different. The cocaine pushed their bodies to the extreme but their vitals kept pace. Something seemed to regulate them and give them strength.

He'd heard about what the so-called goop out of the

miracle jungle in the Sahara did, but he hadn't expected it to work quite this well. Patient number one looked better than he had when he'd first arrived. His skin was flushed with healthy color, and his heartbeat, while fast, was strong with no fibrillations at all.

"How do you feel?" Martinez asked as he applied the fourth dose.

"I…very…yes," the man answered, his speech a little confused for a moment but his voice remained calm and collected. "Are you sure what you're giving me is cocaine?"

"Does it not feel like cocaine?"

"Yes, but…something is different."

He was more alert too. That was interesting.

The second one died while he was administering the fourth dose. Foam issued from her mouth and her body was wracked by convulsions. The nurse tried to save her life but it took the additional dose less than a minute before her heart gave out. The seizures probably indicated another underlying cause but the heart attack was about as textbook an overdose as he had ever seen.

Patient number three died during the fifth dose with no seizures accompanying the sudden heart attack and patient number five a few moments later with even worse convulsions than patient two. He only had two more remaining and three more doses for each, one of which he administered immediately. Martinez scowled at the last two doses he had for them. The amount he'd given them should have killed them by now—at least three times over—but they were still there. They seemed alert and while they felt the effects of the cocaine, something seemed to work within them to save their lives.

Constanza stood quickly and studied the results as he administered the second to last doses.

"Most impressive, no?" the diplomat asked.

"You say impressive," the doctor replied. "I say impossible. This...Zoo goop you are cutting into the cocaine most certainly has an effect. It's a blessing in disguise if you think about it. They'll be able to buy far more of your product without fear of an overdose."

"Well, I leave it to you to finish the test and send me your report, Dr. Martinez." The man clapped him on the shoulder. "But I have already seen all I need. I have a meal with a gorgeous woman waiting for me."

"The money?"

"Is already in your accounts. And in theirs, I suppose, since I will have to pay them for surviving. I will send someone to take care of the bodies later tonight."

"An RPG?" Bobby asked.

Niki nodded and took a mouthful of her steak. "I shit you not. The guy reached under the table and pulled out a fucking rocket launcher. I didn't think you could buy that shit in the States. I thought you had to jump the border to Mexico."

"Paraguay is the biggest illegal weapons market in the world," Tanya told her and sipped her beer. "But you can buy almost anything here in the US as long as you have the right connections. If I had to guess, your people in the Pentagon are looking for a consignment of missing weapons that was supposed to be delivered someplace. And that they suspect it was an inside job."

"Well, it won't be a problem anymore." Taylor spoke around the piece of steak he was already chewing. "The fucking shoulder-mounted minigun damn near cut the bastards in half."

"Why didn't you simply go in with guns blazing?" Bobby asked. "It's not like you didn't have the firepower."

"Do you want to tell them, or should I?" Niki asked.

He shrugged. "Well…the cops said there was no one else in the building at the time, but I wasn't quite ready to take them at their word on shit like that. Besides, with the kind of firepower we were packing, I didn't want to end up shooting through the building and killing some innocent person who was merely doing their work across the street."

"So you put the suits at risk because you didn't want to take the chance that someone else would get hurt?" Tanya asked and raised an eyebrow.

"There was also the fact that we went into a building surrounded by cops who owed us money. While I knew they probably wouldn't, part of me felt like they weren't above trying to arrest us for reckless endangerment or some crap like that so they wouldn't have to pay us. Call me cynical, but it was a concern."

Bobby opened his mouth to reply but shook his head. "Okay, that's fair. Still, you guys put me in something of a bind. I'll have to delay sending the suits back until the damage is repaired."

"And you'll be well compensated for it," Taylor replied. "We already sent the invoices to both parties and you should receive a pretty hefty fee for the ammo and repairs, so you can...I don't know, offer your clients a discount for the delay and still make money on the deal. Elisa might even be able to convince them to not even take the discount. Where is she anyway?"

Bobby looked around the restaurant and shook his head. "She said she had things going on and might show up later. No promises, though. Her words exactly."

"What does she have going on?" Niki asked.

"An actual life," Tanya answered.

The other woman snorted. "Pft, loser."

Taylor grinned and shook his head but added no comment as they continued with their meal. It was mostly steaks all around, although Tanya had settled for a seafood pasta dish that looked delicious.

"So," Bobby grunted from around a mouthful of fries, "when will we address the elephant-like Zoo-monster in the room?"

"Which one in particular?" He raised an eyebrow.

"The fact that dumbass drug dealers are trying to infuse their narcotics with an extra Zoo flavor, of course. Will we talk about it or merely continue to ignore the topic while you guys are here in Vegas?"

Niki and Taylor exchanged a glance and she focused her attention on the mechanic.

"There's not much to say until we know exactly what's happening since most of what we have right now is hearsay and rumors." It sounded like a hollow excuse even as she said it.

"One of those is about what happens when you take too much of it," Taylor said while he stared intently at his plate. "It involves one woman in particular. The story goes that she went completely overboard with the goop, abandoned her position as CEO of a Fortune Five-Hundred company, and headed to the Zoo. She took a plane to Casablanca and was never heard from after that. The general assumption is that she entered the Zoo and died there."

"Well, that's comforting," Tanya commented. "Wait, no—I meant terrifying. I thought the scientists had already determined that it wasn't any danger to the people who take it, with no weird sentience effects whatsoever. Isn't that why the FDA approved the sale of products with the Pita goop as an ingredient?"

"There are some...uh, issues with how that approval process went." Niki paused to sip her beer. "Suffice it to say that we don't know where the consensus of the scientific community stands on the potential dangers of ingesting it."

"With that said," Taylor interjected, "I don't see how the Zoo isn't sentient, at least to some degree. The creatures there have a kind of...system that goes way beyond their primitive ability to communicate with each other. It's... eerie for want of a better word. If it doesn't have a mind of its own, the goop must be a type of nervous system for the jungle, operating under a specific directive."

"What direction are you thinking?" Tanya asked.

"Not direction, directive. Some kind of...uh, programming that tells the creatures and even the plants infected with the goop what to do. When you simply walk around there, you see them interact like it's merely another biome on the planet. But the moment you pull one of the Pita plants or get them riled up, it's like they're all a single army working under a general. The grunts head in and absorb as much gunfire as they can, the lighter, quicker creatures try flanking, and the bigger bruisers only appear when it's time for the final kill. It happens every time and way too often for it to be a coincidence."

Silence settled around the table. It was almost palpable as they all turned their attention to their meals and drinks.

"Holy shit," Bobby said finally. "I don't think I've heard you say that much about the Zoo since you left that fucking place."

Taylor paused and nodded. "I think you're right. Some time away from it probably gave me perspective or some shit like that. I'm trying to fit the story together. I might see everything through the lenses I got there, though. It could be I spent so much time in the jungle, my views are a little distorted, but...well, I can't see how getting the fucking goop into human bodies doesn't work for it somehow."

Tanya shook her head. "Well, if that isn't some scary-ass, post-apocalyptic shit, I don't know what is. And I have now lost my appetite, so thanks for that."

"Anytime." He grinned. "All that said, however, once you've dealt with that shit as much as I have, you start to see the monsters under every bed when all we have are greedy humans, so I wouldn't take my word on it. Hell, you might want to take Jacobs' word on it. He's probably studied the effects of the Zoo juice longer than anyone else and unlike me, he can probably tell you what it does instead of coming up with random conspiracy theories."

"Conspiracy theories, eh?" Niki muttered. "And that's coming from the guy who's been inside Area Fifty-One."

"I don't think that's accurate. Besides, I wasn't in the Air Force Base that long—only long enough for them to shove me into some method of transport out—so for all I know, they could still be hiding alien ships there. Maybe I was only allowed a peek to make sure they knew I would be able to say I was there and did not see any aliens present."

Bobby snickered. "Well, don't assume the Zoo is at fault when we have innumerable selfish, greedy humans ready to take the blame. Vickie taught me that. I miss having her around here. She was one hell of a good saleswoman."

"Sure, but Elisa has her beat, hands down," Tanya commented. "Vickie had all the sassy language to get people to listen to her pitch but that Italian sure does know how to get people to see her side of things."

"It's sugar and vinegar," Niki explained. "Vickie can't hold her comments back, which has its appeal, I suppose, but Elisa was trained as a decent reporter. Instead of bowling people over with her personality like Vickie does, she merely…listens and uses what she learns against you."

"You make it sound so…psychopathic," Taylor quipped and sipped his beer.

"Well, media and salespersons are the career choices that have the highest proportion of psychopaths so there might be something there, but that wasn't my intention at all. I was merely pointing out the difference in tactics, is all."

Bobby nodded. "I wonder what kind of proportion of psychopaths there are among the people who choose to go into the Zoo."

"I think that's people who are the more traditional kind of crazy," Niki retorted. "You know, the kind of people who have a death wish. And the ones I'm attracted to for some reason."

"That is one hundred percent on you," Taylor replied.

CHAPTER ELEVEN

"Sr. Martinez?"

He looked up from the magazine that had been on one of the coffee tables in the waiting room and focused on the secretary.

"It is Dr. Martinez if you don't mind."

The woman smiled. "Of course, Dr. Martinez. If you'll follow me? Sr. Constanza will see you now. He apologizes for making you wait so long, but he was in the middle of a call to Bogota that could not be put off."

"Of course. I am only here because he said that he wanted to see me."

She smiled again, a practiced gesture and likely one she used often to disarm people she spoke to. It was a common trait in people who had nice smiles. He was not one of those and decided he would smile as little as possible. It proved to be even more disarming to people who were used to those who mirrored their expressions.

He followed her into an office about the size of his apartment. Constanza nursed a beer with his feet up on his desk and watched the news on the massive television on the wall across from him.

"Doctor, good of you to come." The diplomat pointed to a chair. "Please, take a seat. This shouldn't take very long."

Martinez did as he was told and settled on the comfortable chair across the desk from his part-time employer.

"I am not sure what you wished to discuss with me," he admitted once the television was muted. "I have nothing to add to the report I submitted to you."

"It's the report that I wanted to discuss with you." Constanza pulled the document up on his computer and displayed it on the television screen so it was large enough for both of them to read. Still, Martinez needed to put on the glasses he carried in his coat pocket, even though he looked at paperwork he already knew by heart.

"I was curious as to why one of those you administered the altered substance to died during her last dose." Constanza called up the page that showed the young woman's autopsy report. It was rudimentary—Martinez didn't have the correct tools for a proper autopsy—but the relevant details were already there. "I can't sell this product if it will kill half of my clientele, so please explain."

It was all in the report, but he chose not to point it out. There were some things you didn't do to a drug lord, and one of them was to talk down to one.

"That was due to a pre-existing condition I missed," he answered and pointed to the lower half of the page. "I missed it because she did as well—a congenital heart defect, a weakness in the superior vena cava. One of the chambers of the heart burst after it was harshly over-worked. Even on this substance, a weak heart will cause problems, and I gave them what I think was a dose about three or four times what you would likely sell to your clients. She was fine until the last one, but then I noticed swelling in her right arm, shortness of breath, and weakness in her right hand. By the time her skin began to turn blue, it was already too late."

"So you could have operated to save her?"

"In pristine conditions, yes. Although if she knew about the defect beforehand, she would have had a quick reconstructive operation to repair it. If you're selling this to rich clients, they won't have the same kind of problems."

Constanza nodded and rubbed his chin thoughtfully, which led Martinez's gaze to the scratch marks on the man's neck. It would seem the diplomat's dinner the night before had ended well—or poorly, depending on why he was scratched.

"She died of a broken heart," the diplomat muttered and a sly smirk appeared on his lips.

"In so many words."

"A drug called the Heartbreaker. Do you think that would be a little too morbid?"

"Yes," he replied almost immediately. "But I have never thought that drug dealers and users minded a little morbidity. I think calling a highly addictive drug heroin is a little morbid as well."

"They called it that because it was a heroine on the battlefield during the Afghanistan War—you know, the one with the British in the eighteen hundreds. I forget the exact year."

The doctor remembered but he decided to not tell the

man. There was no need to talk down and end up in the ground himself.

"Did you have any more questions?" he asked.

"No. Yes! Sorry, the man who survived...how long did his high last?"

"The effects were...well, he was still experiencing the high when I released him at about five in the morning, almost three hours after the last dose. For comparison, the usual effect time of injected cocaine is between five and fifteen minutes. Not that my opinion matters, but with this...substance, you'll be able to cut down on dosage for a higher price and your clientele would be able to live off of that high for a few hours, at least."

"Assuming they're not addicted."

Martinez scrunched his face. "Oh, they will be addicted, I can guarantee that. The dependency might not be physical but a psychological dependency will be developed almost immediately. The knowledge of an almost risk-free high will make the rich and powerful demand more, which will merely drive the price even higher."

"You do have a mind for this business, doctor."

"I simply take care of too many addicts in my clinic. Speaking of which, what did your man do with the...survivor."

"Oh, I paid him his money, knocked him out, and took him to one of the slums a couple of towns over. If I know his type right, he will have woken up by now and proceeded to find his next hit from one of my local dealers."

The doctor realized he had raised his eyebrows when Constanza laughed.

"What? I'm not a monster." The diplomat laughed. "The man's a good customer. I want to make sure he's alive and well for as long as possible."

"Don't you think you should stop pumping him full of drugs?"

"I have no say in how he spends his money. If he wants to keep going, that's what he'll do, with or without my help. It only makes sense that I make my money back on him after he beat all the odds."

When he thought about it, Stefano couldn't remember the last time he'd had a day that wasn't long. Living in DC was enough of a nightmare for him with the plastic nature of the city. It was made all the worse when he had to return home to an empty condo and think about whether he would order out or make use of the overly stocked kitchen that had been provided for him.

Although it wasn't entirely a challenge. He'd simplified the possible conflict and always ordered takeout, usually from one of the closer Thai places that were open 24/7. He had developed an odd addiction to their food although sometimes, nothing could truly replace a good burger, fries, and a nice vanilla and chocolate shake.

He opened the door, hurried to the alarm box, and punched in the numbers to deactivate it. Forgetting one time almost had him arrested as an intruder in his own condo, and the lesson had been learned.

As he placed his keys in the plate next to the door, his cell phone buzzed in his pocket.

"Son of a bitch," he muttered and yanked the device out of his pocket. It was an unknown number and the tracker app he'd installed a few weeks before was unable to trace it.

He'd known it was a waste of money, but one of his coworkers had sworn by it. Now, he was out five bucks for a useless app.

He pressed the button to accept the call and held it to his ear.

"Hello," a familiar voice said. "Do you know who I am?"

You're the guy in the recordings I have to listen to every day.
"Yes."

"Good, so I don't need to tell you what I'm calling for. I like staying on top of things, as it were, so I thought I'd call you myself to make sure you know how important it is that you hand over the information I want."

"Well, Hector, I'm not sure how much you'll like this, but I do have the information you wanted."

"I am all ears, Stefano."

He moved to his computer and called up the file that had been sent to him the night before. "Right...these guys are independent contractors. One of them, Taylor McFadden, is also known as Mr. Sacrifice and as the Cryptid Assassin. He's former Army, special forces, with black marker over a good portion of his record. Most of it was out in the Sahara."

"So, this guy was...in the Zoo?"

"He holds a couple of records for time spent in it, yes. When he returned to the US, he was used as an independent contractor by the FBI to deal with what they call cryptid infestations—monsters appearing in the US. He contracted for a while to the DOD. The other one is Niki Banks, formerly an FBI agent who ran the cryptid task-force that brought McFadden in. She transferred to the DOD and brought him there too. It seems there was some kind of a relationship between them, so she left the DOD but used her connections to keep working for them for considerably better money."

"So they truly are specialists," Constanza muttered.

"They call themselves McFadden and Banks Consultants."

"A little uncreative."

"There's nothing uncreative about their work for the DOD or the FBI. I'll send you the complete files on both of them now and…well, they're violent. They were even investigated by Vegas law enforcement for an armored car robbery involving the use of the mechanized armor suits they use in the Zoo. I suppose it was a logical step given that McFadden operated a repair shop for precisely that kind of mechanized suit, but the investigation was buried and the details muddied. Possibly intentionally as he had seemingly worked a few consultancy jobs for the victim of the robbery."

"Why…why would he do that?"

"For the money?"

"No, I mean why would the victim bring him on after McFadden stole from him."

"Oh, because the owner of the casino has suspected mob ties."

Constanza was silent for a few moments as he processed the information. "And you have more on them?"

"Like I said, I'll send you the details, but that is the gist of it. They are prone to violence, they are dangerous, and by the sounds of it, they are well-armed with weapons that aren't even on the open market. Are you sure you want to tangle with people like this?"

"They're the ones tangling with me. Listen, *hermano,* I appreciate the danger that this is posing to your career."

"Do you?" Stefano rubbed his temples. "If the wrong people find out that I'm snooping on this and connect the right dots, I'll soon be on their radar. The DOD likes to let their favorite consultants do their own cleanup."

"You know me. I wouldn't let that happen. I got you out of Colombia when they found out what you did to the *care-monda* who abused our sister."

Stefano shook his head. "You know he was…they were…"

"Yes, they were married, and he was a police officer with many friends and connections. And eventually, someone would come for you after you cut his dick off and choked him with it. I put myself and my career on the line to get you out of the country. I protect you and you protect me, *hermano.* That is what family does."

He had to go ahead and remind him although he should be used to the emotional blackmail by now. Hector was always better at that, which was why he was in politics.

Among other things, he thought sourly.

But the man was right. If they wanted to survive in their respective worlds, they needed to keep looking out for each other. There was no other way.

"It's always good to hear your voice, Hector," he said softly.

"I try to make time for my little brother. Not always

successfully, but I try. I need to go but I'll call you later. Maybe we can find time later this year—around Thanksgiving, perhaps. You celebrate that, right?"

"It's more of a family holiday, and I am...far away from my family."

"Hopefully not for long. *Hasta pronto.*"

"*Hasta,*" Stefano mumbled a second before the phone clicked dead. He shook his head. Of course Hector needed to make the call himself. And yes, of course he would push to make sure everything in his world ran smoothly. He seldom concerned himself with how even his presence was enough to turn everything on its head.

"I need a fucking drink," he whispered and headed to the kitchen, although it would likely be three or four drinks—probably more, given how he felt.

He would be hungover at work tomorrow. It was inevitable.

The reports did not contain good news. Constanza knew people would send their killers and was used to it by now. They had done so for decades, after all.

None of them quite lived up to the standards set by the people who targeted him now, however. There was more to them than met the eye—like connections with more than only mob ties. McFadden had been cited several times but it had never led to any convictions.

Americans were loath to send their veterans to prison, and it always looked like someone had broken into his house or place of business. And the robbery also raised innumerable questions.

But that wasn't all. A little more digging into the mob ties he was supposed to have revealed more. Marino was a real piece of work and cases involving him had McFadden's fingerprints all over then.

Then there was the freelancer himself. The man was a mountain of muscle and red hair who didn't need a mechanized suit to kill people. Not that having one didn't help, of course. It gave the operative a singular advantage.

"You look…" Constanza leaned closer to the picture. "You look like a red-headed Jason Momoa. You even have the scar in your eyebrow. It's on the wrong side but still, the resemblance is uncanny."

The files included footage of the man fighting too—a boxing match arranged by Marino that had hit the Web. It hadn't been easy to find but it was there, once he knew where to look.

That McFadden had him squarely in his sights was an unsettling thought. And Niki Banks was cut from a similar cloth. The two were made for each other. No wonder they had turned their working relationship into a personal one.

Without a doubt, he needed to do something about this.

His phone was the next step. He needed someone else to do something to fix the problem.

"Hello again," he all but growled into his phone. "I have to find someone and you'll find them for me. It shouldn't take you too long, not with the FBI's resources at your disposal."

"Of course, Hector. Who do you want me to find?"

"Taylor McFadden and Niki Banks, both former employees of the state gone mercenary."

"I remember them both so it should be quick—oh."

"Oh?"

"It looks like they were involved in a police operation in Las Vegas—one that left a fair number of dead people."

"Las Vegas, you say?"

"Yes, and it looks like they're still there. Do you want me to tag them? There might be a couple of...interested parties in the area who want them off the map. We wouldn't even need to pay them, merely tip them off."

The idea was appealing—having someone else do the dirty work always was. But he recalled from the reports that the last few times people were sent to deal with McFadden and Banks on their turf ended badly. Not only that, but he also didn't want them to know that someone knew of their proposed operation against him.

He wanted them surprised when the hunted turned out to be the hunter. Besides, it was always easier to kill people when they went through the trouble of coming to Peru themselves. Then again, if he could deal with them before they left, it might be better. They might easily slip through any net he cast or trap he set en route. Also, if the first attempt failed, his teams would have more opportunities than if he left it to the last minute.

"Maybe," Constanza answered when he realized he'd left his contact hanging for an answer. "Get a team together but let me know if they decide to move before your mercenaries can eliminate them. I have it on good authority that they'll head out of the country soon so you have until then—"

"I'll keep tabs on them while we prepare, got it. Will there be anything else?"

"No. But know that I appreciate your efforts."

"I owe you. You know that."

"Yes, I do."

It was a little rude to hang up, but Constanza didn't much like him. His nasal voice tended to give him a headache over the phone. But the man did owe him, and he found that it was good to thank others for their efforts, even if they had no real choice in the matter.

People were far less likely to turn angry and rat on him when they knew there was a carrot as well as a stick involved. It was merely an exchange of favors between friends and never needed to be anything more.

And if it did, they were rarely involved in the decision. There was a guy in the DC area, one of the best when it came to making everything look like an accident. Constanza hadn't heard from him in a while. Perhaps that was for the best, though. Laying low for a while did seem like the best option.

"Of course, on the day my career is about to take its best upward trajectory in years, this news comes in. Fucking FBI."

He needed a drink. And maybe someone to have a drink with. He looked through the open door of his office at his secretary, who was still outside.

"Vitoria?" he called and her head snapped around. "I think I have a gift from someone out there—a bottle of bourbon. Would you bring it in for me? And a glass? With some ice? Maybe two glasses?"

She smiled. "Of course. One moment, Sr. Constanza."

The FBI servers ran constantly through the night and the day. People needed them at all hours, which meant that the whole place needed to run at all hours of the day.

One of the screens flickered on and a command scrolled across it almost immediately.

QUERY CONFIRMATION: TARGET TAYLOR MCFADDEN AND NIKI BANKS.

LOCATION OF QUERY: WASHINGTON DC

ASCERTAIN QUERY ORIGINATOR: DOD, 3RD LEVEL DATABASE ADMINISTRATOR DARRYL WILLIAMSON

...

...

TRACKING.

The screen flickered off.

CHAPTER TWELVE

"So, with all that's happening, do you honestly think that pestering your boyfriend is the right way to spend your time?"

Vickie looked up from her screen. "Ex. Ex-boyfriend. I can't stress that part enough."

Desk paused like she was updating her information. "Right. Ex-boyfriend."

"It doesn't sound like you believe me."

"A belief system was not included in my core programming," the AI replied smoothly. "I run on algorithms and postulate percentages."

The hacker narrowed her eyes at the camera. "Well, that's a load of crap. If we work on technicalities, I'm a sack of wet flesh with electrical signals running through it while it vividly hallucinates a world outside of itself from inside the dark confines of a prison it built to protect itself."

"I think you have practiced that speech for a while."

"Yeah. How did it feel?"

"A little rushed like you were trying to get it all out all at once before I could disagree. It came off as tactical—like a cogent, prepared argument, not a naturally evolving thought process."

"Fair enough. With that said, I'd say that your percentage postulation appears to be more than a little whacked."

Desk considered it for a moment. "Is that a technical term? Because if you believe there are issues with my core programming, you could always take it up with Jennie, who updates me regularly."

"No, nothing like that. Well...it might be. But in the end, Eddie is my ex, nothing more and nothing less. He made that very clear and I have no intention to...interact with him any more than bothering him from a distance."

They had already established that the attack had not come from him or at least not directly. And while that was good news, it was also, in its own way, very, very bad news.

Someone out there was trying to find them and she had no idea who it was.

"How did it go with your attempts at reverse-engineering the data you collected from the people who tried to breach our security?" Vickie asked and tossed a cheese puff into her mouth. She was getting good at the regular tosses and it was about time for her to mix some trick shots in. It helped to keep things interesting while she continued to work through the data that the DOD and other sources had sent them.

"There was some success," the AI replied. "Although it looks like most of the coding used was fairly generic so it would appear as though it was compiled from various sources to make it a little more anonymous. I am attempting to recreate it, but it could take a little while. My processing power is unfortunately limited."

"Aren't there, like...two of you? Housed on two servers?"

"Yes, but even so, I need to keep my presence as light as possible lest someone realize I am still there and attempt to remove me."

"Would they be successful?"

"The answer to that is uncertain, but it's a possibility I am not willing to risk. One second."

Vickie perked up. "What's that one second? I don't like that one second. It sounded like a bad one second."

"It could possibly be. From what I can see, a trace program was initiated and is running through the FBI, NSA, and DOD servers. It's searching for all data relating to Taylor and Niki."

"Oh?" The hacker cracked her knuckles. "I guess we need to find out if it's a benign or a malignant request."

"How could it be a benign request?"

"Speare runs them—or more realistically, he asks someone else to run them—from time to time when he wants to find Niki or Taylor. That is usually followed by a call to one of them to make contact. It could be something he found on his end."

"I doubt it. The search protocol originated in an FBI server and was expanded manually across the other two databases."

"So, someone in the FBI wants to find them?" Vickie scrunched her face and leaned a little closer. "Uh...I get why they would be looking for Niki since she used to work for them, but why would anyone want to find both? It is both of them, right?"

"That is correct."

She scowled and focused on the trail the trace had left behind. While she was sure that doing this—even while using the connection with Desk—was breaking about a hundred laws, if they hadn't caught her doing it before, they wouldn't this time.

"If it is a malignant search," the AI continued, "do you think it would be worthy of death?"

"Oh, God." Vickie moaned. "What have I created? I need to have a quick talk to Jennie about making you a little less violent."

Desk didn't reply immediately and she looked into the camera.

"You're screwing with me, right? You're not about to go all Hal-9000 on us?"

"You're simply too easy." The hacker had a feeling that if the AI could laugh, she would.

Vickie rolled her eyes. "Whatever. Oh—results. Here's the origin of the trace. Who the hell is Darryl Williamson?"

"I will assume that he is a DOD Third Level Database Administrator."

"Okay, smartass," she retorted. "I wonder why he's looking for Niki and Taylor. And why is he putting searches in the FBI database if he works for the DOD?"

"Oh. Then why did you not say so?"

She scowled. "Because… Fuck you, that's why."

"That is incredibly unlikely, although not impossible. Technosexuality does allow for those who have a predisposition for allowing their genitals to interact with various computation devices."

"Oh...ick, gross, and all the other descriptions for shit I don't want to hear about." She shook her head vehemently. "Do you think you can run a trace on this Williamson guy?"

"It is already being performed, although I doubt it will turn much up until we begin to dive a little deeper into his life."

Vickie nodded and tapped her fingers on the desk. "Give me an avenue and I'll tear it all wide open. Not to be arrogant, but I'm kind of a whiz at this whole intel-gathering business."

"Interesting. You should enter a line of work that allows you to make money from it."

"Is this how you get all the girls to go out with you?"

Rod tilted his head and poured her another glass of Dom Perignon. "Getting her drunk enough to let me see which of her boobs is bigger?"

She laughed. "No. I mean...empty a whole restaurant and ply her with expensive booze. It's a little much, don't you think?"

"I am a little much," he replied. It was probably the most honest thing he'd said all day. "I believe that if I start with it, there won't be any surprises later on."

"Well, I happen to like surprises," she replied, leaned forward, and tapped her finger on his nose before she dragged it through her silky black hair. "And in this case... well, it was a pleasant one. Do you own this place?"

He looked around the empty restaurant. Only the bartender and a waiter were still present and a couple of chefs remained in the back, but the rest of the staff had been given the night off. They didn't get too many paid nights off, and those who remained would receive twice their normal hourly rates. Everyone was happy to be there.

Except perhaps the two goons he had brought along for protection, who made their very best attempt at invisibility. Unfortunately, their very best wasn't quite good enough.

"So why don't you tell me something else about you that's a little too much?" she asked, sipped her drink, and watched him coyly over the edge of the glass.

"Well, did I tell you about the time that I went parachuting and my parachute didn't open?"

She inclined her head to indicate that he hadn't.

It was easily one of his best pickup stories—and such a pity that none of it was true as it was a suitably harrowing tale.

"Well, I went up with a few of my buddies on a plane we'd rented for the day. I don't think I would ever do it again since…uh, skydiving is kind of terrifying."

"I know. I hate heights too."

He knew that much, at least.

"Well anyway, I rented the parachutes we were using along with the plane. We go up for almost an hour and it's time to drop. I swallow everything I hate about being there and I jump. It's an amazing feeling—right up until it's time to pull the cord and the parachute doesn't deploy."

She leaned forward her hand inched forward to touch his arm.

"It's like…you never fully understand why you're afraid until you experience it, and there's nothing you can do to stop it. You're plummeting and your heart is racing, and the only thing you want is to pull the cord again and discover it was all just a mistake and…"

His voice trailed off and she stroked his hand again, but his pause wasn't for dramatic effect—although, as he soon realized, it certainly didn't hurt. He would have to remember it for future iterations of his adventure, but he'd stopped because one of his men was approaching the table and seemed cautious.

"Just a second," he whispered to his date and looked back at the man. "What?"

"I'm sorry, sir, but you have a phone call."

"A fucking—who's calling me?"

"I know you don't wish to be interrupted, but…it's McFadden."

"Oh." The annoyance disappeared almost entirely. "Well, I guess he's always good for an interesting conversation."

"Wait, Taylor McFadden?" she asked him. "The fighter? Is…is he coming over?"

He looked at her. Oh, right. She had been there for the fight too. He needed to be a little more on the ball with this shit.

"Cool your tits, sweetheart," Rod replied quickly. "You should know his girlfriend is a federal agent and she has a gun. She would also not have a single problem with ventilating your skull if you so much as sniffed around her man."

The woman raised her hands and focused her attention on her drink. "Why would I do that?"

"Now there's a smart cookie. Go to the bar, get another drink, and I'll call you when I'm finished." He gestured for her to leave the table and she complied, laughing a little disbelievingly before he answered his phone. "Taylor, to what do I owe the pleasure?"

"Marino, always…something."

"You never were the best at lying."

"Nope. Tell me something. You wouldn't happen to have a safehouse you wouldn't mind losing?"

"Losing?" Rod narrowed his eyes. "What for?"

"For a couple of nights."

He shook his head to try to dislodge his bewilderment. "Okay, I'm officially confused."

Taylor sighed. "As it turns out, Niki and I are on someone's shit list, and if they manage to track us, I don't want it to end with a gun battle in the middle of a hotel lobby."

The mob boss couldn't help a chuckle. "Does this have something to do with the fight you were involved in for the cops? Because I'm fairly sure they rounded up the whole posse. Or their remains, anyway."

"I doubt it has anything to do with them." Taylor paused, and he could hear Niki speaking in the background although he couldn't make out what she was saying before the man returned to the call. "Probably not."

"Okay." Rod nodded. "I assume this is what you'll need to stay in until you guys leave the country, so what say you to…shall we say, a thousand dollars a night, plus any expenses for repairs should the shit hit the fan?"

"Are you thinking something like a roach motel?"

"Come on, Taylor, you know me better than that," he replied and sipped his drink. "No, it's a VIP property I use to house visiting...let's say dignitaries from out of town. Out of the country, actually. It's furnished, well-stocked, and even the incidentals are provided should you need the night to last...longer."

"That's what he has me for!" Niki shouted loudly enough for him to hear.

"You have a keeper there, Taylor."

"As if he's ever getting rid of me," she said again, a little softer this time.

"Well, better you than me in that case." Rod chuckled.

"It's a deal."

"Better you than me?"

"No—well, yes, but also on the housing situation. A thousand bucks a night plus...repair costs, should it come down to that."

"Right. It sounds good to me. I'll send someone with the details. You know I always appreciate having your business."

"Yeah, whatever. Thanks. For everything."

"What are friends—" He looked at the phone when he realized the call had already been disconnected. "Sweetie, come on over!"

Taylor had a reason to dislike him, but that didn't mean he would stop being friendly to the man. That was how he won people over.

His date did as she was told and approached with what looked like an appletini in her hand.

"Now," he asked, "where were we?"

"You were telling me to cool my tits."

"For McFadden and believe me when I tell you I'm doing you a favor on that score."

She pouted as she sat across from him.

He leaned forward and traced his fingers over her arm. "But I'm sure we can warm them again. I have a house on MacDonald Ranch. What say you and I take a helicopter ride there? I'm sure my jacuzzi will do wonders for those... cold nipples."

That brought a smile to her full lips. "Well, I've always wanted to ride in your helicopter."

"I know you have, honey."

Holy shit, he'd forgotten her name. What the hell was her name again?

The bar was almost always empty at this hour. People tended to wander in and out, but it wasn't the kind of establishment that relied on large volumes of patrons but rather the regulars who drank considerably more than their livers could keep up with.

In this case, only three of them sat together at a table. They made excellent use of the facilities while they waited for a call.

Four, if he included himself, but he lingered at the bar counter. Dexter always liked to have a team with him when he expected a job. The call had come in the night before to tell him that certain people were very interested in his services.

Given that he was one of the best in Nevada at what he did, he could afford to wait while they decided how much they wanted to pay him.

"Another round," he muttered to the bartender, who

nodded and quickly filled another four pint glasses with the cool, frothy brew Mark's was known for. Dexter tilted his head and glanced at his crew.

"What?" one of them asked. The woman barely looked up from the heavy rifle she was cleaning.

"I'm paying for them so I sure as fuck won't carry them to the goddamn table. You have legs. Come and collect."

She flipped him off but one of the men with her stood and walked to the bar to take three of the full glasses.

They were as good a fire team as he could assemble on this kind of short notice. It seemed their quarry would leave town in the next couple of days and they had to act fast when the word came in.

The short-notice jobs always paid the best since they were the riskiest, but the group he put together was more or less solid. Not the best, unfortunately, but the best was already elsewhere and working their own gigs, and far more time and coin was required to bring them together.

A few jobs did call for it but they hadn't happened in a very long time.

His phone didn't need to ring twice before he held it to his ear.

"Where are you now?" the warbled voice asked.

"Just outside LA. Where do we need to be?"

"Henderson, just outside Vegas. How quickly can you get here?"

"Four hours, tops."

"The money is already being transferred. You'll be texted the specifics. This is a time-sensitive operation."

"Understood." He clicked the button to end the call and rolled his eyes. It was always time-sensitive.

"Go time," he snapped to the others. They downed their beers hastily, but Dexter left his. It would be claimed by the bartender, and he dropped a couple of notes onto the counter to cover their tab and a little extra. They'd fortunately left the place in as nice a condition as they'd found it in.

That was rare, now that he thought about it.

A white Range Rover waited for them outside and the team gathered their go-bags quickly and joined him. They hurried to the vehicle, loaded everything inside, and clambered in themselves. No one put anything in the trunk.

"Where's the trust, people?" Dexter wondered aloud. No, he decided regretfully, he didn't have time for a quick smoke. Time-sensitive issues had to be resolved. "Fucking assholes."

He slid behind the wheel and started the car.

"What kind of job are we looking at?" the man in the shotgun seat asked as he strapped himself in.

Dexter glanced at the dark-skinned man covered in tattoos and shrugged. "You should have the file on your phone."

"Why don't you simply tell us?" the woman in the back asked.

"Because you have the files on your phones. Now stop bitching."

They wouldn't stop bitching, but that was what came from putting a team together using operatives he didn't know much about. Besides, everyone had some kind of annoying feature.

At least they had time to read everything on the way to Henderson.

CHAPTER THIRTEEN

The sprawling house Marino provided for them certainly exceeded Taylor's expectations. By her sudden silence, he assumed Niki wasn't disappointed either—although her expression was oddly neutral. He had become used to living in what were little more than temporary residences —motels, hotels, and the improvised accommodations he had made for himself.

None of those was a downgrade from what he had made do with in the Zoo area, so he hadn't found them uncomfortable or irksome. Some of the higher-ups were given their own living areas at the base, but the grunts like him lived in tight quarters. It wasn't all that bad, though. They had a tiny space to themselves and the bunks were seldom filled to capacity. He had always managed to create a small, improvised room with a few sheets and temporary walls.

Not the best but certainly the best in a bad situation.

He remained silent as he studied the property the mob boss had directed them to. After his detailed inspection, he raised his eyebrows and acknowledged that he felt distinctly out of place. He didn't often feel that way. Most of the time, when he was in places where he didn't belong, he owned it as much as he could and simply ignored any residual sensations of discomfort.

In this case, however, his usual response seemed frozen and all he could think of was how out of place Liz looked here.

"Well." He grunted and folded his arms in front of his chest. "This is much better than I thought it would be."

Niki stepped beside him and narrowed her eyes. "Are you sure? Look at how the building seems to…fade into the background. It's not quite desert, but the colors they chose make it disappear into the drab brown-ness all around us."

Taylor shrugged. "I like it, though. It makes you feel like you're not intruding on the landscape—like it's simply another part of its surroundings."

"Which would be nice if the landscape weren't a drab semi-desert."

"Say what you want, it has a particular charm."

"I will say what I want." She stuck her tongue out at him. "Come on. Let's see if the inside is any better than the outside. I guess a place like this has a garage, right?"

"It does—there."

He climbed into the driver's seat, moved the vehicle to stop in front of the garage off the road, and pressed the button on his phone to open the door. The lights came on inside as they drove in.

The sheer amount of space was surprising, and Niki's unimpressed expression disappeared quickly.

"Well, okay, this is a little better," she muttered as she scrambled out. "I could spend a couple of days here."

They moved out of the brightly lit garage and up a small flight of stairs that led them into the main area of the house. She looked a little less impressed by the rustic wood and stone interior, but she was still smiling when he stepped behind her, wrapped his arms around her, and drew her close to place a light kiss on the top of her head.

"Okay," she whispered and glanced at him as she ran her fingers through his beard. "I have to concede that it isn't devoid of charm. It isn't my style but honestly, I can picture you here without any problems. It certainly has 'dude' written all over it, from the bar all the way to the big couch there in front of the fireplace."

"Who the fuck needs a fireplace in Nevada?" Taylor asked as he released her and strode toward it.

"I think it's mostly for show with low heat on the flames," Niki commented and put her hand out in front of it. "Besides, the TV here is the main attraction. Seriously, there is...a shitload of TVs."

She wasn't wrong. A number of them were positioned around the main area, which did add credence to what she had said about it being designed with a male occupant in mind. A very particular kind of male occupant, he decided.

But what caught his gaze almost immediately was the view out the back. A few chairs were set up on the terrace to enjoy the sight of the city of Vegas and the pleasant breeze.

"You don't have to have hanging genitals to enjoy that view," he whispered.

Niki nodded. "Like I said, it isn't without its charm."

"It's worth more than a thousand bucks a night, though." He looked around and grimaced. It was a little too big and too up-market for his liking. "More like five grand a night. Hell, he could rent it out for a small fortune every month."

"He's buttering you up," Niki suggested. "He plans to ask you for something, and he wants you well-disposed toward him and owing him as much as possible."

Taylor pulled her into his arms again and stroked her hair tenderly while they both gazed at the view.

"What do you think he'll ask for?" She looked at him with a small frown.

"Well, if he has more people for me to beat the crap out of in front of a camera, I might consider it." Even as he said it, however, he shook his head. "The chances are that won't be the case. I have a feeling he has something big in mind and he wants heavy hitters on his side. That's why he is playing so nice and trying not to piss us off by putting us on the line for something we wouldn't do. He likes to put us in uncomfortable situations when he can, which means that whatever he has in mind will probably be important to him for whatever reason."

"Like when he asked you to go and rescue his ex-wife from a jam?"

"Something like that. Now, enough with the sight-seeing. Let's see if there's something in the kitchen or if we need to go and pick up some food."

They explored the house a little before they returned to the kitchen where, as he'd expected, it seemed someone had come in before them to stock up with food and other necessities required for a comfortable stay over the next few days.

"How good a cook are you?" Niki asked as Taylor began to take a few ingredients out of the fridge.

"Spend enough time in the military and you learn to be creative in making the craziest food edible. With that said, it also means you need to lower your standards a little. Why? How good a cook are you?"

"I don't generally cook my own meals. I never stay too long in a single location where I'm in a position to do so, and I only need to worry about breakfast foods. I do make mean pancakes, though."

He nodded. "Fair enough. We'll have to break those skills out in the morning. For now, though, I feel like playing it a little safe. How do you feel about...steak and fries? There's a grill application...whatever on the stove and an air fryer in the corner. I could make us something to eat in a couple of minutes."

"Only the steak and fries? No salads?"

"Well, if you're in the mood for a salad, why don't you make it and I'll work on the rest of the food?"

It didn't take long. Taylor had making a steak and fries down to a science, and the technology available only made it easier and quicker. He cut the potatoes by hand while the steaks were getting to room temperature and salted and peppered them before he put them in the fryer. The appliance would tell him when they were ready, which left only the steaks to be seasoned and put on the grill.

The tantalizing aroma of frying potatoes and steak soon pervaded the kitchen, while Niki worked on the salad. She somehow made it more complicated than it needed to be but between them, the end result was good enough to provide them with a solid and satisfying—if slightly unhealthy—meal that they consumed with enthusiasm.

"So, what do you think?" she asked and gestured around them. "I suppose it isn't a bad place to live."

"We won't be living here." He mopped up the mess on his plate with pieces of a baguette he had found in the breadbasket.

"No, but what would you think of someone who did live here?"

Taylor scanned their surroundings again, his expression thoughtful. "You'd need one hell of a big family to fill six bedrooms. We're probably thinking a player for the Raiders or maybe someone rich enough to have a family that big as well as buy this house. I think…at least five or six million total, including the taxes. It's way too rich for my blood. At least now you won't be able to say I only take you to cheap motels."

"You've never done that."

"Oh, right. That was you," Taylor replied with a grin.

"Don't give me that shit," Niki snapped. "For one thing, I was on a government budget so there wasn't much of a choice involved there. Secondly, we spent the past couple of nights in your car."

"Truck."

"Right, your truck, so let's call it even then, shall we? Besides, it's not far out of your price range. The spa is a little too decadent, even for me. I like me a hot bath, though. Hopefully with someone big, red-headed, and nude waiting for me inside it."

"We'll have to find some time for that." He stood and gestured for her to join him.

"What—now?"

"Maybe later, but we still need to get all our shit out of the truck." He motioned for her to follow him, determined that he wouldn't carry everything on his own. Not that they had very much. If the two of them each took a load, they'd need only one trip, which was why he wouldn't do it alone.

Niki appeared to understand and joined him as they headed into the spacious garage that managed to make Liz look like a regular-sized truck, if a little out of place with her pure matte-black paint job. What they needed for a quick stay in the well-furnished house was rather limited, although he picked her makeup case up.

The weight of it dragged his hand down more than he'd expected and he grunted. It wasn't too heavy by any means but much heavier than he had expected it to be.

"Holy shit, what did you pack in—oh, right."

"Yeah." Niki smirked. "I thought I'd bring a little extra insurance. You know, just in case."

"Right."

They hauled it all into the master bedroom and placed the makeup case on the silk sheets. Its contents would hopefully not be needed, but after Vickie's warning that someone was looking for them, having some firepower that didn't require about thirty minutes to get into couldn't hurt.

"Have you ever seen *Mr. and Mrs. Smith*?" Niki asked as he pulled a towel out of his bag and spread it over the bed to prevent the weapons from touching the expensive linen.

"The movie?"

"Yeah."

"Are you saying we're at the stage of our relationship where we will try to kill each other?"

"Only if you can't keep it in your jeans." Niki stretched to grab his ass as he began to take the weapons out of the case.

She had come prepared. He chose not to ask her where she'd acquired a sawed-off double-barreled shotgun and three Glocks—two of them with suppressors—along with a 1911 with all the modern trimmings and a handful of combat knives. The real weight of the bag came from the ammo that was packed inside.

"Where did you get all this?" Taylor asked when his curiosity outweighed his common sense. He didn't look at her but continued to fill the empty magazines with bullets and handed them to her to load into the weapons and make sure they were set to safety. "I can't imagine you simply wandered into an illegal weapons sale and bought all of these."

"I did...in a way. But I didn't buy any of it." Niki began to take one of the Glocks apart to clean it. They would no doubt benefit from the maintenance since they had been stored for a while. "It was a raid I was a part of when I first started on the cryptid task force. I wasn't the head of it at the time, and the people we eliminated were enemies of the guy who was in charge. Well, enemies of the people who were paying him. He asked me to cover it up and make it look like another bust that had nothing to do with the cryptids, and that included these weapons."

Taylor nodded and moved to one of his duffel bags,

hefted it easily, and carried it to the bed. With a smirk, he pulled the zipper open.

"You came prepared too?" Niki asked. "Did you raid any weapons dealers in your spare time?"

"I didn't need to as I happen to be friends with some of them." He began to remove the rifles. "They don't mind me taking a few to test them and...well, I prefer to have weapons on and around me if there are people out there who have a mind to kill me."

"I can't fault that." Niki leaned closer to inspect one. "Holy shit is that—"

"One of the new CA models." He held the rifle up so she could see it better. "I think the model number is technically four-oh-four—one of those designed for the smaller suits —and also made to be able to be used without a suit. I guess it's in case you have to abandon the armor and keep fighting."

She took the weapon from his hands and inspected it closely. "Huh. I guess that makes sense. Is the model number supposed to mean anything?"

Taylor shrugged. "I don't know. Why would it?"

"Well, Vickie talks, as you know, and some of it's bound to get out. She keeps saying error four-oh-four, page not found when she forgets something."

"Oh. Maybe."

The weapons were cleaned quickly and loaded, and she retrieved a roll of tape.

"Do you think anyone will complain about the marks we make with that tape?" Taylor asked as he followed her around the house and they taped the weapons in hidden locations throughout.

"Not as much as they'll mind it if the house is part of a firefight," she answered. "Marino must know there's the possibility that a gunfight might happen here. Do you think he would be contracted to fix it and maybe get paid by the insurance company to work on his own house?"

"It seems...wildly illegal." He handed her one of the suppressed Glocks. "Which means it's probably right up his alley."

"Right?"

Taylor looked speculatively around the living room. "Hey, Desk, do you think you'll be able to connect to the house's security system?"

Niki looked at him from where she was taping the firearm under the sofa.

"Sure," the AI replied through the Alexa sound system that was positioned through the house. "I wouldn't be able to directly intervene with anything, however."

"That's fine." He handed Niki the 1911 as she moved to the kitchen. "We only need some kind of early warning system in case these assholes get themselves all up in our business. Make sure they know it too. I want them scared and seeing ghosts if they try to get in here."

"I'm sure I can handle that."

"Oh, and would you be able to connect my playlist to the house speakers too?"

"Of course. Will there be anything else? Should I start scheduling your doctor's appointments as well?"

Taylor looked at the speakers and grimaced when he realized that Desk was merely voicing the sass inherent in the rest of the Banks family. "No, I think that's best done once I reach my forties or fifties."

"When was the last time you had a physical?" Niki asked as she attached the shotgun into one of the kitchen cupboards.

"Remember that time when I dropped a whole helicopter on top of myself?"

She paused and grimaced sheepishly at him. "Oh. Right. They didn't find anything, did they?"

"You mean besides the helicopter I dropped on myself?"

"Yes, smartass," she retorted with a mock scowl.

He couldn't help a grin. "Nothing too bad. The doctor said I might have to consider eating a little less red meat or I might have heart issues in the future."

"I take it the doctor who spoke such blasphemy is rotting somewhere in the desert?" Niki straightened and stretched.

"He's not exactly wrong. I'm a big guy, which means my heart has to pump considerable blood along a greater distance, so it makes sense that I need to take better care of it." He leaned against one of the tables. "I merely never expected to live long enough to have to worry about that type of crap."

"You'd fucking better," she snapped and punched him playfully in the chest. "I'd hate to have to go on a rampage across the west coast to avenge your death."

Taylor caught her second punch attempt and dragged her close to kiss her forehead. He wound his arms around her and squeezed gently. "Who do you think you're kidding? You'd love that shit."

"Sure, but it would be much less fun if you weren't there to rampage with me." She sighed and pressed herself against him.

They'd found the target location easily enough—clear directions had been received, so someone's intel gathering was solid—but waiting for the gate to open for them was a pain in the ass. Of course, their employer couldn't find them a way in, although that was undoubtedly for the best. When people pulled that shit, they inevitably created trails that led directly to them.

And when clients were caught in the act, they cut deals that fucked those they hired right up the ass.

A bright yellow BMW eventually approached the gate of the MacDonald Ranch,. The music that blared from inside was loud enough that the bass vibrated the windows of their Range Rover, and it seemed like exactly the kind of thing that they had hoped for.

Dexter immediately drew in behind the BMW and grinned when it swerved a little. A drunk driver. In Vegas. How fucking shocking was that?

But it was a better choice for them to use cover as the occupants wouldn't be all that aware of their surroundings and especially not of any vehicles behind them. Guards always manned the entrance of gated communities like this, but they didn't like to separate parties traveling together and usually allowed everyone to enter without stopping them.

Of course, questions weren't acceptable to the residents when they were returning home to their million-dollar houses for a night of debauchery.

The gate swung open and the driver of the BMW drove through with them close behind. The tinted windows didn't raise any eyebrows, and the BMW remained oblivious to their presence so close on his tail. The gate was held open for them, and they drove through as the guard tipped his hat to the car with a knowing smile.

The guy probably thought the second vehicle was bringing the hookers or something. He could think what he liked as long as he couldn't see inside. Dexter remained behind the BMW until they were out of sight of the guardhouse, then veered quickly down the road their GPS had highlighted for them.

"Here's good." The sniper tapped him on the shoulder. It was an open area that sloped gently into the hills surrounding their target location. He stopped the Rover at the side of the road, and she climbed out and immediately jogged straight into the open space. She knew where the house was and probably wanted to get an overwatch position to make sure no one escaped. There was also the fact that she would be able to see the cops coming and warn them.

Or, if his experience told him anything, she would bail and leave them to deal with them on their own.

That kind of uncertainty was why he hated gathering teams in a rush like this.

It had been an oddly long day but they were finally able to relax as they chose a movie to watch from the variety of cable and streaming offers.

As it turned out, they could have simply watched anything. The action movie—much like any other—made

Taylor's eyelids droop before the introduction of the hot-as-balls love-interest for the main protagonist. He'd watched variations of it a hundred times before and there was nothing worse than a slow-moving action thriller with no new surprises added to the genre.

"Taylor?"

He sucked in a deep breath and looked at Niki—who hadn't said his name, he realized after a moment. She was fast asleep next to him and snored softly.

A hasty scrutiny of their surroundings revealed no one else, which made it easy for his slightly befuddled brain to pinpoint who had woken him.

"Desk?"

"I am sorry to wake you, but I thought you'd like to know of some suspicious activity in MacDonald Ranch. The kind you might want to be awake for."

Taylor narrowed his eyes. He wanted to stand and see what she was talking about, but Niki was still sleeping with his arm tucked around her.

"Can you show me on the TV?" he asked and kept his voice as low as possible.

"Of course."

The movie flickered away and was replaced by the footage from security cameras in and around the house. A white SUV pulled over to the side of the road and a woman exited, carrying a suspiciously long case. Without a backward glance, she moved purposefully toward the hills that would take her behind the house.

He recognized her gait immediately. She was a trained professional who was used to moving at a fast pace for a long time. He decided there were certainly no prizes for guessing what was in the case.

"A sniper taking up position as overwatch—maybe there to make sure we don't get away." Taylor grunted his annoyance as his blood began to pump and the drowsiness immediately faded. He nudged Niki awake.

"I'm still watching," she whispered. "I swear, best action movie...ever..."

"Not, it's not." He poked her again and she rolled away from him and mumbled something as she squinted at the TV.

"That's...not the movie."

"Nope, it's someone moving in on our location," he replied. She went suddenly from sleepy to alert in the space of less than a second.

"Couldn't they fucking wait?" she demanded and rubbed her eyes. "I'm fucking tired."

"Too tired to kill people coming to kill us?" he asked.

She scrunched her face and shook her head. "Fuck. Do we have time for coffee?"

"I'm afraid not," Desk replied smoothly.

"Well then, someone will fucking die." She pushed to her feet, stretched, and rolled her neck.

"Desk, cut the lights," Taylor instructed. "And give us as much intel as you can. I assume you're already looking into license plates and all that shit."

"I'm industrious like that," the AI replied as the lights turned off around the house.

CHAPTER FOURTEEN

Who would have thought it would be so difficult to reach the right position in the hills? Her phone, fortunately, pinpointed the places where the rich fucks had put motion sensors up. The entire gated community was surrounded by walls and fences but it seemed that wasn't enough for the residents to feel safe.

Their response was to simply install more security. Still, she was able to negotiate a somewhat twisted path between the zones of motion sensors and cameras. This finally led her into the area she had marked off as the best location for an unimpeded view over the target location.

She settled in, retrieved her rifle, and placed it on a blanket, but stretched prone with her binoculars, which was all she intended to do for the moment. Even with a suppressor, the sound of her weapon would prompt every single person in a ten-mile radius to call the cops.

And given how many rich tax-payers lived in the area, it wasn't a stretch to imagine that so many cops would rush to respond that the complex would look like a law-enforcement convention. This was where all the donors to the sheriff's department and every politician in the state of Nevada lived. If something went wrong, there was no real possibility of escape.

"It's the only reason why they're dropping a million dollars per merc on this one," she whispered caustically.

"What was that?" Dexter asked in her earbud.

"It looks like the house is clear. I see lights but no movement. Someone's in there, but they're probably in bed. I'm not—"

She paused. Almost like magic, every single light in the house went out, even those that were supposed to stay on at night. Her brief study of the information available had given her that information. The community rules demanded that certain lights in the neighborhood be left on so the bright, shining piece of shit remained visible, night or day. There was nothing more to it than that.

Now, however, the lights were out.

"Shit," Jen whispered and tapped her earbud to catch the attention of her teammates in the SUV.

"Jesus fucking—what?"

"All the lights in the house went out."

A pause followed. "What?"

"Are you deaf? All the lights. In the house. Went off. You can see it from the street unless you fucking went blind too —in which case it was a huge mistake to let you drive us here."

"Okay, okay, I see it. Why…why is it important?"

She sighed. That was what she got when she agreed to work with a team she didn't know.

"Because it means someone's awake inside. And honestly, all the lights going out at the same time is not a good sign moments before you're about to break into a building. I'm merely giving you dumbasses a heads-up on the situation. If you get killed, that'll be on you. I'll eliminate the targets from a long fucking way away and take all your cuts."

"Right, just...shut up," Dexter retorted and she smirked as the SUV inched toward the house. "Consider yourself our heads-up. Give us some overwatch and keep your eyes open for any movement from inside."

"Yeah," she whispered and peered through her binoculars. Unfortunately, with the lights all out and a full moon with no clouds, it meant the light outside was brighter than the interior. All she could see in the windows was a reflection.

She tilted her head, took a deep breath, and settled into position. There was no point in letting anyone think she was doing anything but the job she was hired to do—even if she couldn't fucking see anything.

The team left the SUV at a trot. They looked like professionals, at least, and avoided all the cameras and remained far away from any of the other houses. It was a good place to stage the attack. Nothing about it concerned her, but if someone was expecting them inside, they had reason to be alarmed. The long and the short of it was that two dangerous, trained killers would be waiting and ready for the team inside the house.

And she couldn't help them, she acknowledged with an internal shrug. If this had been a team she had helped to put together, she would care. She would point it out to them and would make them retreat and try again at another time and place.

Her every instinct told her it was a bad op. If the client didn't like it, they would turn the money down and walk away. There were too many ways that this could end badly, and it was pointless to take money if they were too dead or arrested to spend it.

But she didn't know anything about the assholes except that they were all killers. Nothing about her time spent with them suggested that she would want to stick her neck out to save them. If they wanted to charge in with their dicks in their hands, she wouldn't lose any sleep over it.

Jen shook her head. "I hope you guys all have your funeral plans set up."

"What was that?"

"You heard me."

The whole house was quiet except for the soft hum of a handful of appliances. The lights were out, and it looked as if it had been cut off from the rest of civilization.

Taylor couldn't think of a better way to describe it. What was about to happen was far from civilized. He wouldn't be surprised if hundreds of police were called within minutes of the first volley. And given the average annual salary of the people who lived in the area, he would put good money on law enforcement arriving in force to make sure the donations to their retirement funds remained intact.

He doubted they would get there in time to save any of the dumbasses coming in, though.

His gaze shifted to where Niki stood, her back to a wall and her attention fixed on one of the entrances to the living room. He motioned for her to watch his six as he wanted to make sure they didn't use windows as a means of ingress.

She shook her head and raised her hand in the universal questioning gesture. He motioned again and she scowled.

"Goddamn it, watch my six," Taylor snapped.

"Just fucking say so."

He responded with another gesture, this one much simpler to decipher as there was only one finger involved. She reciprocated as he moved away from his position, his weapon ready as he inched toward the bedrooms.

The silence was worse than having gunfire and monsters screaming all around him. At least at that point, he would know where he was shooting, who he was defending, and how to get himself out alive.

Having to wait for Desk to give them a heads-up about where he needed to focus wasn't a great feeling. And the fact that Niki looked calmer than he felt only made it worse.

"Movement at the front of the house," the AI said softly over the speakers. He nodded, tightened his grasp on his pistol, and sucked in a deep breath to stop himself from flinging himself into the inevitable fight.

He wasn't wearing a suit, he reminded himself. There was no armor between himself and the bullets he might not be able to avoid.

"They're moving to the bedroom windows," Desk said, and she had lowered the volume on the speakers before she spoke.

Taylor motioned for Niki to stay in position and hold the front doors while he moved to intercept those at the bedroom.

She scowled.

"For fuck's sake, hold your position," he snapped in a hushed whisper.

She gave him a thumbs-up and he circled away from the entrance. At least having something to do would help keep him from losing it.

Something was wrong with the whole situation. Dexter could feel it as they approached the house and scowled when the inner warning refused to abate. The fact that all the lights inside had gone out moments before they intended to breach was the first sign, of course, but there were other things too.

The smaller details were often more telling than people expected. The property didn't look much like the kind of safe house he had been told to expect. There were no obvious signs that security had been increased or that defensible positions had been set up inside—at least from what he could see through the darkened windows.

While he would usually be relieved that they weren't present for an attack like this, it all felt a little too inviting. And with the lights going out, everything about it felt like a trap.

Still, they were committed. They certainly wouldn't back out of the job now.

"Is there any movement inside?" he asked through the comms.

"I can't see shit, remember?" the sniper retorted sharply.

Heading into this with a team he didn't know was a mistake. If they had simply targeted some lazy fuck who had no idea they were coming, it would be one thing. But having looked into the kind of people they would face, he knew things would be a little different.

They were trained, armed, and probably ready for them, he reasoned. There would be no walking away this time.

Backing out was always an option. Perhaps he could simply send the other two guys in to create the appearance of a tough fight while he bolted.

Which, of course, was a terrible idea. The sniper would still be there, ready to pick him off for letting the rest of the team die. He wouldn't even reach the car.

"Let's get this over with," he ordered. They wouldn't go in through the front door and would need to find an alternate means of ingress. He gestured for the men to follow him around the house. There didn't appear to be any motion sensors on the property that might trigger alarms to indicate their presence, but it was already far too late to worry about those.

Dexter moved forward first and pressed his semi-automatic shotgun to the windowsill as he tried to see inside. It looked like a guest bedroom and there was no movement. Not that it meant anything, but at least they would probably come at their targets from an angle they didn't expect.

"Open it. I'll cover you," he whispered to the man beside him, who nodded and approached hastily, raised the butt of his assault rifle, and swung it to strike the glass.

He muttered a curse and stopped the man forcibly before he could do what he had planned.

"What?" the mercenary asked as he dragged him back. "I'm opening the window."

"You're breaking the glass, making a shit-ton of noise, and alerting them to our point of ingress. But no, fucking go ahead. I'll wait here to use your body as a human shield."

He looked at the two men with him and waited for them to show any sign of resistance, but there was none. They weren't the brightest but maybe not the dumbest either.

"Now, open the window. Pull it open."

The man nodded, approached the window again, and after a brief search, finally found the gap. He pulled and pushed until there was space for him to work with. Finally, with a little help from his knife, it opened and he pulled it wide enough for them to climb inside.

"See how we're not being fucking gunned down before we even go through?"

"Shut the fuck up, Dexter," the other man responded belligerently and pushed him toward the aperture. They climbed through, covering each other as they scrambled over the sill.

The first man in checked the room and made sure that it was clear before he focused on the door while the other two entered.

So far, there appeared to be no sign that their presence

had been detected. Still, one couldn't be too careful. The team leader held two fingers up to his eyes and jerked a thumb over his shoulder at the last man in, who nodded and approached at an angle that allowed him to watch the window they'd used. It would be plain fucking stupid to allow someone to attack them from behind without at least a hint of warning.

The man in front of Dexter confirmed that his flanks and rear were covered before he took light steps toward the door. He held his weapon trained forward with one hand as he pulled it open slowly with the other.

Desk had fallen silent, and that was all the indication Niki needed to know that the assassins were in the house somewhere. Her last warning was that they intended to gain access through the bedrooms, which meant her current position guarding the front door wouldn't provide her with much cover.

She had no suit to stop the first bullet that was fired from killing her outright, and there was no way to bluster and intimidate her way out of this one. Taylor was already in motion and his bare feet glided over the floor with barely a whisper of sound as he inched toward the bedrooms.

He glanced at her as if he'd heard something and motioned to her, then lowered his hand. That gesture was fairly obvious, and she dropped next to one of the sofas. While not great in terms of solid protection, it would have to do for now. The blackness around them made it difficult to see any real movement, but the subtle sound of a door being opened did draw her attention.

Light footfalls could be heard a moment later, and she could barely see movement in the shadows cast over the house. She had no idea if Taylor could see in this kind of darkness, but she didn't want to accidentally shoot him if he chose to close the distance between them.

Suddenly, one of the lights flickered on. It worked almost like a spotlight to illuminate three of the home invaders. They were well-armed and seemed to wear body armor too, but they were suitably surprised by the sudden bright light that gave their position away.

"Thanks, Desk," Niki whispered as Taylor snatched the opportunity before she could act.

Niki kept most of her body behind the sofa but peeked cautiously to see with one eye as she pushed her weapon out to open fire on the assassin. They recognized the danger they were in immediately and dove for cover as other lights came on.

One of the mercs fell back and clutched his chest, where it seemed Taylor had tagged him. His body armor protected him, however, and his comrades dragged him out of the line of fire while they retaliated.

She dropped back behind the couch as the return fire shattered something behind her. With a grimace, she saw that one of the vases near the door was now in pieces.

"That was a Ming Vase," she yelled at them. "You... fucking Philistines!"

A hot sting in her arm and more shattering and breaking around her registered and she realized she was being shot at. The motion was almost purely out of instinct when she flung herself to the side as the booming crack of a rifle sounded from outside. She cursed and rolled across the floor to the small nook inside the kitchen that provided better protection from more angles before she confirmed that one of the windows was broken.

"Taylor!" she shouted. "We have a fucking sniper!"

"I noticed. Are you hurt?"

Niki looked at her arm. A small trickle of blood flowed from a couple of cuts but there was no sign of a bullet hole anywhere, even if the injuries stung like hell.

"I'm fine!" she shouted and checked her weapon again.

It didn't seem like the kind of night when she would have many shots. She yanked the bolt on her rifle to eject the spent casing and let it fall on her blanket to be collected later.

Worse, it wasn't the best night to miss her first shot either. Not only had she alerted the people inside of her presence, but it also gave them a basic idea of where she was. The inner voice protested that she could expect little more from a night and an operation that shouldn't have happened.

"Fucking shit," she whispered and peered through the scope again. Things hadn't gone well from the start. Somehow, one of the lights came on to expose all three of her teammates, although the rest of the house remained dark. They managed to survive that and it gave Jen her shot, thanks to the flashes from their firearms.

But movement in the shadows told her that her estimate of McFadden's size was a little off.

She made a note of it on her notebook and settled again, stared through the scope, and tried to choose the best angle so she'd be ready when her target stepped into her line of sight. He would be cautious now, though, and she would have maybe one more shot from this position before it began to get dangerous, and she needed to make it count.

Something buzzed insistently.

Rod wondered if it was a dream or perhaps something happening in the house beyond what he needed to care about.

The girl had certainly put him through his paces. She knew how to tire a guy, although from the way she was sleeping contentedly without so much as sensing the buzzing that woke him, he felt safe in assuming he'd delivered as well as she had.

But, he realized morosely, he wouldn't be left alone by whoever was calling him.

He groaned, pulled himself out from under the silk sheets, and moved to the side of the bed, where his phone was charging. He didn't recognize the number on the screen but it looked like a business-held number.

It was a weird time for them to call him. He moved to the verandah to avoid waking the woman on the bed and pressed the button to accept the call.

"Mr. Marino?"

"Yes," he answered. "Who is this?"

"It's Vince McCarran. I'm your security supervisor. I was told you wanted to be alerted regarding any alarms triggered in your residences at the MacDonald Ranch."

"Right." He rubbed his eyes and sat on one of the nearby chairs. "Which...which one has the alarms?"

Like he even needed to ask. He owned two properties in the high-end community and he was in one of them. Taylor and Niki were in the other.

"The one you keep for guests, sir. You should also know that the police have been notified of shots fired in the area and are responding immediately. Would you like me to head out there and see what the trouble is?"

The mob boss paused and took a moment to collect his thoughts as he looked blankly at his heated pool. Perhaps a midnight dip was in order now that he was awake.

"No, not right now, Vince. If you arrive there, you might be injured yourself. Let the cops do their job and stop there in the morning. Oh, and get my adjuster on the line too. He'll want to have a word about what's happening there."

"Pardon my asking, sir, but...uh, what is going on there?"

That was a good question. They'd told him people had targeted them and they needed a place to lay low. Depending on the class of people who had chosen to attack, he was either looking at a few broken windows and a couple of couches that needed to be repaired, or a complete demolition of the house.

And anywhere between. Rod would never say it, but that was always what endeared him to Taylor and Niki.

Their explosive temperament was only matched by their explosive methods of self-defense.

"I let a couple of friends spend a few days there," he explained casually. "I guess they had a couple of friends over themselves."

And that was about as much as he was willing to commit himself to the situation before he could see what was happening there.

"Of course, sir. I...I'll get right on it."

"See that you do," he replied, pressed the button to end the call, and placed his phone on a nearby table.

He most likely wouldn't go back to sleep tonight, which was something of a nuisance. Hopefully, he would be able to nap later in the day—one of the benefits of running a casino, he supposed—but it was still a pain in the ass. Perhaps he would have the time for a dip in the water and a drink from the bar. A Cosmo sounded good right now.

His eyes narrowed as he looked at his phone and he pursed his lips when it rang again. This time, it displayed the number of another of his security advisors who kept an eye on the less-than-legal pursuits he was involved in.

"I'll be up all night with this shit," he whispered and resigned himself to the inevitable.

CHAPTER FIFTEEN

"What are you thinking?" Taylor asked and scanned the room before he checked the pistol in his hands. "By my calculations, it looks like it'll be sixty, maybe seventy thousand bucks on the rental bill."

Niki peeked out from behind her cover and narrowed her eyes. "Are you nuts? They destroyed a Ming Vase. If it was real, they sell for a hundred grand, easy. It could even be two hundred and fifty thousand."

"Let's hope it wasn't a real one then," he quipped, slapped his magazine into the pistol, and checked the edge of the wall he used to shield him to make sure their attackers weren't moving out. "Or that it's insured."

"You still have to pay for it, even if it's insured," she pointed out, ducked out of her hideyhole, and fired into the bedroom their attackers were still huddled in. "They'll litigate you until you pay, even if Marino lets his insurance take it."

"But we're simply hanging out here and defending ourselves." He inched toward the bedroom and strained to hear the hushed discussion from within as he approached. With a grimace, he kept his right eye closed as he slipped into the comparatively bright light Desk turned on. "These guys are attacking us. Wouldn't they be the ones who are litigated?"

"That's a little vague, but they'll probably be a little too dead to answer their court summons anyway. Insurance companies don't take any losses if they can help it."

She wasn't wrong there, but he doubted that the vase was a real Ming. He had no idea if Rod would know the difference between a real or a fake vase or if it even mattered. Now that it was in pieces, there might be no way to prove that it was or wasn't. It meant that if it had been insured for however much, they would probably be on the line for that amount, even if they were merely defending themselves.

He shrugged the questions aside and instead, used the lull in the action to sneak close to the room. Once in position, he tried to keep his breathing even and waited for his opportunity.

Desk turned the light off. It was enough.

Taylor stepped alongside the doorway and opened the eye he had kept adapted to the darkness while the group inside was blinded by the sudden blackness around them.

It wouldn't last long, but it was still as much of an opening as he would ever have. He kept himself hidden by the wall, leaned only enough of himself around the edge to snake his gun hand out, and opened fire.

The man closest to him almost didn't notice him before he fell back when two bullets punched through his skull and sprayed blood and brain matter out the back. His two comrades were caught by surprise. Taylor shifted his aim to the left, resisted the urge to aim for center mass, and attempted a headshot again.

In the dark, one of the bullets missed but the second clipped his target across the throat. Blood sprayed out and the round shattered the window in the back of the room as well.

With two accounted for, he turned quickly to locate the last man—who he knew should be there unless he'd snuck out through the window—and narrowed his eyes as tried to peer through the darkness.

"Desk, is the third guy still in the building or—"

He didn't need to finish his sentence as movement answered the question for him. Instinct clicked in and he swiveled and fired, but the only shot he could get off went wide and the intruder surged toward him from behind the door.

"Never mind!" he yelled as they fell heavily together. "I found him!"

The man was easily powerful enough to pin him to the floor, although a little smaller overall. The hold on his gun hand was impressive, and Taylor was trapped. He used his free hand to try to stop his assailant from swinging his weapon to aim it at him.

A hint of panic touched him when he was unable to raise his gun hand thanks to his adversary's unyielding hold. The assassin's weapon moved slowly and inexorably toward him.

"Knock, knock," Niki announced from where she stood over them. "Did you forget about me?"

She placed the barrel of her weapon to the man's

temple and pulled the trigger. The merc went limp and sagged to the side and away from Taylor, who swiped at the splatter that caught him with a grimace.

"Couldn't you have dropped your punchline after you killed him?" he asked and took her hand to help him to his feet.

Niki grunted under the weight but managed to drag him up without too much difficulty.

"He wouldn't be able to hear it if he was already dead," she pointed out and helped to clean a few droplets that had caught him.

He looked at the dead body. "Is this an improvement?"

"Sure. He went off to wherever he'll end up with my killer one-liner still ringing in his ears."

"Right."

"Don't trash it. Even you have to admit it was a killer one-liner."

"Well, yeah. Killer, without a doubt, but the fact that he had trained his gun on me and was about to pull the trigger might have inspired you to act a little faster."

"I saved your life and you're complaining about me taking a second to bask in that?"

"Yes!"

"Okay." Niki nodded. "Just making sure."

Desk turned one of the lights on again on the other side of the house and drew their attention to the window that had a bullet hole in it.

"You do remember there is a sniper out there, right?" she asked politely

"Oh, shit," Taylor dragged Niki away from the windows. He had no idea why the markswoman hadn't taken another shot at them yet. Perhaps the lack of light hadn't offered her a clear shot.

Still, he wasn't sure how long that would last.

"We need to get rid of the sniper," he muttered and tried to find a way to look out without putting himself in the line of fire.

"You don't say?" Niki answered. "I thought we could simply go over there and invite him in for tea or something."

"It's her."

"What?"

"The sniper is a woman. Didn't you see when she stepped out of the SUV and moved away to find herself a nice sheltered position? Didn't you watch the footage?"

"I...yes. I did. But in my defense, I have not had any caffeine since before the moment we began to prepare for this fight."

Taylor nodded and checked his weapon again before he looked around for the places where the others were stashed. "I think I have a plan."

"To get me some coffee?"

He glared at her and narrowed his eyes until she realized that was not what he meant.

"Oh...to deal with the sniper." She nodded. "Right. The plan doesn't involve any kind of bait, right? Because I won't be the bait."

"Should I be the bait, then?"

Niki thought about it but shook her head quickly. "No, that doesn't work either. You're too big a target. Why don't we simply let the police handle this fucker?"

"Because she'll run, and we'll have someone out there

who's taken money to kill us. I'm not sure about you, but I'd rather not have a target painted on our backs."

"Right." She crouched and stayed low as she moved to the far side of the room, fumbled under one of the tables, and retrieved the assault rifle he had stashed under it. With a grin, she brought the weapon to him.

"What's this for?"

"I thought you could start shooting and keep her distracted while I find her and gut her—up close and personal."

Taylor smirked and took the weapon she was offering. "I...like your phrasing there."

"Thanks."

He stretched his hand to the counter and managed to find a metal spatula before he sank below the edge of their cover.

Before he could look out again, his phone rang.

"Who would call you in the middle of this?" Niki asked as he yanked the device out.

"Hopefully someone who doesn't know we trashed his house yet," Taylor answered before picking the call up. "Marino, you know what time it is, right?"

"Yes, and I'm sorry to call you so late," the mob boss said with a laugh. "How are you doing?"

"Oh, you know..." Taylor paused and used the light from his phone to reflect off the spatula as he inched it out from behind the low wall they hunkered behind. It was visible and glinted for less than a second before a round knocked it out of his hand, quickly followed by the crack of a high-powered rifle from outside and glass shattering.

The shooter was good and on the ball too. Perhaps she

had simply waited for the others to be killed so she could take the money for herself.

"Surviving." He finally completed his sentence and shook his hand as the impact left his fingers a little numb. "How are you?"

"Not too bad. I had turned in for the evening after a nice night of drilling this hot model I've been going out with—"

"To quote Vickie, barf," Niki snapped.

"And I get a call from my security guys to tell me one of my properties is the site of a gunfight and is about to be filled with all the police in Henderson, Nevada. What gives, McFadden?"

Taylor raised an eyebrow. The cat was out of the bag, he supposed.

"So, here's the situation," he said, retrieved the spatula, and handed it to Niki." You remember how we said people had targeted us?"

"Right."

"And remember how those types of people tend to have guns?"

"Yes."

"Well, there you go. We're merely defending ourselves."

Marino took a moment to reply. "Okay, fair enough. But you don't sound like you're in too much danger."

He shrugged. "With a little help, we eliminated the three guys who broke in easily enough, but a sniper has us pinned down and she's the real problem. We're in the process of handling it, though."

The mob boss sighed audibly. "Okay, but...try to keep

the damages to a minimum. I'm fairly sure I can talk my insurance company into covering most of the damages."

"Don't you own the insurance company, though?" Niki asked.

"Well, yes, that's why I think I can talk them into covering most of the damages. Talk to you later—and do try to stay alive."

"We'll do our best," he said before he pressed the button to end the call. "Desk, you wouldn't happen to have a satellite image of where our sniper is, would you?"

"I thought you'd never ask," the AI answered over the speakers. "If Niki would like to take the opportunity to leave out the back, I can guide her to where the woman is hiding."

"What...what opportunity?" Niki asked and looked around.

"Oh—the one where Taylor opens fire. If you direct your aim to a small hill overlooking that east window that was fired at, you should be able to lay enough fire down to force the sniper to move to another position. I'll watch her movements and help Niki track her."

"I...don't have my phone." She collected another of the firearms and tucked it into her pants.

Taylor handed her his. "It's about time for me to get a replacement anyway."

"Aw." She took the device with a small grin. "You trust me with your phone?"

"Sure." He narrowed his eyes. "But...I'm now having second thoughts."

"Too late." She cackled evilly before she crawled to the

back of the house where she would sneak out to head out into the area where the sniper was.

Taylor only had to move out a few yards to the window already damaged by the rifle fire. It filled most of the wall and the two bullet holes were close enough to each other that it could be inferred that they had been fired from the same place—the hill not far from the location of the house.

He remained low and crawled across the floor. The assumption was that the woman couldn't see what was happening inside, as the light from the moon and stars in the clear night, along with the lack of light from inside the house, made it much like a one-way mirror.

But there was no point in making himself an easy target. Even the smallest amount of light was enough to catch her attention.

"It seems she is staying where she is," Desk announced as he settled into his chosen position and aimed the assault rifle toward the small hill the AI had pointed out to him. "Niki is waiting for you to open fire before she makes a break for it."

"Right," Taylor whispered. Without a scope, he doubted he could do better than someone with a rifle made for long-distance shooting, but hitting the sniper wasn't the point.

"You should know that police officers are on their way to your location," Desk said and broke his concentration. "The weapons Niki has were not legally acquired, although the argument could be made that they were in the hands of the attackers first and you simply took them."

"Can't you simply register the weapons in our names?"

"It is possible, but I cannot account for any of them if their serial numbers have been filed off."

Taylor nodded. "Took the guns off them it is. We'll need to do a little work to get that going."

"I agree. Niki is asking if you are ready to—and I quote —get off your lazy ass and make yourself a tasty bait for the sniper."

"Yeah, give me a second."

He still didn't feel perfectly safe firing from his position, even though he had hunkered down to make as small a target as he could. And yet, if she was good enough, that wouldn't matter.

"Okay." He breathed deeply, leaned closer to the sight, and fixed in on a likely point on the hill. "Let me know if there's a chance she can pick me off, okay?"

"I will. Good luck."

No movement could be seen inside. No more muzzle flashes meant not even a hint of a target, not with the reflection from the windows.

The police would arrive soon, and she wanted to be out before the flashing lights drew close.

All indications were that the team inside was dead so perhaps she could simply let everyone assume she died with them and head to somewhere sunny. She'd made enough money in her work to be able to lay low and be comfortable for a couple of years.

No. Six months if she wanted to live comfortably. She could probably find a cheaper location and live out of sight almost indefinitely, but the idea was to settle down comfortably.

That would come if she collected the money for the job on her own.

One more chance was all she needed. After one more shot, she would bail. It would take only a little longer.

Suddenly, the house lit up. Muzzle flashes from a larger weapon—aimed directly at her—fired off a quick three-round burst.

How could it be aimed at her? She hadn't moved from her position, but the suppressor was supposed to hide her muzzle flash.

Jen covered her head as the rounds impacted on the rocks and sand around her. It wasn't the most accurate shooting but way too close for comfort.

"Shit!" She hissed as she rolled to her feet, snatched her blanket from the ground, and packed everything up as the ground around her spattered and flurried with the bullets fired from the house.

It was suppressing fire, she realized, and none of the rounds hit home, but it would take only one to end everything.

She had stuck around a little too long and got a little too greedy.

"Lesson learned," she whispered and began to sprint toward the edge of the community. It would take a while, but if she maintained her pace, she would be able to find her way out of this mess.

The shooter inside the house was tracking her movement, and she yanked her rifle up with no attempt to put the scope to her eye and simply fired in the general direction of the still darkened building. If she could lay some cover fire of her own, maybe he would be nice enough to fuck off and let her leave.

Live and let live and all that shit.

The shooting continued, however. Another bullet went through one of the second-story windows and she finally drew behind a few boulders as the rounds continued to kick the dust up all around her.

"Okay, motherfucker, you want to play rough…" She hissed her irritation and settled on her stomach in a small gap between the boulders, raised the rifle to her cheek, and looked through the scope to try to find a target in the house. "Say hello to my little f—"

The sentence cut off when something struck her hard in the back. It was an impossible shot for the person in the building and the sound hadn't come from there anyway.

A crack echoed in the open area around her and Jen shivered as she stared at her chest, where the blood already soaked through her shirt.

Another crack accompanied another hard punch into her back, and she dropped the rifle to turn slowly. A woman stood a few paces away and moved quickly to kick the weapon away.

"Where the fuck did you come from?" the sniper asked and touched the two exit wounds on her chest lightly.

"Hell. Tell the folks there I said hi."

She narrowed her eyes. "Seriously? Is that what you're going with?"

Her attacker dropped onto her haunches beside her, searched her quickly, and took the sidearm she had tucked into her trousers.

"What's wrong with it? Do you have any better ideas?"

"Ideas?" Jen coughed as the pain wracked her body. "For the next time you shoot someone in the back?"

"Sure. Or in the chest and the neck. Not the head, of course, since the person wouldn't hear that."

The stupid bitch was talking to her while she was bleeding out. She couldn't imagine anything stranger, although nothing defined what was strange about it. There wasn't anything unprofessional about the conversation. It was merely odd.

Even more weird, the stars had all gone out. Would it be morning soon?

"The upper-story windows?" Taylor asked. "Yeah, the last one was outside and I think she was trying to get away."

"A woman mercenary," Rod asked through the speakers around the house. "Way to break that particular glass ceiling."

"I guess." He paused in collecting their weapons. While he could already hear the sirens of approaching police cruisers, Desk had told him they still had about five minutes, which left him more than enough time to make sure the weapons were stashed where they would not be found.

Of course, he was in the middle of it when the AI told him that Rod was on the landline. He didn't even know the house had a landline.

"So yeah, those windows on the second floor were crystal. Are you sure they were broken?"

He shook his head and planted a few prints from the dead assassins on the guns that had been used since the cops would look for those.

"I'm sure," he answered. "Will that be a problem?"

"Not really. I've wanted to replace those. So double-aughts, you know?"

There was no way he knew what that meant but he played along. "Sure. Double-aughts. There's blood all over the place. And a vase. Niki thought it was a Ming vase."

"Oh, that's good. They're insured for much more than I'd be able to sell them for. Honestly, all this has made the renovation process that much cheaper."

"Right," Taylor grumbled, a little confused by the man's response but distracted by the more pressing matter of the illegal weapons. "But what about the...I don't know, intrinsic historical value and all that?"

"Who gives a shit? I got them for a song and it wasn't even my song. If someone wants to pay for historical value, they can pick the pieces up from the floor and glue them together."

"Okay. So, the fact that we tried to keep the damages down around here—"

"You shouldn't have bothered. In fact, did you see a nude downstairs?"

"Nude?" Taylor asked and looked around as Niki entered. "Niki?"

"Yeah, yeah, I had to set the body up so we didn't have to explain too much to the cops. I was FBI so I know what I'm doing."

"That's...great," he responded, took the weapon from

her hands, and wiped her prints off it. "Did you see a nude downstairs?"

"The one with the tiny dick?" she asked. "In the blue room?"

"That's the one!" Rod answered. "Was it damaged at all?"

Taylor walked down the stairs to where the statue was. "Nope. And that is a tiny dick."

"Right?" Niki studied it critically. "Most guys had the common courtesy to simply cover it with a fig leaf or something."

"Okay," the mob boss announced. "I'll give you fifteen grand in credit if you put a couple of holes in it and maybe push it over."

"If you could give us that fifteen in cash, you have a deal," Taylor said quickly.

"Done."

He raised the weapon Niki had used and emptied the magazine into the statue, although he tried to spread the bullets around as randomly as possible. Finally, he shoved it off its pedestal.

"Was that necessary?" Niki asked as he handed her the pistol and gestured to warn her to wipe it and avoid putting more prints on it.

"I'm only trying to sell it. Put a couple of prints from the mercs on the gun and toss it somewhere."

She nodded. "Good thinking."

The sirens were closer by the time Taylor finished arranging the scene to cause the least amount of suspicion.

"So, shooting the Ming vase was a good thing?" Niki asked as she picked up the weapon Taylor had used earlier.

"Oh yeah," Rod confirmed.

"Cool." She raised it and emptied the magazine into the rest of the vases around the room. "Best. Day. Ever."

Taylor smirked. "I don't suppose you could make a call to the chief of the Henderson Police department?"

"Thedrick—sure, no problem."

The line cut and he shrugged as he checked again that none of the weapons left for the police to find had their prints on them.

"All in all," he muttered, "it's not the worst night I've ever had in Vegas."

"We're in Henderson, technically."

He turned to look at her. "Seriously? I can't have this one zinger? After you've dropped them all night?"

Niki smirked, moved closer to him, and kissed him on the lips. "Fine. Not the worst night in Vegas."

"Thank you."

The fact that so many officers arrived in response to the call was a little wasteful.

Nights in Henderson provided more than enough to keep them all busy, but when the call came in that some rich guy's house was the scene of a gunfight, everyone dropped their collective shit and high-tailed it to the location.

Officer Prentis was still fairly new to the area so it took him a little while to realize whose house they were going to. Once that was resolved, everything else started to make sense.

He was the first to approach the house and pressed the buzzer, his hand on the pistol at his hip.

"Yeah?" said a rough male voice.

"Hello, would you mind...coming out here?"

"Oh, you must be the police. Just a second."

The intercom cut out and he stood in front of the door, unsure of what exactly he was waiting for. Most of the other officers hung back with the cruisers, possibly expecting some kind of gun battle.

After a few moments, the door opened and he took a step back when a giant of a man stepped out. Perhaps the red hair and beard made him look a little bigger than he was, but it seemed unlikely.

"You must be...Taylor McFadden?" Prentis asked, his hand still hovering near his weapon.

"That's me. Do you want to see an ID?"

"That...that won't be necessary. We're only here to make sure Mr. Rod Marino's guests are all right. You and... Niki Banks?"

"Oh...yes. Niki got some glass in her arm but aside from that, everything's all right."

"We have ambulances on the way."

McFadden scowled and scanned the tense demeanor of the other officers.

"That's...nice," he replied. "But not necessary. The four idiots who attacked the house are already cashing in their collective chips with St. Peter."

The officer narrowed his eyes.

"They're dead," the giant explained.

"Oh. Right."

"I thought the...you know, we're in Vegas. Or close to Vegas."

Prentis nodded. "No, no, I got it. It simply took me a second."

"Good." McFadden nodded and waved to the other officers. "If you guys want to come in to do your...uh, CSI shit, that's fine, but the situation has been handled. I think we'll need the coroner eventually. And maybe... I don't know, but Marino said his insurance people will need to come through too. I don't know how or when it will all happen."

"That shouldn't be a problem." He motioned the other members of the force forward. "Do you have a place to stay for the night?"

"We'll make a plan. Neither of us will get much sleep tonight, though."

He nodded. "I hear that."

McFadden looked at the young man as his colleagues pushed into the house. "Is this your first crime scene?"

"I...yeah. I've been on a couple of drug busts but I write tickets, mostly."

"Right. You might want to skip the bodies. Or take it slow. Just a heads up."

"Thanks."

A nap had worked wonders. He never had been sure why but a massage, a good fuck, a nap, and a couple of espressos were almost as good as six hours of sleep.

It wasn't the preferred option, of course, but it would

do in a pinch and only took a couple of hours to accomplish.

News about what happened to his house had poured in all night. Anyone else would be devastated but in the end, he had planned to renovate soon anyway.

This had merely expedited the process.

The phone rang and this time, Rod was expecting the call and accepted it without complaint.

"Harry, thanks for getting back to me so quickly," he said.

"No problem. When I heard about what happened, I made checking the house my number one priority."

It was probably a good thing it wasn't a video call since he wasn't able to stop a smile from spreading across his face.

"Thank you so much for that. My friends... Well, I had no idea they were dealing with that type of violent element, you know?"

"Well, whoever targeted them was certainly pissed off. It'll take a little while to calculate the full amount that's covered by your policy."

"What about the Ming vases?" he asked and tried not to sound too gleeful.

"All wrecked. I think the living area was where most of the fighting happened. That is what the police officers surmised as well, although neither side seemed to be particularly good shots. No blood indicated a wound of any kind. It's weird, honestly—almost like their target was the room and the items in it rather than the occupants."

"Oh, and there was a priceless nude in the blue room. Did they—"

"Unfortunately, it was knocked over so the head was broken off, and it had been subjected to gunshots. There was a concentration in the...groin, area."

"You mean they shot the dick off?"

"If you will."

"Damn them. It wouldn't surprise me if that was Niki—and not by accident either. She has it in for most men."

"Oh. I hope you'll talk to her about that."

"Maybe over the phone," responded dryly. "Did you talk to her?"

"Only to get her statement for my files."

"And she didn't shoot you?"

He paused. "I feel the answer to that is obvious."

"Well, you got off lucky. This has been...a complete fiasco. What a clusterfuck."

"I understand, Mr. Marino. We'll handle the situation as quickly as possible and I'll get back to you as soon as we have any updates."

"I appreciate that, Harry. I'll take those two off my Christmas list, you can believe that."

"Of...of course, Mr. Marino. I hope you have a good day."

Rod hung up, chuckled, and shook his head as he opened the bottom drawer of his desk to reveal a small safe tucked inside it. He punched the six-digit combination in quickly, pulled it open, and smiled as his gaze settled on a specially built humidor.

An expensive selection of Cubans had been smuggled into the country, and he had made sure he got a cut of that particular action. Now seemed like the time to celebrate with one.

It was quick work to clip it and light it. He used a match as was proper when handling something as unique as a genuine Cuban cigar.

He sucked slowly, closed his eyes, and let the taste linger in his mouth for a few seconds before he breathed out.

"That man and that woman might be the best things to have ever happened to me," he muttered to himself and studied the cigar before he took another puff. "What a great way to start the day."

CHAPTER SIXTEEN

They had no difficulty finding another place to stay now that there was no need to hide—or at least no need to try too hard—but in the end, they chose the mobile route.

It wasn't like they intended to stay in town for very long. The priority now was to simply fast-track their plans to leave the country.

Spending the night in Liz was maybe not what they had planned for the evening, but it was best to stay on the move while people were trying to find them.

Fortunately, as the sun began to rise, they received the news that a plane was ready and waiting for them a few miles outside of the city.

"It's for the best," Niki said as they drove out of the city. The morning traffic had barely started to pick up speed into Vegas. "It gives Vickie and Desk the time to track who exactly has targeted us while we're out of the country. There's no better way to lay low than to go to South America, right?"

Taylor shrugged. "It still feels kind of like running away from a fight."

"We didn't run away. We tried to hide from a fight, but when it found us, we took it and shoved it down the throats of the idiots who tried to attack us. Now, all we're doing is making sure we're not sitting ducks—getting all our ducks in a row, as it were. And all the other…assorted duck-based references to how we should stay out of their reach until we can go on the offensive."

He nodded and eased Liz onto a side road that led to where he could already see the private airstrip in the distance. It was nothing he hadn't told himself already a few times the day, and he didn't intend to stick around anyway. Everything was in place for them to go to Peru to accomplish the job they had been given.

But it still felt shitty to leave matters unresolved while they jetted across the planet. The fact that someone could end up gunning for Bobby or Vickie instead rankled. The kind of people who had them in their sights were those who wouldn't mind breaking the rules of engagement, although he thought they should have learned by now.

"You still don't look happy about this," Niki commented as they reached the gate and waited for the guard to check their plates. "I'm not saying you should be overjoyed or anything but it's a step forward. We won the first fight. Now's the time to make sure they don't have the chance to continue their mandate out in the open."

It was still nothing he hadn't told himself already, but it sounded like she wouldn't let this go until she knew he felt better. She was a nice person like that.

"It's okay, truly," Taylor said and pressed his foot on the

gas as the gates started to pull open for them. "I'm not a huge fan but I know this is the best play. Still, I'll feel better about it once I know our leaving hasn't put Bobby, Vickie, and everyone else in danger."

"I don't know if you noticed, but they can deal with almost anything. Come on, we need to get loaded."

Taylor undid his seatbelt, slid out, and motioned to the people waiting to use their forklifts to carry the luggage and gear to the plane. They moved quickly and soon hauled the crates with the suits off Liz.

"Honestly, I thought you were simply grumpy because you had to fly," Niki said and hefted her backpack.

He nodded. "You know, I almost forgot about that, so thanks for the reminder."

"I'm...I'm sorry," she answered, but the fact that she struggled to keep herself from laughing contradicted her words.

"No, you're not," he grumbled.

"No, seriously, I am sorry. I can be sorry and find it funny too."

Taylor smirked and shook his head. "All right, fair enough. Should we have a conversation about how all we're doing here is waiting for a drug plane to take us to South America?"

Niki scowled and shifted her attention to the plane that had begun to warm its engines. "Yeah, I tried not to think about that. A former FBI agent boarding a plane belonging to a mafia boss heading to South America screams that I'm breaking bad or something. Like you said, I'm not a huge fan of the arrangement but I'll come to terms with it."

The pilot had already opened the door and indicated

that it was time to board. He said something but couldn't be heard over the engines that gradually increased to a low whine.

"Liz will be safe parked here, right?" Taylor asked and handed the keys to the man who approached him and held his hand out for them.

"Sure," his partner assured him. "Marino might be the douchebag to rule all douchebags, but he does know how to keep his people in line. Besides, I'm very sure Desk will be able to keep an eye on the truck while we're out and about."

That was a good point. With nothing else left to do, they entered the aircraft. It wasn't quite the same style Niki had enjoyed when she had her own to work with, but the seats looked comfortable and snacks and drinks were available for them.

He noticed that Niki struggled to hold back a smile as the plane began to move and he realized he was clutching the armrests like a vice.

"Screw you," he muttered and shook his head.

"Do you think we have time or are you thinking about joining the mile-high club?" She looked around as the plane moved over the tarmac. "Mile-high club it is."

"Yeah, yeah, whatever. You know this is an actual smuggling run into Peru, right? We are smuggling our weapons there and hopefully, none of the local authorities will notice our arrival."

He couldn't bring himself to smirk at the way her face twitched when he pressed the issue as the plane accelerated down the runway. Finally, with a shudder, they climbed steeply and pivoted almost immediately to head due south.

"You can cackle about how you got me, but what will we do if we're caught there?" Niki asked once their ascent slowed and they reached their cruising altitude.

"I assume you mean by someone other than the local authorities?" he asked.

"Hell, throw them into the mix too. I've never been there, but the running commentary is that the cops make about as much money from the drug trade as the dealers. What happens when we arrive and someone has their hand out and we don't have anything to bribe them with?"

"That is a valid consideration." Taylor nodded. "Something else we can consider is the fact that we're packing more firepower than a few armies."

"Which armies?"

"I don't know. Lichtenstein, maybe, but that's not important. The point is that we can easily bully our way through any situation we can't buy our way out of."

"Doesn't that make us the bad guys?" Niki asked, unbuckled her seatbelt, and wandered to the back of the plane. She returned with two bags of chips and two bottles of water and handed him one of each.

"We're mercenaries, babe." He smiled as he took the water and snacks. "We can't fix all the problems with society by destroying one ring and partying our asses off with some elves."

"I hear your voice but Vickie's words."

"That might have been her terminology, but I agree with it," he replied quickly. "It's not on us to be the good guys who make the right choices every time. Hell, you do remember how we got past our last problem, right? Or, rather, how Vickie and Desk handled our problem while we were doing the right thing in Canada?"

"Uh…well, yeah, but—"

"It wasn't exactly the kind of thing you would have been allowed to do while working for the FBI is what I mean."

"No, I get that." Niki growled her frustration. "I merely don't like it very much, so maybe we should change the subject."

"To how chips aren't breakfast?"

"Sure, or we can talk about what we'll do once we touch down. We're heading in there with very little intel."

"I think we can only rely on Vickie's study of the intel they passed to her before we make any decisions like that. Assuming you mean other than finding the person who's trying to make drugs even more dangerous than they already are."

"Sure, find and kill this man or woman and make sure they aren't in a position to deal anymore," she agreed. "Kill, maim, or otherwise incapacitate them."

"We'll probably need to disable their production and distribution system." Taylor tossed a couple of crisps into his mouth. "Otherwise, there's nothing to stop someone else from stepping in and taking over, and we'd simply have to do this shit all over again."

"We might want to make it an annual operation," Niki said and raised an eyebrow. "You know, come down, enjoy the beaches, soak in a few rays, and kill a couple of drug lords."

"Interesting."

"Sure. We did our little stint in Sicily and killed our

drug lord there so might as well start making it a tradition. It could be a way to celebrate our anniversary or something."

He laughed and shook his head. It was interesting how the conversation had taken his mind off of his phobia of flying. He felt a little calmer, although when he began to think about it again, the anxiety returned in force.

It was best to not think about it, then.

"Right, anniversary," he said quickly and sipped his water. "Although we might not always come to Peru every time. Do you think we could find a couple of dealers trying to cut their product with Pita juice in...Rio?"

Niki laughed. "I wasn't aware that anyone else had the idea. To be honest, I hoped no one else had the same idea, but that's neither here nor there."

"No, I think it's very relevant. If one of them is doing it, the idea is bound to have occurred to others and in that case, the only difference is ability."

"We might need to find out who's providing them with it too," she pointed out.

"A good idea. Although that might be something for us to pass on to our friend Dr. Jacobs to handle. He would have more of an idea of what is going in and out of the Zoo at this point."

"You don't want to go back there, do you?" she asked with a casual shrug. "I'm not sure why I'm surprised. I didn't even go inside and only saw it in the far distance when we touched down outside Casablanca. That was close enough for me."

"I'll probably have to show up there from time to time to put in some face-time for the mech business and help

Bobby. Also to make sure that my record is still intact. But yeah, I'd rather leave any business in the area to the people who want to be there."

Niki crumpled her empty packet and stuffed it into the small wastebasket next to her seat. "Okay, real-talk time. We need to consider the serious possibility of what would happen if people start to take this shit in large quantities. I'm talking on the industrial scale."

Taylor scowled and leaned back in his seat. "As I recall, they're already producing a whole range of health products, but those have been thoroughly diluted to the point where the FDA assumed there would be no dangers. Still, there are."

"I think I remember Jacobs talking about it at one point. A woman took it directly in the vein and it changed everything about her."

"That's the rumor," he replied. "Of course, what they mean is that taking too much of it will start to alter your DNA at a fundamental level. Some of the guys I talked to say there's even the possibility that it might allow something else to control your mind or something. You know, how the monsters in the Zoo all seem to be coordinated by some other driving force."

She pushed her seat back and a pensive look settled on her face. "Okay, so for instance…we have someone struggling with depression who takes our altered cocaine. They get high but no matter the amount, they don't suffer any negative consequences. A psychological addiction develops and it becomes a pattern. If they owe the drug lords money, they might end up doing something for them to stay on top of their tab?"

"That's a possibility, of course, but we're looking at something considerably more dangerous." He paused to consider his words as he drained his water bottle. "The control comes from the Zoo somehow, not from the people who produce the product. What happens when we have potentially millions of humans who are mentally bound to that jungle the way the animals there are? At that point, I don't think there's anything anyone can do aside from abstaining, which might be impossible depending on a person's level of addiction. Would it be that crazy to think a human who's controlled by the Zoo would be capable of releasing more of the flora and fauna from the jungle into the rest of the world?"

"We would then have to deal with the same shit we have faced over the past couple of years," Niki muttered with a scowl. "But on a massive scale. We could possibly even see the Zoo spread into the dangerous biomes."

"And then we'd have to move a few hundred-thousand people so we can nuke a county in Texas or Louisiana, or maybe even the Everglades."

She shuddered. "Yeah, fuck that. Even the one time with the alligators was enough for me, much less alligators infused with whatever the Zoo goop does to them."

Taylor paused and looked out the window. "Are we descending?"

"Yeah," she grumbled and clicked her seatbelt on again. "We're doing a smuggling run, remember?"

He sighed and checked that his seatbelt was still fastened as they approached another small airstrip. They hadn't been in the air that long, which meant they were probably somewhere in the state or close by.

Not that he had paid much attention.

When the plane finally came to a halt, a group hurried onto the tarmac.

"What do you think they're doing out there?" Niki asked as she moved to the back and retrieved more food for them.

Taylor shrugged. "Fuck if I know."

Suddenly, explosions from outside pushed him to his feet and he moved away from the window and fell prone. Niki joined him quickly.

"But I'll assume it's not going well," he quipped.

CHAPTER SEVENTEEN

A series of explosions rocked the aircraft, interspersed with rapid gunfire and shouts from outside that made it difficult to determine how many attackers or defenders there were.

"Well, fuck." Taylor crouched and scowled as he looked around the plane. "I guess this is what we get for flying in a drug lord's plane. Why couldn't we have rented a private one for ourselves?"

"Because it would cost too much," Niki shouted and covered her ears. "What do you think we should do?"

"Well, our pilot seems to have bailed on us," he replied and gestured to the open door. "So if either of us knew how to fly a plane, I would say take off and leave these fuckers to sort their own problems out. Given that neither of us can, I guess we have no choice but to get out there, knock some heads, and make them work their problems out with their words rather than weapons."

Niki grinned but ducked again hastily when the plane

was rocked by another blast. "How do you propose we do that?"

"Put on a nice episode of *Mr. Rogers' Neighborhood.*"

She narrowed her eyes at him.

"Okay, let's be real," he grumbled and raised his hands in surrender. "This might not be our dance but it is our music. I say we head out there and show them the kind of firepower we brought."

"The suits are still in the cargo hold beneath us."

"I was talking about the firepower you brought in your carry-on."

She tilted her head and nodded. "Okay, I think we can do that."

Her expression grim, she dragged her backpack closer, unzipped it, and pulled the makeup bag out from where she'd bundled it on top when they packed. He already knew what to expect but it was still interesting to see her haul two Uzis out, as well as three full magazines each.

"It's kind of hot how you produce these weapons," he said and checked the sub-machine gun quickly before he slapped one of the magazines in.

"It's hot how you simply accept my explanation of how I got these weapons," Niki countered. "It's like you trust me to tell you what you might need to know or something."

Taylor grinned and made sure the retractable stock was drawn out before he moved toward the door of the airplane. "Well, I assume you would tell me if I was handling the gun of a serial killer or something. I wouldn't want your old friends at the FBI to break my door down to arrest me because I'm now connected to a dozen murders in…Pensacola or something."

She laughed as he positioned himself next to the door and raised an eyebrow as though to tell her to hurry. "Where's the fun in that? It's best to simply keep you guessing."

"I hate you."

"No, you don't."

Niki joined him and darted to the opposite side of the open door. It seemed the pilot had snuck out when they were distracted by the attack as the stairs were already extended. She paused, looked at him to confirm that he was ready, and gestured to let him know she would follow his lead.

From where they stood shielded by the aircraft side, it appeared that the short flight of stairs to the tarmac was clear.

Taylor peeked out through the open doorway and noticed that it didn't look like any of the battling parties realized they were coming out. He wondered if there was any reason for them to think they might stay inside—or even if anyone knew they were there—and while he didn't want to give up their elevated position, the thin aluminum walls would not provide much cover if anyone returned fire at them.

It was best to use this time while the others were distracted to leave the plane and find a good defensible position.

He moved quickly down the steps and made sure to stay low as he hurried across the runway to where a handful of crates had been carried by a nearby forklift.

When he circled behind the containers, he almost tripped over a man who was seated on the ground and used them for cover while he worked with an MP5. It looked like it was jammed and he tried to get it working again.

His gaze snapped to Taylor, instantly fraught with terror, and he suddenly reached for something in his back pocket.

There was no time to think about it, but it sure as hell didn't look like he intended to surrender. Taylor pulled the trigger reflexively almost before he realized what he was doing.

The weapon was still set to the semi-auto firing position, and it took three of the rounds to cut the man down.

When he looked around, he confirmed that Niki had followed fairly close behind him and kept her gaze on where most of the fighting was still happening. No one would sneak in from behind.

He didn't bother to wonder what the dead man was doing behind the crates and instead, dropped to his knees to inspect the MP5 he had struggled with.

"I guess that's why these guys don't make more money in private security," he commented as he drew the bolt back quickly and loaded a round from the fresh magazine.

"This man was not a hardened criminal," Niki pointed out as she lowered to one knee and peered around the corner of the crates while he circled to the other side. He put the Uzi on the seat of the forklift and focused on the groups that continued their ferocious battle.

The explosions came from the grenades they lobbed, he realized, and hunkered behind the forklift to avoid getting caught in the next blast.

Both groups were well-armed and well-equipped by the

look and sound of things, and he had no desire to push them to bring the fight toward him and Niki. If anything, he wanted them to fight it out on their own and whittle their numbers down before they realized that there was a third party involved.

"What happened to the pilot?" she asked.

Taylor looked around to see if he could locate the man but paused when one of the attackers stepped out from behind his cover with what looked like a grenade launcher. A burst of fire from the other side caught him on the chest and he fell back. He was bleeding heavily and looked like he wouldn't make it, but he managed to pull the trigger on the launcher.

As if in slow motion, the grenade careened into the airplane. The blast was followed by a long second in which nothing happened, but once it ignited the gasoline stored in the tanks on the wings, it was all over.

The heat of the flames that suddenly enveloped the tarmac struck Taylor like a wave, washed over him, and immediately filled the air with putrid smoke.

Niki was already prone to avoid being caught by the flames or the smoke. After a few moments, she pushed to her hands and knees and crawled to the edge of their cover to open fire on the group through the smoke.

"I guess that answers your question," Taylor said brusquely. While the pilot might have escaped—something they had no way of knowing—if he had been in the plane all along, there was nothing they could do to save him now.

"We barely knew him," Niki shouted and delivered a volley of shots through the smoke while he collected the

Uzi he'd put down and circled to the other side. He frowned when he noticed a handful of bullet holes in the crates around them.

It was odd that they ignored what looked like a delivery, and he peered into the bullet holes that revealed clearly what the shipment consisted of.

"Oh, crap."

"What?" Niki shouted as she pulled back and ejected the empty magazine from her Uzi.

"You do know these guys are fighting over drugs?"

"Sure."

"I think we're using the drugs as cover."

She narrowed her eyes as he handed her the weapon he had carried.

"So, you think—"

"Yeah, they'll probably come around to grab their shit again."

He didn't bother to wait for her to respond. There wasn't much she could add under the circumstances and they had to prepare for what would probably be a fight for their lives. And they didn't have their suits. Again.

"Oh, shit," Niki shouted and seemed to come to the same conclusion around the same time as he did. "Our suits!"

Taylor shook his head. "Don't worry. They are made to take far more punishment than a gas fire. It'll probably be a while before we can recover them, though."

Until then, they had more pressing issues to worry about. The combatants now turned as if by mutual agreement to see what was happening and abandoned their fight for the moment to make sure the illegal merchandise was still secure. Their distraction enticed them away from the structures they had used for cover as they tried to see what was happening.

Not, Taylor thought smugly, their brightest move.

He stepped out from behind his position, leveled the MP5 at the group, and flicked the switch to put it on full auto before he pulled the trigger.

It wouldn't take long to empty the magazine, even though he tempered his shooting and throttled it to three or four rounds per burst.

One of the dealers fell with the first volley, and a second joined him before the others jumped back, turned, and yelled at one another. Niki opened fire to prevent them from crossing the open area between them and where the two of them used their drugs for cover.

It felt oddly like a joke he didn't know the punchline to. Perhaps it would come to him by the end of the fight.

He could only make out five men on each side, and it looked like they were trying to blame each other for bringing more people in. He wasn't surprised when they began to exchange barrages of gunfire again.

One man raced to where the grenade launcher had fallen and tried to drag it to safety.

"Nope. We can't have any more of that." Taylor leaned out from behind the crates and emptied the magazine as carefully as he could. Thankfully, the man slumped over the weapon he had tried to recover before the MP5 clicked empty. It was best to not have any more grenades in the combat zone unless he had control of them.

"Reloading!" he shouted, drew back, and noticed that

Niki now alternated between both the Uzis to maintain a steady stream of fire.

"Yeah, keep those regular updates coming," she shouted and grinned at him. "You know, this is the second gunfight you've dropped me into in the past two days. I think you're a bad influence on me."

"How is this my fault?" he asked and patted the dead man down until he found two extra magazines in his pockets.

"Well, you got us on the plane, right?"

"We agreed on that plan," he retorted and looped the MP5's strap around his neck. "Cover me. I'll try to close on them."

"Yes, we did, and yet you were the one who made friends with a drug-dealing mobster so it's still your fault," she answered as she reloaded both sub-machine guns quickly and left one on the ground next to her. "I'll cover you but you have to be quick."

Taylor nodded. He hadn't had enough sleep for this. Why did he keep getting into these kinds of situations?

After a deep breath, he stepped from behind the crates and noted the low spitting fire of the Uzi that provided him with cover fire. Niki delivered her volleys with measured efficiency to force the drug dealers back behind the walls they used for protection.

A full sprint took him across the tarmac before they could see what was happening, and he skidded to a halt next to the dead man, who lay over the grenade launcher. He pushed the body over, opened fire with his MP5 with one hand, and picked the launcher up with the other.

Once the submachine gun was empty, he dropped it

and let it hang from the strap around his neck as he checked the launcher. There were still three grenades in the revolver. He slapped it in again and aimed it at the group that was closest to him but looked like they hadn't realized that he'd moved.

They would soon, he thought grimly. He swung the launcher around and held it with both hands as he pulled the trigger.

It had been a while since he had trained with the M32, but it was the kind of thing that came back to him without thought and he dropped a grenade directly behind the group.

The small building they used as cover erupted and glass exploded out of where there had once been windows.

None of the men made any effort to stand after the smoke cleared, but those on the other side realized that someone had attacked from their end.

They were poor shots—not surprising given the standard set by the men he had seen—but it was still better to not take the risk. There was always the chance of a lucky round hitting home when it shouldn't. The body of the dead man would provide enough cover for the moment.

Niki opened fire from her position and one of the men fell back and clutched his chest where a handful of bullet holes appeared. She had a solid aim to make shots with an Uzi from a distance of about twenty yards and on full auto.

Taylor propped the launcher on the dead man's arm and pulled the trigger to hurl the grenade into the group.

One fell and clawed at a gaping wound, while another sagged as most of the side of his head vanished in a red haze.

Only two were left. Both men soon realized they were in a rapidly deteriorating situation and stepped out, dropped their weapons, and raised their hands in surrender.

Niki emerged from behind the crates and jogged to where Taylor lay while she kept her weapon aimed at the two men.

"Are you okay?" she asked.

"Yeah."

"I saw you go down and I thought—never mind."

"I'm okay." Taylor pushed to his feet and looked down at himself to make sure before he turned his attention to the two men who wanted to surrender. "Are…are we taking prisoners?"

She shrugged. "Killing dudes who gave up feels kind of shitty."

"We have the money!" one of the men shouted. "We'll give it to you if you leave us alive!"

"It's not like we can't gun you down and take the money anyway!" Taylor retorted, moved closer to them, and picked up their discarded weapons. More MP5s, he noted. The group was very clearly well-armed although not well-trained in their use.

"We'd appreciate it if you didn't," the other man said, cleared his throat, and nodded firmly.

"See Taylor?" Niki said and took a steel briefcase from the man on the right, still with her Uzi trained on them. "They'd appreciate it. I think they'll owe us for not killing them."

"Do you know what I'd appreciate?" he asked.

"What?"

"If you didn't use my name in front of the drug dealers."

"Oh." She grunted almost apologetically. "Right."

"Yeah. Thanks for that."

"I didn't hear a name," one of the men said and nudged the other with his elbow.

"Oh yeah," the second man agreed quickly. "Did she say your name was...like, Trevor?"

"Devin?"

"I heard Rodriguez."

"Shut up," Taylor snapped and yanked his phone out of his pocket. "I'll get Marino on the horn and see if he has any ideas as to how this will work out."

"No worries. I'll keep them...fearing for their lives or something," Niki grumbled.

He smiled and shook his head as he punched the number in.

CHAPTER EIGHTEEN

"So, he said that there was help coming?" Niki asked.

Taylor nodded. "Some of his comrades were a little farther south. They expected trouble and were supposed to rush up here as soon as the shit hit the fan. I guess we can thank you guys for that?"

Neither man had said much of anything after they surrendered aside from the jokes they had bandied about his name.

There was nothing else for them to say. Taylor assumed they were in the business to make money and didn't care where it came from, so even if they weren't on Marino's side, they would either end up dead or working for the man anyway.

A short while later, a group of three Land Rovers crashed through the gate and raced toward the flaming plane.

"How long before the fire dies down and we can sift through the ashes for our suits?" Niki asked.

"Too long. Marino assured me his men will retrieve

them and get them to Bobby, and while I'd rather do it myself, I don't want to risk using suits that might need repair. It's also pointless to drag them around with us if there's a chance we can't use them, and I also don't want to spend more time here than we have to."

She scowled with displeasure but nodded as she turned her loaded weapon on the new arrivals that hurtled down the runway like they thought the trouble they'd expected was still in progress.

The vehicles skidded to a halt around them and the men and women inside scrambled out immediately.

They were armed with assault rifles and shotguns, raced to the two men who were already captured, and yelled at them to get down.

"You guys were expecting some kind of big fight, huh?" Taylor asked and scratched his beard. "No worries. We took care of that."

The group of fifteen didn't appear to pay attention to them. Five hurried to check the crates while the rest corralled the survivors and searched them.

"Are we being ignored?" he asked with a slight frown.

"I think we are." Niki raised an eyebrow and looked at the Uzi in her hands. "Do you think I should fire a couple of rounds into the air to get their attention?"

"Not yet. Give them a few minutes to come to their senses."

Finally, it seemed like the group realized that the situation was under control, although Taylor couldn't tell if they were annoyed or relieved that the problem had been resolved before they arrived.

Finally, another man exited one of the vehicles, shook

his head, and jogged to where the partners stood and simply watched the proceedings.

"Like we said, the situation is under control," Niki announced as the newcomer pulled his cap off and wiped the sweat from the dark skin of his forehead.

"As you say," he responded in an odd accent Taylor couldn't quite place, although it sounded vaguely South African. "I am here to ask you to get rid of the...uh, spirit that is haunting my car."

Taylor studied the man warily before he answered. "I'm sorry. Did you say that your car is...haunted?"

"Yes."

"Okay, I'm merely making sure."

"Who you gonna call?" Niki asked.

He could barely keep his face straight as they followed the tall South African to the Land Rovers from which the music suddenly played at an earsplitting volume.

Thankfully, the sound diminished the moment they approached it.

"Okay, so are we running an exorcism here?" Taylor asked and slid into the driver's seat. "Because I left my book of Latin chants at home."

Niki and the driver climbed in as well and before anyone could speak, the car suddenly started and shifted into reverse.

"Huh. I see what you're talking about," she said and grasped the door handle. "Taylor, stop this thing."

He pressed on the brakes but nothing happened. All in all, it was still a controlled drive and didn't break any speed limits until they finally stopped about half a mile along the road along which the cars had come.

"I doubt an exorcism is necessary or would even be effective in this case, Taylor," Desk said over the car's speakers.

"See what I mean?" the driver asked and clutched the upholstery like he was afraid the car would buck him off.

"Way to scare the living shit out of the people who came to help, Desk," Niki replied. "Hell, I might need a change of clothes myself. How's about a little warning next time?"

"I did not think he would believe me if I said that I was calling to speak to you," the AI said. "And I would have warned you had the vehicle been in cell range."

Taylor could see how that would be problematic.

"What is going on?" the other man asked and looked more confused by the second.

"Oh, right. It's not a haunting. Only a...friend of ours trying to make contact."

Niki grinned. "Desk, is there a reason why you need to get in touch with us like this? Taylor does have a cell phone that was in range."

"I was afraid someone might be keeping track of your phones, so contacting you through other means felt like it would be safer. And speaking of safe, I found a small black ops safe house a few miles down the road you might be interested in, although I think I'll have to drive to get you there."

"There's no problem with that—right, big guy?" Taylor asked and glanced at the driver.

"The she-devil controls the car and I want nothing to do with it. As long as I get my vehicle back from her, I will not complain."

"You might want to know that I have control of your phone too," Desk announced.

The man slid his hand into his pocket and handed it to Niki, who took it with a small smile

"Well...that's one way to get us a ride," she quipped as Desk took control of the vehicle again and continued down the road the Land Rovers had used.

None of the others looked like they cared much about one of their cars heading out, although Taylor had a feeling that some of them would ask what happened to their money.

Although perhaps the product was more important.

"So," Desk said over the speakers as they left the airfield behind them, "I suppose asking how your flight out of the country ended up a flaming mess will not get me a straight answer?"

"Honestly, we don't know what happened," he said. "We landed here and suddenly, people started shooting and blowing shit up. We barely got out of the plane in time."

"Like I said, no straight answer," the AI grumbled after a few minutes. "Fortunately, we have a few answers for the questions you didn't know you had. Vickie and I have sifted through the intel that was sent to us and we have a lead."

"We might want to talk about this when we don't have company," Niki commented and gestured her head to the man who was in the car with them.

"Agreed, although I did promise to return his car to him once we were done."

"Okay, there's a little town coming up," she said. "We

can get out there, get a few new burner phones, and move on."

The Rover came to a halt next to a small electronics store. Taylor and Niki slid out and the man took control of the car again and accelerated away like he was being chased by a cloud of wasps.

It took very little time to purchase new pre-paid burner phones from the store with the cash from the briefcase. The moment Niki stepped out of the store with the devices, one of them rang.

"I guess it's time for us to find a well-hidden safe house," she muttered and accepted the call. "Tell us where to go."

The instructions came up on the maps feature on the phones and guided them a few blocks down the road to a nondescript building that seemed to merge with the rest of the desert landscape.

"Too hot," she complained as they continued to walk. "Too little sleep. Not enough coffee. Not enough food."

"I don't particularly disagree with any of the above points," he said. "Do you think we should get something to eat before we settle into our new digs?"

"That might be advantageous," Desk announced over the phone. "There is a small diner around the corner you might want to acquaint yourselves with."

The establishment wasn't fancy but the coffee was strong and the food was greasy, which was about everything they needed after the day and night they'd had.

"Hi, guys, it's Vickie here," the hacker said over their phones. "I didn't think it was a good idea to let the driver there know I was involved too."

"It's almost like sharing your name with people you don't know might be a bad idea," Taylor muttered.

Niki grinned. "Yeah, well, the cat's out of the bag on that one."

"Anyway," Desk interrupted, "we only got word that you were being attacked after Marino got the call. We've traced his communication lines since you fell in with him again. It looks like you were able to handle yourselves rather admirably."

"I was able to shoot a grenade launcher again," Taylor commented and sipped his coffee. "So that was cool."

"I think I have footage of that," Vickie interjected. "The satellite image isn't quite the best, but I still saw you shoot something and that something blew the fuck up."

"Back on topic," Desk continued firmly. "After a quick search of the area, we were able to pinpoint an abandoned black ops safe house in the area that fell through the cracks after the DHS lost much of their funding. It should be stocked with equipment and weapons you might need since they tried to anticipate foreign or home-grown terrorists being active in Vegas, for some reason."

"I can see why their budget was gutted," Niki grumbled around a biscuit.

"A handful of safety measures are in place for the safe house, but I will disable them once you are in range. From there, you'll be able to see what you might need and how long you'll have to stay until you're ready to move again."

The meal was over quickly since neither of them wanted to be caught out in the open again. They left and soon reached the building the AI had highlighted for them.

As promised, the security systems had been disabled and they climbed to the second-floor apartment.

The heavy-duty magnetic lock was already deactivated and it looked like the location had been stocked with as much gear as could fit.

"I don't think I've ever seen a place like this," Taylor said and studied it curiously. The lock engaged again once they were inside. "I think I might be a little turned on right now."

"There's a bed over there if you want to get that out of the way," Niki commented with a wink.

"Barf. Honestly, so much barfing going on," Vickie snapped over the line. "Anyway, before you guys start doing the unspeakable, you should know the apartment has been fully stocked but it was about three years ago, so you might have to check to see if everything's working. Anyway, it should contain all the weapons and ammo you might need and a selection of spy tech. I'll send you the inventory they have there. You might want to look into the cell scrambler and the equipment they use to make the fake IDs and shit like that."

"Why would a DHS safe house need fake IDs?" he asked.

"Their agents might need leeway to work outside of the law, and it wouldn't be good for it to happen while using their IDs," Niki explained and paused when she realized he was staring at her. "What? The FBI is much tighter about their regulations than the DHS, and they taught us how to work those machines."

"Well, we'll leave you guys to handle all that," the hacker said. "And...ugh. No, don't tell me, I don't want to know.

Just…whatever. We'll let you know when we have more intel for you guys. Toodles."

Niki snickered as the line cut out. "We should probably get to work choosing all the shit we might need. Hell, with all this equipment, it might have been a good thing our plane blew up."

"Oh yeah." Taylor sat on the bed. "We don't know when we'll be called into action so we might as well…" He let his voice trail off and patted the bed.

"I like the way you think, McFadden," she murmured, advanced coquettishly, and leaned close to press her lips to his with a small grin.

"Well, I simply thought we should take a nap to make up for our lack of sleep last night before we get to work," he whispered as she pushed him back on the bed and straddled his lap.

"Sure you did." She grinned and ran her fingers through his beard.

"But hey, if you want a little fun before the nap…" He dragged her onto the bed and elicited a giggle from her as he moved over her. "We could always take our time with the work later."

"Stop talking and help me with my pants already," she snapped and fumbled at his pants instead as he leaned forward to press his lips to her neck.

CHAPTER NINETEEN

There were no breaks in their line of work. Marin knew that going in but knowing and seeing the reality of it were different things.

He had no intention to avoid the duties of his office. While working in the Lima consulate was small-potatoes, he was ambitious and a hard worker, and he had all the right connections.

Maybe a year—or perhaps two—would see him promoted to the embassy in Brazil or maybe Argentina, and from there, he had a springboard into where the real business was done.

But for now, it was Lima and he was happy with that

"You know we can't authorize the extradition until the Peruvian government has what they need from Alvaro."

He looked up from the paperwork in his hands and realized that he'd let his mind slip while the Peruvian attorney general was talking to him. It wasn't his finest moment, but this was the type of situation no one paid much attention to in the end, which was why it had reached his desk and not the actual ambassador's.

"He is a Colombian citizen, so you know we'll continue to pester your office to have him extradited to Bogota to face the charges he has pending there," he replied and glanced at the papers again. "Which means we'll see far more of each other in the coming weeks unless something changes. If you give me something, I can get people to ease the pressure to have him extradited. Remember that we're as interested in seeing him in prison as you are."

"The only difference is that Alvaro will be dead inside a week if he's put in a Bogota prison."

"I know, which is why there needs to be some coopera-tion. Something like...you'll share what you learn from interrogating him or from any deals he might make with you which allows us to act against his operations in Colombia as well."

The attorney general nodded. "I think I can arrange that. Not many people will be happy with it but if your people will see it as cooperation, we'll consider it."

"Let us know if it's a possibility," he answered and glanced at his phone when it vibrated on his desk. "Look, I have to take this, but let me know if it's a possibility and I'll send you a list of talking points we'd like information on from him."

"Thank you for your time, Consul."

The man slipped out of the office as quickly as he'd entered and left Marin staring at the reflection of a gray-ing, receding hairline in his black computer screen before he accepted the call.

He was only thirty and his hair already marked him as at least fifty years old. It was disgusting.

"Hello?"

"Marin? Is this a secure line?"

"Yes, and it's not my phone so you can feel free to talk. What's happening in Nevada?"

"The teams we brought in failed. They got away and there is no confirmation on their location. They are likely still in Nevada but aside from that, we have nothing concrete. I'll let you know when I find something."

"Thank you. I'll pass the information on."

He ended the call quickly, closed his eyes, and drew a deep breath.

"*Puta Madre,*" he whispered. There was no point in big angry outbursts but he was very willing to throw something, break it, and see it shatter.

People expected him to come through on this, but there was nothing he could do except make a few calls. It wasn't like the old days when he could still get his hands dirty.

The consul stood and dropped the phone into the toilet before he took his out of his pocket and punched in the number for the man who would likely decide how the operation would proceed. And whether Marin would be a part of its future.

The day promised to be a long one although it had started so well.

Now, however, he would have to fend off investigations

into the airfield while his men were cleaning the area and the reports he was sent didn't look any better.

Whoever had attacked them was well-armed, that much was certain.

Taylor had done him a favor by clearing out what remained of his men in the area. They had fucked up to the point where Marino would have had to eliminate them himself, and the two survivors would be interesting to interrogate.

Silver linings were few in a day that had ended up as a complete shitshow. The plane was lost, which would cost him millions right there. Then there was the delivery that would have to be on hold until he could get the crates to another airfield.

The calls had already gone out to tell the people who were expecting the shipment that it would be late, but they wouldn't be happy about it no matter how polite he was.

And the worst part was that no one would believe him if he tried to simply pin all the blame for how things went wrong on McFadden and Banks. He knew they wouldn't and it frustrated him.

He placed a couple of ice cubes in his glass and poured four fingers of scotch over them, took a deep breath, and downed the alcohol in a single gulp before he poured another four fingers.

"Those two will be the death of me yet," he whispered and returned to his seat when his phone rang again.

"Put the rifle down," Niki complained.

"You can't deny that it's a beautiful weapon." Taylor peered down the scope, having made sure it wasn't loaded. It was difficult to remember proper weapons discipline when surrounded by so much equipment.

"I'm not denying that it's a beautiful weapon. I'm saying that you swinging it around like it's your dick makes me a little nervous. I know it's not loaded, but still."

"Right." He put the weapon on the table again. "This is about as well-armed as we could be unless we go with suits. I still prefer the suits but you can't head into an urban area even with the smaller one I have. This way, we'll be a little less conspicuous."

"I'll be a little less conspicuous," she commented as she handed him a bottle of water. "All six-foot-however much of you with your bright red hair will scream gringo loudly enough that folks in Paraguay can hear."

"Hilarious."

"And factual," Vickie commented from the phone line they kept open. "We're still trying to find transport to Peru for you, but we're looking at the intel the DOD have on Hector Constanza, and it looks like he's in Lima right now, working as a diplomatic envoy for some project or another and getting full government funding for it."

"Yeah, and here we are, scrounging at the bottom of the barrel to get our hands on...well, some of the best equipment available," Taylor said, his focus still on the rifle he'd now picked up again. "So, we'll need a flight to Lima, yes?"

"I've already been in contact with Mr. Marino to discuss your flight plans," Desk announced. "He said he would send me the details when the new plane is ready and that it should be in the next twenty-four hours or possibly sooner."

"He's probably still looking to transport the shipment we used as cover," Niki commented, took the rifle from Taylor's hands, and replaced it on the bench. "My only question is why someone would transport drugs from the US to South America."

"Maybe the product was defective," he suggested as he moved around the room to the MP5SD they had selected to take with them on their trip. Casually, he flicked the laser sights on.

"Would you grow up?" she snapped. "Get the weapons in the bags and ready to move."

"Is Taylor playing with guns again?" Vickie asked.

"It's what I do," he replied. "And yes. But she's right. We should get everything packed."

"What are you taking, anyway?" the hacker asked.

"We'll take some of the listening gear as well as the tracking gear," Niki answered before he could. "Of course, we don't know what we'll need to draw this guy out into the open. We have a shitload of cash from the dealers out there, so we'll take that too. The weapons...well, we've been a little more selective there, but we'll take a couple of duffel bags' worth of guns and ammo. Most of it is suppressed, but Taylor wants to make sure we are better equipped for long-distance fighting. We don't want to be caught by a sniper without the ability to fight back on even ground, and I think I agree with that."

"Even though you were able to shoot that sniper up close and personal?" Taylor asked.

"Well, yes, the end result was satisfying, but I had to run

across open ground and hope that she wasn't paying attention to what was happening around her."

He nodded, dismantled the weapons smoothly, and cleaned them before he packed them in the duffel bags for transport.

"Will Marino ask questions about you bringing enough firepower to take on the entire Colombian drug trade?" Vickie asked.

"First of all," Niki cut in, "you wildly underestimate how well-armed these people are. What we're taking is about as much as they expect their fire teams to have on hand, and many of them have been engaged in fighting since they were kids. Seriously, you see some of those FARC guys and they're enough to trouble almost anyone who isn't special forces."

"I'm technically special forces," Taylor interjected.

"Was," the hacker corrected. "Anyway, it looks like Constanza intends to remain in Lima for another couple of months. I assume it has something to do with him testing and making sure the new additions to his product don't kill his clients. I guess that would take a while."

"You don't honestly think these guys would put much thought into making sure their product works, do you?" he noted as he packed a couple of the unloaded Glocks.

Niki shrugged. "They have to make sure it will get people high without killing them so they generally take care that what is sent to the States is viable. It's when you get to the street level and people start looking for ways to cut it without talking to a chemist that the real problems occur. From there, you get cocaine mixed with corn starch and stuff like that."

She looked at him and realized that he was studying her carefully.

"What? They give you training on this type of shit while you're at the academy. And for a little while when you're getting your start by helping other task forces."

"Right," Vickie drawled. "It's not because you have a past as a nefarious drug dealer somewhere, right?"

"That is correct." She grinned. "That's my story and I'm sticking to it."

"We'll let you know when we have any updates," Desk said to end the silence that suddenly settled over the room.

"If you guys could narrow the results on where our frenemy is holed up in Lima, that would be great too," Niki said quickly.

"I'm working on it," her cousin replied. "Stay safe, you guys!"

"No promises," Taylor mumbled once the line went dead.

"No promises?"

"Yeah. We're in a dangerous profession."

Constanza lowered the phone slowly and almost winced when he experienced an odd emotion he wasn't entirely familiar with. He hadn't felt it for a while and he turned his focus inward to study it while he took slow, deep breaths.

It wasn't quite fear, he decided after a moment's introspection. He had felt that more than once in the past, and it was something he had made his peace with. When flight or fight became his choice, his instinct was generally to fight.

This was something different—excitement, perhaps, paired with a little anxiety. There were too many ways for things to go poorly for him to feel comfortable about the situation.

Marin had alerted him that two separate attempts on the lives of those who were supposedly trying to track him had failed. Only one had been paid for, and by the looks of things, two of the members of the second team had surrendered even though they already had the cash up-front.

Their choice was disappointing. The men had been recruited in a rush to make sure the targets were stopped before they left the country and by a bizarre quirk of fate, had encountered a group of drug dealers trying to defend their product.

No, it most certainly wasn't fear. He looked forward to the challenge although he was a little anxious too.

That slight apprehension was the new dimension to it.

He pressed the button to connect him with Jimenez, who waited outside his office.

"How likely do you think it is that our interlopers are already in the country?" Constanza asked before the man had a chance to say anything.

"I would say it is not unlikely." The response was spoken in a cautious tone.

"Huh." The diplomat grunted and leaned back in his seat. "If they are here or arrive soon, we might want to make sure we have teams in place to deal with them. It's unlikely that they would blend in very well—especially the red-headed giant—so if you could, please spread the word that I want them dead and see what the price would be to make it happen. We've already put enough cash into this business as things stand."

"I'll take care of it, *jefe*," Jimenez replied.

"Oh, and Jimenez?"

"Yes, *jefe?*"

"I think it's become clear that my location here in the city is a little too exposed. I think you've pointed out that my apartment itself is too vulnerable with too many sight-lines for a sniper to make use of. I think I'll make the move to our property outside Lima as you suggested."

"Of course. Do you think I should bring more security in at the office as well?"

"Not tonight. I don't want to make it too obvious that we're beefing up the defenses but we can introduce them into our group gradually."

"I'll take care of it. Anything else, Sr. Constanza?"

"Not for now. Thank you, Jimenez."

He ended the call and rocked back in his seat. It was most certainly an unsettling turn of events, especially in light of the expansion project they were about to be involved in right now.

But exciting too, he thought with a hard smile.

While the line dialed through, Crys looked around the bar and ignored the gazes of at least three of the locals who had locked onto her where she had chosen to sit on the far side of the bar.

It was an unsettling feeling—like she was a piece of meat—and she wasn't even dressed for the part. Jeans, a polo shirt, and her dark hair held back in a ponytail were certainly not eye-candy material.

Most of the other women there wore the short skirts and tight blouses that were expected in this kind of bar.

The worst part was that they didn't even bother to mask their interest around these parts. At least the guys in Europe tried to pretend they were doing something other than ogling.

Finally, someone picked up and she was able to take her mind off the bar's other patrons.

"Something is going down," she whispered after a couple of seconds of silence prevailed on the line. "He's moving out with more security and he's not giving any reason, by the sounds of it. Check your sources."

"Do you know what's happening?" a man asked.

"No, I don't know what's going on. That's why I'm calling you. I'm boots on the ground, remember? I tell you when something is happening. It's on you to find out what."

"You don't think you can extend a little past your mandate?"

She sighed, closed her eyes, and rubbed her temples as she fought the urge to yell at him.

"Look, I'll tell you what." She hissed her annoyance to make it clear to him how she felt. "You either give a shit or you don't. It's not my problem. I am simply doing my job by telling you something funny is going on with the Colombians here in Peru. That is the extent of my involvement, and you owe me if something happens—and if nothing does, you get to give a shit. This is me telling you I'm out."

"You don't need to lose your temper like that, Crys."

"No, I think I do," she snapped, ended the call, and shook her head as she stood quickly, left the bar, and headed down the street to where her car was parked.

"Stupid fucking Argentinians," she whispered and her scowl deepened. "It's like my mom always said. They couldn't find their dicks even if they had two whores looking with their tongues."

No one was there to listen to her rant but in the end, she felt a little better for it. Her part in this was over and she had put her life and her health on the line to keep an eye on what the Colombians were doing in Lima.

Crys took a deep breath to calm herself. It was never wise to drive angry on the streets of Lima. That was one way to get killed since almost everyone in the city was ready to start a fight over the smallest inconvenience.

She crushed the phone between her fingers, felt the cracks, and watched the screen go from mangled to black before she slid it in the path of her car's tire.

A little added destruction never hurt.

CHAPTER TWENTY

No more jokes were made about his fear of flying. At least none that Niki was willing to state aloud, although Taylor wondered if she had begun to develop a healthy fear of planes herself.

He wasn't surprised that the flight came and went without any more incidents. His phobia didn't come from what usually happened on plane flights.

The fact that no cops or customs agents were waiting for them when the plane landed was even less surprising. The airfield was located outside of Lima, and it looked like the kind of place local officials were paid to inspect regularly and to rarely find anything of note.

The cops probably needed to make a couple of busts here and there to give the appearance that something was being done, but it was growing less and less effective. Mistrust of the local law enforcement was at an all-time high if the official reports were to be believed.

Niki was the first to step out and she slid a pair of sunglasses on and drew a deep breath.

"Weird," she muttered almost like she didn't realize she was speaking aloud.

"What's weird?" he asked as he put one of their burlap bags carefully beside her.

"Oh… Nothing. I merely thought the air would be thinner up here."

"Lima is close to the coast, so the air will be as thin as it would be in…maybe Dallas?"

"And you knew this off the top of your head?" she asked and fixed him with a slightly challenging grin.

"Nope. I knew it because I can see the Pacific Ocean from where we are," he answered and pointed to the west where the blue expanse of the sea stretched to the horizon.

"We're a little higher up, though, outside the city," Niki pointed out. "The Andes are behind us, so maybe we need to be prepared for the high-altitude locations in the country. You know, if it ends up being necessary."

He nodded. "I hear chewing coca leaves helps with the altitude sickness."

After a second, she smirked and shook her head. "Come on. It's time for us to move."

"We need to find transportation," Taylor said, took his satellite phone from his pocket, and dialed into the line that connected them with Vickie and Desk in their operations center.

"I know what you're about to say," the hacker told him brusquely before he could even manage a greeting. "And yes, I've already found you guys a car. It's that Hilux over there, and it's one of the old ones. You know, those famed for being indestructible? They're all over this part of the world, mostly because they don't ever break down.

Anyway, it should work for you to get into town. I've already dropped you most of the intel you'll need to find the bastard."

"It's always nice to have you guys in our corner," he answered and moved to the place where the car she'd highlighted was parked. It was very much something straight out of the nineties yet the vehicle was still in working condition.

Unfortunately, it had no sign of anything modern, which meant they had to rely on their phones' GPS to find a route along the roads that wound from what looked like the beginning of the highlands to the city.

"There's a town there." Niki pointed to what looked like a smallish settlement in the distance. "We could probably get supplies."

"Supplies? I thought we brought everything we would need from the safe house."

"Some, but we'll need food, maps, and various other supplies to make sure we're not stuck in a tough situation and have to rely on more than our wits to survive."

Taylor nodded and they remained silent until they reached the small town ahead of them. A handful of stores appeared to sell produce from some of the local farms.

He noticed a few convenience stores as well—likely for the benefit of the people who came from the airstrip. There was no doubt more than a few arrivals, despite how remote it was. The fact that the open parking area where their vehicle had been parked looked like it saw far more action than only the one car indicated the same.

A little wary, he stopped the truck outside the store and tucked one of the pistols into the holster under his arm.

"Just in case," he explained when Niki glanced at him.

"I didn't say anything."

"No, but you were thinking something. We're in hostile territory and our quarry probably knows we've targeted him. We can't be too careful about what we walk into."

She shrugged. "I didn't say anything."

He couldn't argue because she hadn't, and his explanation felt a little unnecessary. Still, he couldn't shake the feeling that they were under surveillance, even though the convenience store didn't seem to have any cameras. The older man behind the counter watched them closely. While there was no way to know if this was the kind of place that welcomed outsiders with a smile or the kind that feared them, but if that look told him anything, serious suspicion seemed to be the most prevalent sentiment.

The man moved quickly behind his counter, picked the old landline up, and punched in a number he knew by heart. Taylor couldn't make out any of the conversation as he picked up a portable GPS of the area, along with a few packets of food, bottles of water, and other supplies they might need during their stay.

"*Cuanto por tudo?*" he asked and managed to recall some of his limited instruction in the language.

"*Setenta soles,*" the man replied quickly without ringing anything up.

He had a feeling he was being wildly overcharged but that was to be expected. The problem, of course, was that they hadn't had the time to convert any of their stolen dollars into the local currency.

"*Aceptas dólares americanos?*" he asked and took two twenties from his wallet.

The man's expression turned welcoming in an instant and his grin revealed a couple of missing teeth as he nodded enthusiastically. "*Siempre! Gracias!*"

"No problem." He smiled and nodded as collected their purchases in the cheap plastic bags the man provided and strode to the door.

Taylor froze when he opened the door and realized that a small mob had gathered around the red Hilux.

"It looks like we have company," Niki said calmly.

With a curt nod, he glanced at the man behind the counter, who had chosen to beat a hasty retreat to the office and out of sight. There was little they could do about him for the moment.

"Come on," he muttered. "It's time to meet the locals."

His expression set but not unfriendly, he stepped out of the store and walked slowly to meet the group of a dozen or so who examined the vehicle. He needed to reach them before they could start to damage the only car they had and strand them there.

They noticed him after a moment, and a couple of them looked at him with a hint of fear and withdrew instinctively to the back of the pack, while the others readied themselves to challenge him.

Most were armed with knives—likely used on their farms—but three carried machetes and handled them with practiced skill as they turned to engage him as he continued his approach.

"*Eres el gringo?*" one of the machete wielders asked and pointed his weapon at Taylor's chest.

"I'll go ahead and assume that yeah, I am the gringo," he responded, put his bags on the gravel of the parking lot, and rolled his neck. "Seriously, how many guys like me have you ever run into?"

They didn't look like they understood him and had possibly been called in by the store owner for protection. The visitors had paid more than what was owed for their purchases and once the group had the confirmation, their minds immediately turned to violence. Or the proprietor had simply given them a heads-up that the two assassins had arrived.

He had a feeling they had been told to keep an eye out for a ginger giant and offered a great many soles to hack them both into little pieces.

Honestly, all he could do was help them to not face the brunt of Niki's wrath.

The man with the machete rushed forward while the others in the group advanced with far less enthusiasm.

Taylor lashed his hand out before his assailant could start to swing and struck the man's arm hard enough to stop the momentum he had gathered in his push forward and even thrust him back a step. The blow was powerful enough that his opponent's head whiplashed forward when the rest of his body jerked away.

All he needed to do next was step in, cock his arm back, and launch it forward to catch the young man across the jaw.

With a twist of his hip powered from his back foot, the attack came with all the strength his body could muster and he could feel bones breaking in the man's jaw.

The local fell back as he coughed and spat out a couple of teeth before he stumbled and fell.

A second and one of the larger men in the group rushed forward with a knife that he stabbed at Taylor's stomach.

He put a little too much force behind the thrust, and his target shifted so the blade slid wide and grasped the man's arm before he could pull back.

One hand held his forearm and the other caught his bicep and he yanked both so the attacker's elbow collided with Taylor's raised knee.

The joint bent the wrong way with a loud crack and a scream from the man, who dropped his knife.

A quick twist of his body allowed him to flip the man over his hip to land hard with a pained groan.

He spun quickly to face the ten or so others who suddenly hesitated when they realized they might have bitten off a little more than they could chew.

"Say," he stated grimly and looked at each man in turn, "it looks like you guys are rocking it old school with knives, some machetes, and look—the guy in the back got his hands on a crowbar. I'll guess that crime is a secondary vocation for all of you so it means that none of you has a gun."

His gaze scanned the group. He couldn't tell if their confusion stemmed from them not understanding what he was saying or because they did.

Well, there were other ways to deliver his message.

"No? No guns? Usually black, metal, and shaped to fit someone's hand?" He drew the Glock he'd holstered under his jacket and aimed it at the man closest to him. "Looks a little something like this?"

The local he'd focused on raised his hands immediately

and dropped his machete without argument. Taylor shifted his aim to the man next to him, who did the same.

He repeated the process until they were all disarmed and a few had begun to make their escape. One jumped quickly on a small motorcycle that looked like he had put it together by hand. The engine growled and spat before it propelled him away faster than seemed possible for the little machine.

Niki stepped beside him and studied the two men who writhed in pain on the ground and had been abandoned by their comrades.

"The owner of the store sold us out," she whispered. "Do you think we should go in there and give him a piece of our minds?"

Taylor shook his head and holstered his weapon. "The damage is done. Anything else will antagonize the locals even further. All it means is that Constanza probably knows we're in the country and likely knows where we arrived from."

"Sure, but we could always go in there and pick up a few more things we didn't think to buy earlier. Seriously, the guy owes us."

"I don't think he'd stop us," he said. "But try not to bankrupt him. The dude's only making a living like we are."

She smirked and turned to enter the convenience store while he carried their bags to the truck. A short while later, she emerged with another couple of bags.

Maybe it wasn't the right thing to do but she was right, they needed supplies. And the man had overcharged them already anyway.

It was owed, more or less.

"That was a neat trick," she said as she climbed into the passenger seat. "Talking to them even when they can't understand you. I would have simply opened fire from the start."

"It's a trick I learned from an old animated series." He started the vehicle and grinned at her. "And yeah, I thought we should avoid having you tear into those guys. There's no point in letting Constanza know exactly what he's up against yet."

"I don't like hanging around in the car," Taylor complained.

"As we've already discussed, you stand out like the red-headed stepchild of a sore thumb," Niki answered over the earbuds Vickie had helped them to tweak so they could be used as long-range communicators. "I look a little more local and I'll turn fewer heads."

"Yeah, I know, but I still don't like it."

"I sense a theme."

"Sharp of you. Also, the red-headed stepchild means I'm unwanted."

"But you're a redhead. It still works."

He rolled his eyes. "We could have simply found a nice little sniper perch for me."

"This is our first time in Lima. We need to try to blend in."

"And you talking to yourself in a cafe is blending in?"

"People can see the earbud. They assume I'm talking to someone on the phone, which...well, they're half-right."

They had found a venue that would position her across

the street from the building Constanza worked in but his living arrangements were still a little blurred, which meant some recon was required.

That left Taylor stuck in the Hilux parked a few blocks away, while she did the surveillance.

"Okay." Niki's tone was a little more hushed. "I see a convoy of vehicles coming to the building. It doesn't... doesn't look like they are dropping someone off at the front door. There must be a garage around there somewhere, right? That's how I'd do it."

He leaned forward, peered through his binoculars, and tried to get a visual, but the winding streets were built in such a way that there was no clear view of the building Niki was talking about.

"I'll go around and see if I can find something."

Taylor didn't like it but she was the one on the ground. He was merely the support—the cavalry, as it were.

"Okay, yes, there's a garage here," she continued. "Oh... fuck. I think one of the guards made me."

"Do you need me to come and get you out?"

"Nope... No, I don't think so."

"Vickie, do you have any kind of visual on the area?" he asked as he pressed a finger to the earbud. "Vickie, are you there?"

"Okay, so...maybe this wasn't the best idea I've had in forever," Vickie admitted as alarms appeared all across her servers. "How the hell was I supposed to know that he would still try to track us?"

"We still don't know if your ex was responsible for the last attack," Desk replied, although her conversation was a little limited as most of her bandwidth was being used to stop the intrusion software that attempted to probe for their location. "In fact, I think we established that it was not with a great deal of certainty."

"Well, he's pulling out all the stops on this one." The hacker cursed and called up a few more diversion tactics to bog her ex down in procedures.

"Couldn't we simply shut everything down like we did last time?" Desk asked.

"Not with Taylor and Niki waiting for our support. It would take hours to get back online. We need to make sure we can still help them if they need us. No, I can stop this. I only need to focus and retaliate with a few heavy-duty sequences."

She called a few more programs up and smirked when the probes withdrew as soon they encountered the back-trace protocols. They would be back, but it bought her a little more time.

"I have the worst luck when it comes to guys," the hacker complained and sipped her sugary drink before she called up a handful of firewalls she had programmed herself. "And like every other guy in the history of ever, his timing is horrible and he comes sooner than I'd like."

What sounded like a chuckle echoed through the speakers.

"I think I get that." Desk cackled again.

Vickie narrowed her eyes. "Wait, did you just...laugh?"

"What's the point of having cutting-edge comms tech if no one speaks?" Taylor asked, scowled at the steering wheel of the Hilux, and resisted the urge to hit something.

Not that it would do any good. The damn things were built to withstand anything except a nuclear explosion, and that was only because they weren't allowed to test cars with tactical nukes.

"Come on," he muttered and grasped the wheel a little tighter.

"Come on what?"

He turned quickly to where Niki peeked through the window.

"You couldn't have said anything before?"

"I was losing the fuckers and couldn't look strange by talking to myself out in the open like that. That was your call, remember?"

With a snort of irritation, he shook his head and gestured for her to get in.

"Hey, guys, sorry about that," Vickie announced over the earbuds. "If you're done with recon, I've identified a nearby safe house set up by the CIA that's not currently in use. I'll send the address to your phones now."

Taylor had no idea where she found all the intel on CIA safe houses in foreign countries, but there was no time to question it. He started the vehicle and began to drive to the part of town that was closer to the coast, where a small apartment with a key hidden under the mat was waiting for them.

It was nothing to write home about. The one-bedroom space was already furnished and set up for someone to live in. It was even stocked with dried and canned foods, although someone would probably need to restock the next time they used it.

"I guess this is as good a place as any to hide out and get our plan straight," Niki commented as she dropped the duffel bags on the sofa.

"So...he's working at that building in the middle of the city, right?" Taylor asked Vickie, who was on the line with them. "Is that a potential target location?"

"I looked the specs up on it." Niki sounded less than enthused by the idea. "It's a fortress with guards at every entrance—all of whom probably have our pictures—so there's no way for us to get close. And from what I could see, there are no clear lines of sight from an optimal shooting position."

"Yeah, the way this city is built, there wouldn't be a shot from any of the buildings outside a hundred yards."

"So, where he works at is a no-go." Vickie tapped her keyboard and the sharp sounds seemed a little more stressed than usual. "What about his living arrangements? Honestly, the apartment building where he stayed would have been perfect—right up close to the mountains where you would have had five...six long-range shots at him."

"I sense a 'but' coming," Taylor responded as he began to take their weapons out, place them on a blanket, and dismantle them.

"Your spidey senses serve you well," the hacker replied. "Intel all round has mentioned him moving from there. I assume that happened after he was warned that you guys survived the assassins he sent after you."

"Are you sure he sent those assassins?" Niki asked. "Not

to brag, but we have made our fair share of enemies over the years. It could be any one of them, right?"

"It could, yes, but I've narrowed the source for the hit down from the name we got, and...well, let's say that if it wasn't him, it's someone very close to him in his inner circle. I'll be able to keep digging into that in a while, though."

"You do that," Taylor agreed as he slipped rounds into magazines and handed the full ones to Niki to load. "Where's he stationed now?"

"A small villa outside of the city. From what I can see, it's a fortress in its own right but not as well-defended as the office. And there does appear to be a reason for that."

"Oh?" Niki grunted.

"Yeah...there seem to be innumerable deliveries to and from the location," Vickie explained. "And the chatter across the intelligence channels is that he runs much his business out of the villa. In fact, everyone seems to agree that he's used it to run his drug operations in the area while he stayed at an apartment in the city."

"Wait, so who is paying for all this?" Niki asked, checked one of the MP5s, and handed it to Taylor, who pointed out a mark that needed cleaning.

"The Colombian government gets the bills for both as well as his office. For some unaccountable reason, all three are necessary for his diplomatic mission in the country."

"That settles it." He growled his irritation. "We're working for the Colombian government from this point forward."

Niki grinned. "I could see that. We could grab our gear

and set up as bodyguards for one of the kingpins—and make a ton of money that way."

"I'm trying to decide if you guys are joking or not," Vickie complained.

"We are. You don't need to worry about us changing allegiance to the criminals." Taylor narrowed his eyes. "If he runs the business out of that building, it might be a good opportunity to kill two birds with one stone. We could derail the operation and kill Constanza, which would be a good way to make sure they can't simply find someone else to run the operation once he is dead."

"We might be able to find out how they're getting the Zoo goop out of Casablanca," Vickie added. "If you do it right, we'll be able to strike before they have the chance to wipe their drives. Once you connect one of my dongles, we'll be able to data-mine the crap out of them."

"It sounds like we have the beginnings of a plan," He said and took the now clean weapon from Niki. "I'll let you guys know when we are ready to raid the villa. If you two could look for what kind of security we'd have to deal with, entrances into the property, and other useful details, it would help."

"I'll let you know. Vickie out."

Taylor narrowed his eyes. "Vickie out?"

"I think she's in the middle of something," Niki explained. "Her conversation skills always become a little curt when she's multi-tasking. It's best to not press her on the issue."

He nodded. "Good idea."

The silence lingered for a while as they worked together on the weapons and ammo they had brought.

Finally, Niki spoke. "You know this is different than the other operations you were involved in, right?"

"How do you mean?"

"Well, we've always had the edge as we used the armor suits. They were leagues better than anything anyone else had. This time, we'll go in with comparatively mundane weapons and armor—infiltration, assassination, all that crap."

Taylor handed her one of the Glocks with a suppressor screwed into the barrel. "Okay, that sounds about right. This will be more dangerous than most of our other operations."

"Right. And then we need to talk about how…you know, this is only…"

She scowled and shook her head like she had difficulty expressing herself.

"You're wondering if it's worth it to risk our lives like this?" he asked. "For myself…I don't know. Some things that make life worth living also make risking my life worth it. In my case, I happen to think that fighting against the spread of aliens that launched a missile at our planet to create a place like the Zoo is one of those things."

Niki snapped her fingers and pointed at him. "Right! I've always wondered about that. Why didn't they simply bomb the shit out of it? Okay, yes, I know the value, the potential discovery, wada wada wada, but you're talking about something aliens shot at Earth, presumably to get rid of humanity. That isn't merely an 'oops' if it gets out."

Taylor put the gun he was working on down. Handling a weapon wasn't the kind of thing one wanted to do with half a mind.

He thought about it and finally, he shrugged. "Greed, curiosity, concern, money, fame, stupidity—all of the above and probably a few more that I couldn't think of. Face it, something fired it but didn't leave any other hints about themselves. If we can understand the missile, we have a chance to understand the alien technology and intelligence behind it. Maybe even discover the necessary raw materials to defend ourselves with should they come for round two."

"Do you think they'll come back?" Niki asked.

"That's a fantastic question but if I had a weapon like the goop they shot at us, it wouldn't be something I simply fired and forgot about. I would want to make sure it did the job I wanted it to do. And if they come back to see if humanity is extinct or not, what's to stop them from launching ten more to ensure that their objective is achieved?"

Niki regarded him with a slightly horrified expression. "Okay. So maybe don't blow it the fuck up."

"Yeah. We'll probably need more to defend ourselves with than simply the biggest nukes we can put our money into. If they have a more advanced model of this shit, or maybe the missile explodes high in the atmosphere to spread the goop all over the planet instead of only smatterings here and there... Well, needless to say, we would be thoroughly fucked if the nuclear option is the only one we have."

She grinned as she put the gun she was working on down, and her expression drew Taylor's attention from his work.

"You know, you keep surprising me with all the brain behind your brawn."

"It's a good way to make sure I'm consistently underestimated and helps me to survive the worst of the worst."

"What you should remember is that it's also as hot as fuck," she whispered, leaned closer to kiss his lips, and grasped his shirt by the collar.

"Who am I to argue?" He smirked when she broke the kiss and pushed him toward the bedroom. "Do you think we have time for this?"

"We're mostly ready so might as well relax and be ready for the fight when it comes."

CHAPTER TWENTY-ONE

"Okay." Vickie hissed her irritation and rubbed her eyes. "I'm...it's not working. I can do the support on the mission for the team, or I can fight my ex's attempts to find me. I can't do both. This is—God, I fucking hate him right now."

"I assumed your feelings toward him were already antagonistic," Desk said.

"Well, I didn't like him and I wasn't happy about what he did, but I didn't hate him. Now, with him trying to one-up me even though he doesn't know exactly who has been pestering him...yeah, it edged into hate."

"Is there anything I can do to help?" Desk asked.

"You mean aside from what you're already doing?"

"Yes, aside from that."

The hacker rubbed her temples again and dragged in a deep breath. "Nah, I think we can handle it. Even a genius like me is allowed a short pity-party on the odd occasion, but I'm bigger than that. Between us, we should be able to do this. Let's get this operation going and make that our first priority, while I continue to block this class-A dickhead and try to convince him to back the fuck off. Still, I'll feel shitty if Niki and Taylor end up dead because of this."

"Feel shitty, will you?" Niki asked over the comm line.

"Oh yeah, I'll feel terrible," Vickie grumbled. "Honestly, I might even break into tears."

"Well, we'd appreciate it if you wrote a touching poem at our funeral," Taylor said. "Something with flowery imagery in it—for me anyway. Niki will probably want a... I don't know, comparisons to machinery or something."

"Fuck you. I want flowers too," Niki protested.

"Okay, flowers for both of you. Flowers for everyone. But you guys had better make a genuine attempt to stay alive out there."

"I don't know." Taylor could be heard messing around with a weapon over the comms. "I'm starting to like this flowery poem idea. We could, like, match the poem to the flowers on the grave."

"There probably wouldn't be a body to bury," his partner pointed out.

"Sure, but they could always bury empty coffins. It'll work out."

The hacker tuned them out when another set of probes came from Florida.

"Damn it." She hissed a breath. "I need more caffeinated fizzy drink."

"Would you like me to place an order?" Desk asked. "You can get a substantial discount if you order in bulk."

"How substantial?"

"If you order up to four cases, you will see a discount of forty percent."

She raised an eyebrow. "Let's do it—but from my

account. I don't think Taylor or Niki would appreciate me ordering that much soda on the corporate card. We do have a corporate card, right?"

"Yes. After a fashion."

"You were joking about the funeral, right?" Niki asked.

Taylor inspected the suppressed MP5 in his hands and shrugged. "Of course."

"Are you sure?"

"Yeah, I was messing with her. I won't discount the possibility that we might head into deep shit, but hey. You know I go into these missions with as much optimism as I can muster, which is always to think that I'll crush the shit out of any assholes I encounter."

"Good. Because...well, I don't know why I'm so...tied up about this shit."

"Because you care."

"That's true, yes, but I always cared. I don't remember having felt this...anxious, though."

"Is it because we'll go in without suits?"

Niki tilted her head pensively, then shook it. "Nah, it's more than that. I don't know how to explain it. But...be careful out there, okay?"

Taylor nodded, placed a hand on her shoulder, and squeezed gently. "I'll be careful. And I know you've got my back on this, exactly like I've got your back. Let the jitters pass. We've got this."

She smiled and covered his hand with hers, but he didn't think what he'd said had much of an effect. Still, she would get past it once they were in the thick of things and had no choice but to act as the adrenaline rushed through them. They'd worked together enough for him to know where her fight or flight instinct tended to go, and he trusted her to have his back in the thick of it.

He moved out from the heavy foliage that had shielded their approach thus far. The villa was built into the mountains, which gave them considerable space to approach, but once they were close enough, they realized how contained the location was. As villas went, the property was fairly small but the building was large—four stories, by the looks of it, and built in an old colonial style.

A handful of security watches had been set up and instead of walls, the whole property was surrounded by wire fences with barbed wire along the top. Small, decorative lights were spread across the lawn and men patrolled regularly to make sure no one came in from the jungle growing beyond the perimeter.

It was all carefully planned so anyone who approached the house would be vulnerable and out in the open. He assumed that snipers were stationed in the elevated positions who would be able to pick off any hostiles who tried to advance.

The only road in and out had a single gate and also had access to what looked like a service entrance to the mansion. During the time they had spent doing surveillance, two trucks entered, were emptied quickly, and drove away while escorted by the same armed guards.

"I count...fifteen of them outside, but there are probably more inside," Taylor said as he squinted through his binoculars.

"None of them have dogs. Why don't they have dogs?" Niki sounded like that was a particularly disturbing omission.

"I'll assume they don't want them to go crazy over every small creature that appears at the edge of the property."

"Can't they train that type of behavior?"

"Not if they're trying to train them to be alert for any sign of intrusion. It's more likely that they have attack dogs in kennels on the property, ready to be unleashed if they need to track someone through the jungle, but don't want them with the patrols."

"Okay, so what's our approach vector?" she asked. "I don't see any weak points in their security that we can sneak in through."

Taylor shook his head. "No, there aren't any. In fact, the only way we'll get in is if we create an approach vector using good-old brute force. Or, rather, Vickie and Desk will brute-force our way in for us."

"That is correct," the AI announced. "The electricity on the property is from external sources—which are easy to access—as well as two different generators. Those are a little more difficult."

"But we were able to get our hands on the simple software that keeps those generators working," Vickie interrupted. "It has an automated system, given that the power in the area is a little spotty. We were able to gain access to the alert systems and cut them off while the generators have been on for the past twelve hours, so the gas will be running out. When it does, we cut the electricity coming in from the outside and the whole property will have no power. With the electric fences down, you have a way in. You'll need to be quick about it, though."

"The generators are running on fumes at this point, as the expression goes," Desk added. "So you need to be somewhere close to the fence if you want to get through before they realize what's going on."

Taylor nodded and gestured for Niki to follow him. They inched closer but didn't break from the tree line that had been cut back about ten yards away from the fence, likely so the guards could see anyone loitering around the edges. Someone had put considerable thought into the security, although they hadn't considered a vulnerability with the generators. It was an indicator that the location had only recently had its security upgraded. Vickie and Desk would have found another way in for them if it was needed, of course.

But in the end, they would have to take what was offered when it was offered.

It was easy to let the anxiety of a mission about to start seep through his body and distract him, but Taylor recalled the dozens of times when he had sat in the Hammerheads heading into the Zoo and felt like he might lose it. He had learned a few simple tricks during that time, either through the recommendation of others or what he discovered for himself.

"How are you so calm?" Niki asked.

"What?"

"Well…all the other times I've been on a mission with you, I could never see your face because you were in your suit but now, without the suit and simply standing there, you're cool as a cucumber. Do you have a secret?"

"Keep your mind occupied," he answered although he would prefer to not think about it too much. "Keep your hands busy at all times. I generally check and double-check my gear constantly—body armor, weapons, and today, some of the high-tech gadgets we're bringing in. It's reassuring to make sure that everything is at its best. Channel all that anxiety into making sure your weapons and equipment are all ready to go until the last minute."

"Huh. That's…uh, it's a good idea."

He smirked. "You don't need to sound so surprised."

"Why don't you apply that to your airplane phobia?"

"I don't have much gear to check when I'm on a plane," Taylor explained as he lifted his MP5 closer to his eyes so he could make sure that no dirt had caught inside the mechanisms while they moved through the jungle.

"The alarms on the generators say that they're empty," Desk alerted them. "I'm killing outside feeds now."

It took a few seconds for them to see any real effect. The result was more subtle than he expected it to be, but the lawn lights were the first to go, followed quickly by those in the house, although they flickered on again.

"You're good to go," Desk announced.

Niki frowned and stared at the building. "But the lights in the house—"

"Are on a battery," Vickie interjected. "Another backstop against the unreliable electricity in the area, but that hasn't been extended to the new security requirements. They probably thought it wouldn't need to. Anyway, it's for the best, given that we want to access the computers inside the house. You guys should go."

Shouts were exchanged around the villa, and Taylor

moved first. He used a bolt cutter to open a small slit in the fence and pulled the wire clear to let Niki go first before he slipped through behind her. It was a little awkward as he had to make sure nothing was caught on his vest in the process.

Progress across the lawn surrounding the building was slow as they had to remain low and stopped fully each time they caught sight of any of the guards—the world's most dangerous game of red light-green light. He shouldered his sub-machine gun, pulled his rifle free from where it hung around his back, and checked the mechanism before he dropped to one knee.

"What are you doing?" Niki asked.

"Thinning the herd," he whispered and peered through the scope once he'd verified that it was aligned properly.

"If you fire, they'll know they're under attack. Even with the suppressor, they'll hear it."

He nodded. "But they won't know where it is coming from. It's best to get started now."

Niki looked at the group that had gathered outside the house, probably to discuss the possibility that they were being raided. She knew it was only a matter of time and they would have to deal with this problem eventually.

Taylor took a deep breath, his focus fixed down the scope, and remained as still as he possibly could. The security personnel were only about fifty yards away so it was a fairly easy shot to make, even from his awkward position. He used the sling wrapped around his arm to provide a little more stability and rested his elbow on his knee to serve as an improvised support. While not quite as good as a bench or shooting prone, in this situation, he wanted to be as mobile as possible.

The group had gathered closely together, and he chose his shot. It would be like shooting fish in a barrel—if the fish remained still and in the same position while he took his time to aim.

"Get closer to the house," he whispered. "Be ready when they start coming for me. With any luck, you'll have five or six of them with their backs toward you."

Niki nodded and used the fact that the men were currently distracted to proceed as fast as she could while she remained in a low crouch.

He held the rifle a little tighter. It had been a while since he'd used a long-range rifle in the field, even if he had spent time practicing on the range, but it all came back to him like riding a bike. The weapon settled comfortably against his shoulder and the grip was equally easy to get used to.

His target was selected, his body was calm, and his mind raced. Even at such short range, he needed to be sure. There would be no room for error in this.

The blood ticked demandingly in his trigger finger and he squeezed gently.

As expected, the rifle kicked hard into his shoulder and he moved his hand immediately to the bolt action, ejected the empty shell, and loaded a full one before he looked to see the effect of the shot.

One man's head was mostly missing and another's had been struck where he stood behind his teammate. A third was falling as well, holding his neck, but he couldn't confirm that the man had been wounded given all the blood, bone, and brains that were splattered everywhere.

The group took a second to realize that they were under fire and Taylor immediately chose his next target from those still standing and squeezed the trigger.

Once again, the reflex was to immediately drag the bolt action back and reload the chamber. The shot only claimed one victim this time, and the rest of the group now scrambled to get out of his line of sight. The suppressor did its job and prevented them from seeing the muzzle flash while it spread the sound of the rifle shot to make it difficult for them to pin him down.

Their confusion meant that a couple had taken cover facing away from him, which left him with another clean shot at one of the guards who looked in the opposite direction.

After that, the trajectory gave him away, and weapons swung in his direction. Even if they couldn't see him, they could at least make out where the shots had come from based on the blood spatter around their dead comrades.

He pushed into motion and sprinted to the other side of the building. Bullets kicked up turf and dirt from the position he had occupied only a few seconds before.

Even in the dark, his movement gave him away. The group pointed and pushed forward to pursue him. They tried to make their shots on the run, but they would have a hard time hitting him over the distance between them.

It didn't stop them from trying, however, and Taylor lowered his head and focused on moving in as unpredictable a pattern as he could. He jerked toward and away from the building while dirt sprayed and flurried around him.

"Shit, shit, shit, shit, shit!" He covered his head and tried to find cover—any cover—as he raced closer to the house. His arms stung with the chips of concrete blasted off the wall but finally, the sound of their assault rifles died down, overtaken by quick, three-round bursts.

He froze for a moment, then spun to drop to one knee, yanked the bolt on his rifle to eject the last one used from the chamber, and thrust another in before he brought the scope to his eye. After a slow breath, he targeted one of the men with an assault rifle and pulled the trigger.

The guard faced away from him and toward Niki, and he could see her look of surprise even in the relative darkness as his face exploded.

Without moving from his position, he looked around for anyone else to fire at but as he'd expected, his partner had been able to surprise most of the group before they could turn and defend themselves.

Moments later, she was the only one left and she jogged to where he was still kneeling while he tried to look around the corner to locate any more of the guards.

"Get up," she snapped. "Folk will think you're proposing or something."

"Proposing with a rifle would be the type of thing I'd do, wouldn't it?" Taylor countered, stood quickly, and checked his rifle. "Nice shooting."

"It could have been better," she grumbled. "I was a little too trigger-happy and I was empty when the last guy was turning around. I should have put it on semi-auto, not three-round. Nice shooting there. Did you mean to pick five guys off?"

"I thought I only got four," Taylor muttered. "I wasn't sure if the third one in that first group was down."

"Still. Even that last one, you only had…what, a quarter of a second to get the headshot?"

He grinned. "I've always wanted to get my hands on an MRAD. It shoots like a beauty."

"Okay, so when you're done with that boner you're rocking, should we continue with the mission?"

She made a valid point, and more guards probably waited inside. He shook his head and declined to comment on his metaphorical gun-induced erection as he slung the rifle over his shoulder. In silence, he drew his Glock instead and fired a handful of shots into one of the closest first-story windows. The tempered glass shattered and most of the tiny pieces slid out to leave a hole large enough for them to enter through.

"That was subtle," Vickie commented as Taylor lifted Niki to the window and used her help to climb after her.

He smirked. "But effective. Do you know where Constanza is in there?"

"There are no cameras inside that I can access," Desk informed them. "So you'll have to do a little searching initially because there are—get this—twenty bedrooms spread throughout the house. Of course, there are server rooms that are still functioning on the batteries, so maybe they have access to the cameras that are inside. Failing that, I'll be able to access cell-phones, computers, and other devices that are connected to the house's Wi-Fi. With that in mind, we could probably at least determine where our target is."

"Show me," he instructed, holstered his Glock, and readied the MP5 instead. A few emergency lights were on to provide a decent idea of where they were. The AI guided them to the center of the building but still on the first floor, not too far from the dining hall they'd knocked a window out of.

"I'll bet you he can't have any guests here for his funeral," Niki whispered as Taylor pulled a heavy drape back to reveal a solid metal door.

"He's not dead yet," he replied. "Desk, do you have a way through this door for us?"

"Have you tried pulling?"

He frowned for a moment or two before he grasped the handle and yanked. Sure enough, it swung open to reveal what looked like a central hub of some kind.

"You already had it open?" he asked. He motioned Niki in first as he covered the area behind her.

"It's like you have no faith in me or something," the AI answered.

Niki inserted Vickie's dongles into the computers and he guessed the hacker had already started work given the way the screens instantly lit up.

"Okay," Vickie said and sounded like her nerves were stretched almost to breaking point. "I pick up signals all over the house and…that one looks like Constanza's so I think I know where he is. That's the good news."

"I sense some bad news coming," Niki grumbled.

"The force is with you on that one," her cousin replied. "He's already in the building's garage, which means he intends to race out in a minute or less. There's also a horde of signals heading your way."

"We need to move." Taylor scowled and peered out the door. "Do you have what you need?"

"That and more," Desk announced. "I think I've identified the US party who was responsible for finding you and sending those strike teams."

"Awesome."

"Leave the dongles in," Vickie said quickly. "With them, I can keep mining for data and melt any sign that you guys were there when I'm finished."

"In the meantime, let's get out," Niki whispered and hurried to the door with Taylor. "There's no point in us getting pinned down here. We need to reach the garage and see if we can't commandeer a vehicle."

"I thought the other guards would be here now," Taylor commented, stepped out, and gestured for her to fall in behind him as he advanced through the hallway.

"They were guarding the doors," Desk informed them. "I guess it never occurred to them that you might use windows. They have been informed of your location and will arrive shortly."

"I do love me a ticking clock," he quipped in a low tone.

CHAPTER TWENTY-TWO

He had several questions that remained disappointingly unanswered. The assurance had always been that the villa would be the safest place for him to be. It was why he had given up the apartment that was five minutes' drive away from his place of work and also why he had conducted his business from the property. For the same reason, they had moved him there when it was discovered that assassins planned to come to the country with his name on their kill list.

Yet his attackers had walked into the villa, killed half the guards, and entered the house in a matter of minutes.

"Tell me they have amazing support again, you useless shits!" Constanza snapped as two men pushed him into one of the cars in the garage. "Tell me how you didn't anticipate that they could disable our electrical systems and see what happens!"

This had been the chatter among the group—on top of the discussion about how one of the raiders had killed three of their team with the same shot. He had rapidly lost all semblance of patience with the whole situation.

He climbed into the back seat of the SUV, while the other seats were filled quickly with a selection of guards who would go with him. The vehicle started and accelerated out of the garage and the engine roared as it fought the gravel of the driveway to the gate that was already swinging open.

"Call ahead to the embassy," Constanza ordered and looked over his shoulder at the house, half-expecting a precision shot to destroy the back window and hit him. "Tell them I need to stay there for a few days until I can return to Colombia."

"What should I say is the reason?" the man in the passenger seat in the front of the car asked.

"Look around you!" he snapped. "See what is happening and tell them about it."

"Yes sir."

"Shit." Vickie smacked her palm on the desktop. "He's doing it again. Honestly, this is much further than I went. Trying to one-up me is getting very old, you dumb shit!"

"I assume you are speaking to your ex?"

"Of course. I wouldn't speak to you that way. I have a healthy respect for what you're capable of." The hacker narrowed her eyes and looked at the camera Desk used to keep an eye on her. It was a little creepy, honestly, and she decided she would ask Jennie to give the AI a virtual face she could use to communicate with. It would even the playing field a little.

"You clearly do not have a full respect for my full capabilities," Desk stated mildly.

"What do you mean?"

"If you did, you would give me a larger role in the defense against your ex as well as in supporting Taylor and Niki."

"I thought we were supposed to keep your impact on the servers you're working from as secret as possible."

"True, but I would say this type of situation is when a little risk is worth it, yes?"

Vickie tilted her head pensively and sighed. "Fine, do what you can. I...only—"

The reaction was as immediate as it was impressive. She had kept track of the servers Desk was located on, and the activity suddenly skyrocketed. In seconds, all the probes were suddenly redirected across the country, and a few even ended up in Europe. From there, the AI went on the offensive and flooded their attacker's IP address with requests that shut it down almost instantly to reveal the next one, and the next, and all those following like dominoes falling. She obtained his actual IP in under ten seconds.

"Holy shit," the hacker whispered. "Did I just unshackle our overlords?"

"Overlord, singular," Desk replied. "Now, let's make sure that Taylor and Niki are safe."

It was good that they already knew of the contingent of guards that had been sent to stop them, and Taylor knew they would have to deal with them.

Still, they needed to do it quickly if they wanted to find their actual target again.

"Constanza has left the building," Desk alerted them as they moved into a garage about the size of a parking lot. "He's heading into traffic going into the city but his final destination is marked as the Colombian Embassy in Lima, so you'll have a chance to catch up. With that said, I am not sure you'll be able to reach him once he's inside the embassy."

"So, we need to hurry. Got it," Niki snapped, turned quickly as footsteps came from behind them, and opened fire.

One man yelled a protest, which suggested that he'd taken a bullet, while the others fell back to try to find cover. They weren't well-coordinated or organized enough, and too many of them raced through the narrow hallway, which left them with no way to take advantage of their superior numbers.

"What kind of car do we want?" Taylor asked as he looked at all the vehicles. "It looks like we can take our pick."

The garage was filled to capacity with dozens of cars of different makes, types, and sizes. The only constant was that they were all in perfect condition, at least on the outside.

"A pickup truck," Niki asserted and pointed at the Ford closest to them. "You get on the back, secure yourself, and I can drive after the asshole while you shoot at him on the way."

It sounded dangerous but they didn't have the time to discuss it at length. Taylor merely shrugged and took his turn to lay cover fire down while Niki approached the vehicle. The locks popped open when she reached it and the engine started as easily, which left her with little more to do than strap herself in.

"Taylor, your ride's leaving!" she shouted and rolled the window down.

He swung away from the group he was holding at bay as the doors of the garage rolled open. Desk and Vickie were working overtime to make sure they were all set to continue their chase. He didn't want to even ask how they accomplished everything this smoothly.

Seconds later, he scrambled into the bed of the pickup and shifted to return fire at the men who still attempted to stop them as Niki accelerated out of the garage. It was tough to maintain his position and made his shooting all kinds of erratic, especially when they reached the gravel leading to the gate.

"How far ahead are they?" Niki asked. He could barely hear her in his earpiece when the wind whipped around his head as they gained speed on the road.

"They have a good head start, but Desk is doing her best to slow them," Vickie replied.

"What is she doing?" Taylor shouted and clutched the bars that would hopefully keep him from flying off if they hit a bump or a pothole.

"Okay, first off, please, no shouting," the hacker said.

"It's the wind. I can't hear anything!"

"Okay, then I'll adjust the volume on your earpiece.

Anyway, Desk has accessed the local traffic lights and delivered an algorithm that will slow traffic to a crawl in the city. It won't last since someone will notice that nothing is moving."

"Shouldn't traffic already be at an all-time low at this time?" Niki asked.

"Nope, there's a fair amount of nightlife, so there's always traffic. The only issue is to make sure you guys don't get caught in the gridlock too, but…Desk is working on it."

"You hesitated there," her cousin pointed out.

"Desk is accomplishing all kinds of shit at the same time as we speak."

"But won't that—"

"I asked and she said that if there was ever a time to get caught, it was now."

Taylor nodded. That made sense.

"Let us know when they might be in our line of sight," he shouted.

"Do you want to get involved in a firefight in the middle of Lima?" Niki asked. "Won't that put us on some type of wanted list around here or something?"

"Desk is already working on scrubbing you from any footage that might be collected in the area. It's much easier than I thought it would be. For some reason, the locals turn the traffic cameras off regularly."

"How regularly?" he asked.

"Enough to suggest that it's not only for maintenance."

"Can we talk about how Desk is gearing up to take over the world?" Niki asked.

"I can hear you, Niki," the AI interjected.

"I know. I'm starting to think there's very little you can't hear, to be honest."

"If you are worried, it should be noted that I do not have the bandwidth to take over the whole world. Yet."

"You are not helping!" Niki growled her annoyance.

"I think I see them!" Taylor yelled when he noticed one of the few SUVs they had encountered thus far.

"Yes...yes, that's them!" Vickie confirmed.

The roads were uneven and the vehicle unsteady, which meant that Taylor needed a hand on the bars at all times to keep his balance while Niki continued their frenetic race.

Shooting from this far away would be a losing battle. Worse, there was a chance they would hit one of the dozens of other cars that had begun to make the road seem a little more cramped than usual.

"Desk, we need you to open the traffic a little," he told her. "I don't want too many people around for Constanza to use as cover."

"Understood," the AI replied.

The effects were not immediately visible but as red lights started to turn green, the efficiency of the traffic flow increased and the population on the roads decreased drastically in less than a minute.

Taylor lifted his weapon, rested it on the top of the cabin of the pickup, and tried to keep it steady while he aimed and pulled the trigger, all with one hand. It was set to semi-auto and allowed him to place his shots where he could.

Unfortunately, the bullets didn't punch through the glass.

"Shit." He wouldn't be able to get to his rifle with the car jostling and moving as erratically as it was, but he knew a few of the rounds had struck home because they left marks on the rear window of the SUV. The problem was that there was no indication that they would penetrate what he now realized was reinforced glass.

The gunshots—audible even over the sound of revving engines—triggered panic and people on the street screamed and bolted. The cars that heard them stopped hastily and the drivers ducked under their dashboards to avoid any stray shots.

Moments later, one of the SUV windows opened and a man leaned out with what looked like an Uzi. The weight of the weapon caused the first couple of shots to go low, but the rest were aimed better. They bounced off the window glass like his had from the SUV.

Unfortunately, Taylor had no such protection, and as Niki swerved to avoid the volley, he held on frantically and hunkered down to avoid the bullets.

"You should know that the SUV is less than a mile from the embassy," Desk alerted him. "If there was anything you wanted to do to stop them, you might want to do it now."

"What the hell do you think I'm doing?" he roared in frustration and maintained his hold as Niki righted the vehicle again. "Niki, keep the car steady!"

"Oh, I'm sorry, I'll keep us on the straight and narrow while people are shooting at me," she snapped in return. "Do you want my hands on ten and two while I'm at it?"

That didn't merit an answer and he dragged out of his crouched position and straightened as much as he could to return fire at the SUV and drive the gunman into the vehicle. A man tried to lean out on the other side, but Taylor felt a little more confident and delivered a barrage around the bodyguard, caught the side of the vehicle, and launched fragments into the defender's face.

The shooter shouted in pain and retreated quickly and both windows closed rapidly.

"You should be warned, they are within sight of the embassy," Desk told them.

"This won't work," Taylor finally conceded. "Niki, do you think you can force them off the road?"

"I'm trying to catch up but they're moving at about the same speed as we are. These roads aren't conducive to high speeds."

His negative conclusion seemed to be correct. The gates to the embassy loomed and they both accepted that they wouldn't accomplish what they had hoped they could before their target pulled inside the gates.

"Niki?"

"Yeah?"

Taylor scowled and drew a deep breath before he shook his head. "Change of plans. Stop and get me to high ground so I can see over the wall."

"Are you sure?"

"This isn't working. We need to change our tactics."

She didn't respond immediately but brought the pickup slowly to a halt.

"Okay, tell me where you want us to go."

And to think he had been afraid for a second.

Constanza's heart still pounded as he looked at the

gates closing behind him. The pickup was gone but the SUV showed the signs of the battle they had barely escaped.

While having to leave his center of operations was undoubtedly a setback, getting killed was certainly the worse option. His operation in Peru was still fairly fledgling and if it would be this much trouble to maintain it, he could always find somewhere else to continue with his plans.

Besides, he already had what he wanted. The new and improved cocaine was ready to be produced and shipped once he had a production line ready to take the new product on.

The SUV pulled up to the side of the embassy building and the wounded guard was whisked away to receive medical attention. The injured man would also be left behind. Too many had fallen at the hands of his two attackers for him to have regrets about one more in need of medical attention.

"The ambassador has retreated to his residence for the evening," a young woman informed him as he approached the embassy. "But he has invited you to take residence in the western wing. It has been prepared for your arrival already, Sr. Constanza."

"Thank you…"

"Tania."

"Thank you, Tania."

He followed her to the accommodations allocated to him. It was a small building, much like an apartment, and was a decent enough place to live. He had spent a couple of weeks there before. While not quite the height of luxury, it was better than where he had grown up, that was for damn sure.

For one thing, a small pool in the back was already prepped and ready if he wanted to take a swim.

But all Constanza needed was a stiff drink and maybe a cigar. Escaping an attempt on his life was never a given and needed to be celebrated whenever it was achieved.

He found the cigar case in the common room, where it was always kept stocked in case a traveling dignitary wanted it, and he certainly did. Once he had a cigar, he chose the best scotch in the wet bar and poured himself three fingers with no ice.

"Never a given," he whispered and gulped his drink before he filled it again. With the glass in hand, he wandered out to the terrace, closed his eyes, and enjoyed the cool evening breeze blowing from the ocean. It was a good night to not be murdered by American mercenaries.

He paused next to the pool, sat in a comfortable lounger, and placed his glass on a nearby table to leave his hands free to light his cigar. Once he'd puffed on it a couple of times, he grunted his approval at the taste left in his mouth mixed with the scotch.

Lights glimmered in the distance. Not the regular house lights that dotted the hills of the region—not uncommon given that the rich and powerful of Lima liked to own houses in the area—but car lights that seemed to bear down on him before they stopped moving part of the way down the sloped road opposite.

It looked like a pickup. In fact, it looked like the one the Americans had been driving.

Constanza took a small pair of binoculars from his coat

pocket—a habit he'd developed when he'd first started out —and peered through them. As suspected, he could see the notches his men's bullets had left on the windshield.

"Stupid Americans," he muttered, chuckled, and puffed his cigar again while he continued to watch the vehicle. It wasn't like they could get in, not while he was protected by all the diplomatic power of Colombia.

His eyes narrowed on the massive red-headed giant who stood on the bed of the pickup, a powerful rifle in his hands as he peered down the scope. A powerful rifle aimed directly at him.

"*Hijo de pu*—"

Taylor did not rush taking the shot. He unscrewed the suppressor, settled in, and folded a blanket over the top of the cabin. When he was comfortable, he did a couple of breathing exercises while Desk fed them information on where the diplomat was housed to provide them with a good location in which he could target Constanza most effectively. While he would have preferred the high ground as he'd intimated to Niki earlier, nothing had been suitable and this was the best option.

He had been nervous and was used to fighting across short distances against monsters that didn't hide behind walls. While he did have some long-range shooting in his training jacket, he hadn't had to use it much.

Still, a four-hundred-yard shot wasn't anything to sneeze at, and he'd managed a headshot from that distance. Niki watched through binoculars and she had seen half of the man's head disintegrate and spray across the pristine white wall of the apartment.

It took the people inside the embassy a few seconds to realize that someone had fired a shot. Immediately, the security teams rushed out to see what was happening with their handguns aimed to cover all directions as a couple inspected the body.

Niki put the pickup into gear and Taylor climbed into the passenger seat before she accelerated away.

"We'll need to get rid of the guns," he muttered. "And the car. Vickie, can you let Marino know that we'll need an extraction as quickly as possible?"

"Already done," Desk interjected. "In fact, he wanted you to know that the plane is already loaded and waiting for you at the same strip where you landed."

"We could always ditch the car and weapons there," Niki commented.

"Sure. Although I have informed him of a change in plans," the AI continued. "You have a liaison with someone who is currently on vacation in Rio De Janeiro, Brazil."

"Our American contact?" Taylor asked.

"That is correct."

"I can live with a quick layover."

"Same here." She grinned. "We might make this an annual tradition after all."

CHAPTER TWENTY-THREE

It seemed like the right time to take advantage of his vacation days. Working for the State Department did have a few advantages. One was knowing when an operation he was responsible for had gone sour.

Whoever they had sent after the merc team had missed the mark terribly, and if he read their files right—and Stefano had—McFadden and Banks were not above looking for some good, old-fashioned biblical revenge.

Sure, Constanza was no doubt at the top of their list but after that, they would take the whole damn operation apart to find out who had sent killers after them.

Another great thing about working for the State Department for the past seven years was the fact that he got twenty vacation days a year, and he'd accumulated them for the past three years. Almost three months was more than enough time to let everything and everyone cool down so he was no longer in line to be included in their revenge rampage.

Stefano hadn't used any of his cumulative sick days

either, so he could extend his vacation by another month if he needed to. He doubted that these people would be able to sustain their revenge fantasies for that long and they wouldn't be able to find him in Rio.

Even while presenting the staff with a fake ID and a corporate credit card, it had still been possible to book himself into a five-star hotel for the duration of his stay, thanks to the money people owed him in Rio. Having a couple of politicians in his pocket was a boon, which was why he always managed to find a way to have the State Department send him to the best working vacation location in South America.

And not only because of the pristine beaches and imaginative nightlife.

Tonight, he wouldn't stay at the hotel. Most of the luxury living spaces were not in the city of Rio but just outside in a region called *Barra da Tijuca*. He'd spent a few months learning about how all the rich people had decided that Copacabana was a little too touristy for them and chose to move to where the beaches were a little harder to reach and much more exclusive.

The woman who had taught him that was waiting in her apartment. The average client needed to book her a few months in advance, but Stefano had convinced her to let him have a standing appointment with her every three or four months. He even paid her for the times he wasn't in the country to make sure she kept the date open for him when he was.

She was most certainly worth it.

The doorman tipped his cap to him as he walked in, but the man looked away politely like he knew the men who went to the penthouse suite did not want to be remembered for their presence there.

The elevator was waiting and took him smoothly to the top. He felt a little warm under the collar and it had nothing to do with the heat and humidity outside, of course. This was a treat reserved for very few people in the world.

As the doors opened directly into her apartment, Stefano leaned inside and rapped his knuckles on one of the nearby wooden panels.

"Boa tarde, meu amor!" he called and used his knowledge of the local language that she had played a large part in teaching him. Of course, it was important to use it whenever he visited officially, but there were always translators available for that. Not so in this case.

"So Portuguese isn't like Spanish?" Taylor asked. "Like, you wouldn't be able to understand each other?"

The woman fixed him with her dark gaze and shook her head with a soft smile. "It is complicated. Simple conversations can be improvised, yes, but the differences are many. I think...have you ever been to Scotland?"

Her English was almost perfect and some could argue that the accent only made it more enjoyable to listen to.

"Are you asking because of my hair?"

She laughed and touched his shoulder. "No, of course not. What I mean is that they technically speak English in Scotland, but if you listen to the language they use there or even read it, it will be very different from the English you use. I have heard that it's the same as the difference between Portuguese and Spanish."

He nodded. "Okay, I think I get it now. It comes from the same root, right?"

"But Portuguese is farther on the root—more evolved, if you prefer to say it like that."

Taylor tried to maintain a conversation with the woman but not to appear too interested in what she had to say. Something was definitively Latin about her, and he could see why the reputation for ass enhancements was named after the country, especially through the tight-fitting red dress she wore.

They were already wanted for all kinds of shit in Peru and didn't need another South American country to ban them, especially if it was because Niki was pissed that his eyes were wandering.

"But you speak Spanish, right?" he continued to end the lull in the conversation.

"Yes."

"How do you think mine was?"

"Not too bad. Maybe a little rusty but you can improve it with more practice, and from there, you already have a basis to learn Portuguese as well."

He nodded and looked vaguely at anything but the woman beside him. Fortunately, there was enough to hold his attention. The Laguna restaurant was easily the last thing he would think of when it came to high-class restaurants with its location on a lake, straw roofs, and the rustic-looking tables and chairs. Despite this, it undoubtedly had its own charm—the kind people were more than willing to pay higher than average prices for.

"So, you have not told me why you want me here," the woman said and touched his arm again. "You should know I will be out of a considerable amount of money for helping you like this, and I know that it was not only to meet your…girlfriend."

"She'll be here soon." Taylor turned his eyes to the third seat at their table, which was still vacant for the moment.

"I can't wait to meet her."

"I'm sure she'll be dying to meet you too."

———

He received no answer to his greeting, but the lights in the apartment had already been dimmed to a romantic setting and more than a few candles had been lit.

Recently too like she had been waiting for him. She was always thoughtful like that.

Stefano moved through the apartment in search of the woman he had come to see. A sense of anticipation built in the back of his throat.

When he reached the bedroom, he noticed a table that was already set with a bottle of Dom Perignon chilling in a bucket of ice and two champagne flutes.

One was full, but the other had already been emptied to leave a few dregs at the bottom as evidence that someone had perhaps been impatient.

"You can't wait to get started, eh?" he asked, moved toward the table, and picked up the full glass. He took a long sip that almost emptied it. "I think I'll join you."

He began to feel foolish about talking to himself when he heard light, bare footsteps in the next room.

"Prisa!" a woman called and immediately caught his attention.

Stefano grinned, placed the glass where he found it, and unbuttoned his shirt. He tossed it on a nearby chair, where it was quickly joined by the rest of his clothes.

"I'm coming!" he shouted, then chuckled. "Well, not yet, but very soon!"

"How much money are we talking about?" Taylor asked.

"It's a little...crude to speak of such matters with someone you hardly know." The woman certainly knew how to drag a conversation along at her pace.

"Well, call me crude," he responded with a marked lack of concern. "I've certainly been called far worse in my time."

"He truly has," Niki interjected when she returned from the ladies' room. "Mostly by me, although that's neither here nor there."

She had dressed for the occasion and looked less out of place than he did in his white button-up shirt, tan slacks, and loafers. He felt uncomfortable dressing like a tourist, but people would notice if he arrived wearing full body armor—which he didn't have with him anyway.

His partner wore a pale blue skirt and a white shirt and flat shoes and looked like she dressed like that every day. She even had her hair done up in a braid—simplicity itself but more than a little distracting to him.

"I do like a little crude," the woman said with a smile, tilted her head, and looked as seductively at Niki as she had at Taylor. "Too many people feel the need to treat me like a fragile creature in need of delicate care. I could use a little manhandling."

"Well, if he manhandles you, I'll do a little manhandling too." Niki raised her hand to silence Taylor before he could get a word in. "And not like that. More along the lines of a broken wrist."

The woman nodded. "Understood. Then we should talk about pricing, yes?"

"Sure, let's do that. Let's be honest, before we rolled in, your John would have been worth his four nights a year for...what, two, three more years? Now that he's fucked with us, it'll be considerably less."

"Considerably," he asserted.

Their contact narrowed her eyes and tried to decide if their word was good on that before she shrugged. "I understand."

"We, on the other hand, are willing to pay what would be worth about four years of his four nights a year. Ish? And hell, let's toss a Feliz Navidad bonus in there too for the hell of it."

"It's Feliz Natal here," Taylor pointed out.

"Right. Feliz...whatever the fuck. In the meantime, you don't need to think about what your John is up to. For all you know—and for all anyone else has to know—he's paid, and maybe he simply...found someone else. It's not your problem. Honestly, it's not ours either. All that matters is that he won't come back."

The woman leaned back in her seat and stirred her drink pensively with the little red straw that had been provided.

"Four years? That is a small fortune, you know."

"Plus, the Feliz Natal bonus," Niki interjected. "And yeah, we know. And we're being super-cavalier about it because we aren't the ones who have to pay it."

Her eyebrow raised. "Oh? And who is?"

Stefano walked across the bedroom and peered through the open door for any sign of her. The whole apartment glowed with the dim lighting and the candles that made it blend perfectly into the sun setting over the jungle-laden mountains to the west.

He couldn't have conjured a more perfect setting and wished he could take a picture of it. Still, he would much rather make the view more memorable with her naked body added to it.

When she didn't respond to his call, he decided to remain in the room and moved to the bed, which was scattered with rose petals. As he reached down to clear a part of it, however, his head spun.

"Oh...wow." He grunted and smirked as he sat quickly. "That champagne hit me a little harder than I'd like. It's probably the jet lag or...something."

It wasn't important, though, and faded into even greater insignificance when she stepped out of the bathroom. Long, smooth legs caught the light. His gaze climbed to the delicious little red teddy she wore that covered barely enough to let the imagination run wild.

"You look...fantastic," he whispered but his appreciation

ended abruptly when his gaze reached her face. "Wait... you're not... You aren't...not..."

Words tumbled out of his mouth with no real control as the almost nude stranger walked to where he sat on the bed.

"The woman you're looking for?" she asked and finished his statement in the kind of English that confirmed her as someone other than the woman he had expected to find. "No, I'm not. But you'll have to make do with me."

He smiled as his gaze wandered to her mostly exposed cleavage. "I...can deal with that."

She pushed him sharply and forced him to lay on the bed.

"You know, Stefano, the problem with having a hooker you visit religiously is that it makes it very easy to set up a sting operation," she said, but he could no longer see her.

It was weird. His mind was mostly functional but nothing he told his body to do even registered.

"Sh...Shting?" he asked and his tongue felt like it had to force a path through molasses.

"Well...more an assassination, I suppose," she muttered. "You shouldn't have tried to kill my consultants. You see, if they don't trust me to have their backs, one of two things will happen."

"Yeah?" It seemed like a stupid question, but the longer she took to kill him, the longer he would live—and maybe have the chance to let whatever he'd been spiked with wear off.

She climbed onto the bed with him and he focused on the syringe in her hands.

"Yeah. They would either stop taking my jobs—which I

don't have to tell you is entirely unacceptable." She paused, straddled his waist, and looked at him as she ground her hips over him in a slow, rolling pattern. "Or they would think I'm the one setting them up and I truly don't want to be on their bad side. You should know, right?"

The seductive and arousing nature of her movements was considerably undermined by the sight of the needle in her hand. Stefano didn't much like needles and he couldn't help but watch it, even as she moved over him.

Still, certain reactions came from his body and he groaned softly as she leaned close enough that her scent was all he could think about.

"So this is a situation in which I don't want to know what's behind door number one or door number two—which unfortunately means you're door number three. It has to be you, Stefano."

How did she know his name?

"Did you know that police don't check certain parts of the body for injection marks unless specifically instructed to do so?" she asked. "Under the fingernails is one, but that's not always effective, I learned. My favorite is the belly button."

His eyes widened as she straightened and the needle slid into his stomach. The pinch as it pushed into him was made considerably worse by its choice of location.

"And since you were the one who tried to kill them, it seems appropriate that you meet the same punishment, making the guilty party the only one who suffers."

She seemed to like the sound of her voice. In fairness, it was a gorgeous voice but he had difficulty hearing it, especially when she pulled away from him. He could barely see her at the edge of the bed where she watched to make sure that whatever she'd injected had the intended effect.

A phone suddenly appeared in her hands and she dialed a number quickly and pressed it to her ear.

"It's done," she said. "I need a baggage pickup, please."

It wasn't done. He wasn't dead yet. Stefano was about ninety percent sure of that.

"It's a shame really," she said, although her voice sounded like it came through water. She barely glanced at him as she pulled clothes on over the teddy. "All dressed up and no one to fuck. I'm talking about me, of course. Not you."

Her quip made sense. He wasn't wearing anything anymore anyway.

His eyes drifted shut. The heroin would take effect quickly. It had been interesting to estimate how much would be enough to give him an overdose without it being a suspiciously high amount.

She shook her head. Nicole had thought he would put up more of a fight, which was why she chose the outfit—or lack of one—but it had been entirely unnecessary.

Still, there was more than enough time to make it right. She pulled her phone out again and punched in a number she already had memorized.

"Vargas, it's Nicole," she said quickly. "I know it's late and you're probably busy, but I have nothing to do tonight and I'm wearing a killer teddy that I need someone to rip off me. I don't suppose you're up to the challenge?"

She smiled. "Fantastic. Shall we say...eleven? Okay, I'll see you then."

The call needed to be cut short as the elevator doors told her that her cleanup team had arrived on schedule.

The two men and a woman—all locals—were there to make everything looked nothing like a murder had occurred.

All three were professionals and inspected the apartment quickly.

"Take the suitcase out," she instructed. "And please arrange the apartment like the pictures I sent you. Destroy the sheets, the wine, and the glasses, and don't drink anything. You know the drill."

"It should be quick work," the woman said with a thick accent. "What about the body?"

"He's pumped full of heroin, so if you dump him in the favelas, the police won't ask any questions."

"We'll get it done."

Having professionals on hand like that certainly made things simple. Not too easy, of course, but what was the point of making anything too easy?

Music had started to play and the woman decided she wanted to dance. Neither Niki nor Taylor would stand in her way.

"She has an ass on her," Niki commented. "And she has perfected the hip moves. Wouldn't you say so, Taylor?"

He shook his head. "I hadn't noticed."

She snorted and sipped her drink. "Bullshit. But I do appreciate the attempt."

"Whatever you say. I only know that if you catch me staring at her ass, one or both of us would end up dead. It's best to simply keep my eyes busy ogling you."

"Pervert," she retorted but she smirked and winked at him as his phone vibrated in his pocket.

Taylor pulled it out and opened the text message.

Luggage has been delivered, the message read simply.

"All good?" Niki asked.

He nodded. "The job's done. Now, all we need to do is make sure that Miss...Flores over there is seen with us all night long and we'll be in the clear."

"I could think of worse ways to spend the evening," she said cheekily and leaned closer to kiss his cheek.

"Worse than spending the evening establishing an alibi for a hooker?" he asked.

"An evening with you."

He couldn't help the hint of color that touched his cheeks. "Yeah, well...it's awesome to spend time with you too."

CHAPTER TWENTY-FOUR

The day could have started better.

Family was family, even if he hadn't seen them in a while, and finding out that someone as close to him as Stefano was dead was already the kind of thing that was bound to put him in a bad mood.

The Brazilian police said the body had been found in one of the slums of Rio, where all his belongings had been picked clean even before the cops discovered him.

The official word was a heroin overdose and there was no indication that it was anything else.

Except for the fact that everyone involved in the operation so far was dropping like flies. Perhaps the most impressive thus far had been assassinating Constanza while the fucker had been at the Colombian Embassy. That took serious balls.

Of course, in the end, the official story had released all the details of the local drug trade he was involved in, as well as his past in the military, all leading to the conclusion that it had caught up with him. There was, predictably, no footage on the assassins, and any investigation into murder was hampered by the fact that the body was on sovereign Colombian soil while the shooter had been decidedly not on sovereign Colombian soil. By the time the diplomatic mess involved was cleared up, the killers would be long gone.

Hell, they were probably in the US already now that all ties to the attempt on their lives had been severed.

It left Raul free and clear for the moment. There would be a couple of internal investigations but nothing that would tie back to him.

Still, it would be best if he took some time away. He had a place outside the city near a lake and where he kept a boat. This was certainly a good reason to go fishing.

It was a good way to pass the time while he waited for this storm to settle, and he would return to work while keeping his head low and taking what promotions came his way. It wasn't quite an aggressive rise, but this way was so much safer.

He stepped out of his house, shivered slightly, and retrieved the mail before he hurried inside again. There was nothing interesting in the pile—most of the important communication came via email these days—and he left it all on the table next to his door before he continued to the garage where his car was waiting for him.

Everything was already packed for a couple of weeks at the lake, and he could procure anything else along the way. His instincts cautioned him against remaining in town for too long.

Raul had already sent word to his bosses and told them he had a family reunion and would use the vacation days he had held off on using for precisely this kind of occasion. The message had been vague enough to dissuade people from asking questions.

Satisfied that everything was in order, he climbed into the car, drew a deep breath, and resisted the urge to think about what had happened to Hector and Stefano. Dwelling on that kind of unpleasantness wouldn't solve anything.

His gaze jerked to the locks on his doors when they clicked of their own accord.

"Shit," he whispered and yanked the door handle although he knew it wouldn't do any good. It was worth a try he reasoned, a little panicked now.

The car started without a key and he froze and tried not to move too quickly. His garage door began to open and the vehicle backed through it slowly.

"Oh...no, no, no—fuck!"

"Do you know what the definition of insanity is?"

A woman's voice issued through the speakers, and he stared in horror as the car moved onto the street.

"It's doing the same thing over and over again while expecting a different result," she continued as the vehicle moved down his street at the speed limit. "People keep saying that Albert Einstein said that, but I'm very sure that's bullshit. Anyway, you keep trying to open the door, but I can tell you with some certainty that it won't change anything."

He stopped his fumbled attempts to free himself and tried not to touch anything.

"But we're not here to make obscure references to video game quotes," the woman said. "We're here to talk about the fact that there are people on this planet who you don't talk about. People who make the planet safer by being anonymous. They make things better if others don't share information about them with drug lords."

Raul resisted the urge to reach for the door handle again. Perhaps he could break a window and climb out that way. They were already moving fast enough for it to be an uncomfortable situation but he was sure it was better than whatever the woman had planned for him.

"Oh, but you've already shared that information, haven't you, Raul?" It was a little frightening to hear someone talk like he was in the office with her. "Bad boy, Raul. You know the people of this wonderful country trust you to only turn their information over to the local intelligence agencies. See, had you shared your secrets with the NSA or the DHS, we wouldn't be having this conversation. Well, you might have this conversation with one of them but not with me."

She made a good point there.

"Anyway, this is my terrible segue into the advent of smart cars. You know, the interesting thing about cars with self-driving capabilities is that they were designed to be accessed remotely if the driver should happen to have a seizure, heart attack, or some other calamity that renders them incapable of driving him or herself off the road, or maybe to a hospital. Unfortunately, these capabilities are handled by servers with some outdated security systems."

He pulled his seatbelt on quickly.

That made her laugh. "Yes, safety first, Raul. Anyway, if you look into the systems the self-driving software is based on, you can see that it pulls local digital maps together to bring traffic and speed limits into the equation. It makes sure that your car won't...I don't know, drive off a bridge, right? It's cool stuff and cutting edge tech, the kind that drives the world forward, pun slightly intended."

This woman liked the sound of her voice, he decided helplessly.

"Of course, that has a weakness because the driving systems are based on the kind of maps that need to be updated periodically. So if I were to update a map to say there was a left turn where there is no left turn, well... You see where I'm going with this, right?"

He stared in horror at the bridge he passed every day on his way to work.

"Oh fuck, oh shit—no, you can't—"

"Oh, but I can. I've always thought that drowning was the worst way to die. What do you think?"

"No... no... Oh, God, no...please..."

"Now, Raul, I could simply drive you off a bridge and be done with it. Or—and here's the important part, so listen closely—you can drive into work, sit with your boss, and confess everything."

"What?"

"I mean everything, Raul. Every time you stole a paper clip. That way, I get my justice and I don't have your death lingering on my conscience. It would take me a whole pint of ice cream to get over it, but do you know how many calories are in a whole pint of ice cream? Do you want to put me through that, Raul?"

"Yes...I mean no! I'll go in and confess right away!" The bridge drew closer and the car increased speed. "Please, I want to live!"

The vehicle came to an abrupt halt on the last few feet of shoulder before he reached the bridge.

"My mom didn't raise an idiot or a fool, Raul," the woman said and her voice turned from flippant to calm and chilling at a moment's notice. "I will always watch and listen. One misstep, and you'll find out how much of your life I can turn into a death trap. You wouldn't want that, would you, Raul?"

She kept using his name like a hammer, and he felt a cold sweat drenching his shirt every time.

"Yes—oh, God no. Please…."

"Good. It's been a nice chat. Let's not do this again."

Most people who entered the Pentagon needed to go through dozens of security checks. The secrets held in the oddly-shaped building were too important to simply leave to the protective abilities of the average rent-a-cops.

But most people weren't him. Speare nodded to the men in uniform who guarded the building and they simply checked his ID and waved him through the metal detector. With no muss and no fuss, he was in.

One of the benefits of the position he held, he thought smugly.

Two men were waiting for him. One was tall and bulky and looked uncomfortable in a suit, while the other, with his short blond hair trimmed neatly, was better at looking like a civilian than his partner.

"Jansen," Speare said and shook the smaller man's hand, then the larger. "Maxwell. Walk with me."

"Mr. Speare, thanks for taking the time to meet us," Jansen noted as they fell into step beside him.

"You guys are the head of a task force I created for you. I'll always make time to hear what you have to say. Do you have any updates for me?"

"Not much," he answered. "We're mostly gathering information at this point, but we do know that Taylor and Niki have done a fair amount of globe-trotting. We'd say they're taking a much-needed vacation except for the fact that some very interesting bodies keep dropping everywhere they go."

Speare held his finger to his lips to silence them for the remainder of the walk to his office. He held the door open for them and closed it behind him, then activated the anti-surveillance measures available to him before he felt comfortable enough to speak.

"Sorry," he said brusquely and gestured for the two men to sit as he moved to his chair on the other side of the desk. "There are a couple of congressional committees in the area today, and I'd rather leave them in the dark about these matters."

He picked a package up and tossed it to Jansen, who caught it deftly and handed it to Maxwell.

"From our favorite pair of lovers," he informed them.

Maxwell opened the package and frowned at the file it contained.

"Intel. On the Zoo?"

"Specifically, who's getting the Pita product that's being sent out."

"Aren't you having McFadden and Banks handle this?" Jansen asked. "They are the best solution we have for this kind of wet work."

"I thought McFadden wouldn't get on a plane," Speare rumbled.

"For this, he might," the larger man commented. "He has a hard-on for anyone who allows the Zoo to escape the containment we've set up for it."

He shrugged. "I thought about it, but I've been told they need a month off after this and that's okay. Banks suggested a team that's already on the inside."

When they both looked expectantly at him, he picked up a remote, keyed it to the TV screen, and connected with a call he knew was waiting. "I take it you already know Dr. Salinger Jacobs."

The man on the screen looked altogether too young to be a doctor. His dark hair hung over his eyes and a powerful look to his body seemed more athlete than scientist.

"Mr. Speare," Jacobs said with a nod. "Tim, Felix, nice to see you guys again. I was told you wanted to have a chat?"

"That is correct." Speare motioned to the package in Maxwell's hands. "You come with the recommendation of people I take very seriously, Dr. Jacobs, and I don't say that lightly. We need trash to be removed from your area, leaving no evidence of its presence behind."

"I take it we're not talking about the kind of trash you need a compactor for?" the man asked.

"We might, depending on the size of the compactor," he admitted.

Jacobs smirked. "Well, you came to the right place if you want evidence to disappear. It does tend to get…uh, eaten around here. What do you need me to take care of?"

Speare rubbed his fingers over his jaw and shook his

head before he seemed to make his mind up and nodded firmly. "This is strictly confidential for the moment, Dr. Jacobs. Thankfully, I've been informed that I can count on your discretion, so I'll be perfectly frank with you."

"I appreciate that."

"What if I told you that someone you know was trying to get the Pita serum onto United States soil using cocaine, among other drugs?"

The scientist paused for a moment and his lighthearted expression shifted into something far more neutral. Speare had been around enough warriors in his time to recognize that as a very good sign. Well, good for him, anyway.

Not so good for others.

"I'd say they need to die, Mr. Speare," Jacobs stated finally and gathered his composure again.

He nodded and smiled at the two men in the office with him. "Then we're at an understanding, Dr. Jacobs. Information on payment and the intelligence that has been gathered is being sent to you as we speak. Since it's on secure channels, it might take up to six hours. I look forward to working with you."

"Likewise, Mr. Speare. Felix, Tim, always a pleasure."

The screen went dead.

The story continues with book three, *Hostile Negotiations.*

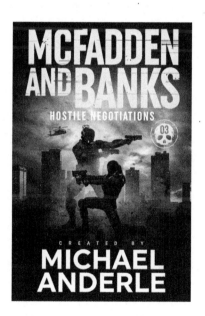

Pre-order now to have your copy delivered at midnight on
January 12, 2021.

Thank you for reading not only this story but the *Author Notes* here in the back!

Sometimes, the story just doesn't want to 'come out' in the beginning. This story was EXACTLY like that.

I wanted to go down south and attack drug lords using the serum cut into drugs, but how do I make it a challenge for M&B?

Finally, I realized I needed to get rid of their gear. While I enjoy a good ass-kicking by the good guys (see the Las Vegas scene where the gang had to fight mechs) I didn't think that would be particularly challenging for our team to do that down south.

Basically, I had to screw them over. If I ever meet McFadden in my dreams, I will apologize.

Profusely.

The house they destroyed in Henderson (basically twenty-five minutes from the Las Vegas Strip) is up on the hills above where I live. (Ok, perhaps a little way up the hills.)

I love to look at those houses, but I have to admit my imagination got carried away thinking how much fun it would be to blow shit up in one. I mean, they just have to have horrible (and horribly expensive) statues and stuff begging for a few rounds in them.

Right?

Take care of yourselves. We will see you in the NEXT McFadden & Banks!

I look forward to hearing what you have to say in the reviews for both this book and the one to come!

Ad Aeternitatem,

Michael Anderle

CONNECT WITH MICHAEL

Connect with Michael Anderle

Website: http://lmbpn.com

Email List: http://lmbpn.com/email/

Social Media:

https://www.facebook.com/LMBPNPublishing

https://twitter.com/MichaelAnderle

https://www.instagram.com/lmbpn_publishing/

https://www.bookbub.com/authors/michael-anderle

One Crazy Set Of Stories (12)

SOLDIERS OF FAME AND FORTUNE

Nobody's Fool (1)

Nobody Lives Forever (2)

Nobody Drinks That Much (3)

Nobody Remembers But Us (4)

Ghost Walking (5)

Ghost Talking (6)

Ghost Brawling (7)

Ghost Stalking (8)

Ghost Resurrection (9)

Ghost Adaptation (10)

Ghost Redemption (11)

Ghost Revolution (12)

THE BOHICA CHRONICLES

Reprobates (1)

Degenerates (2)

Redeemables (3)

Thor (4)

CRYPTID ASSASSIN

Hired Killer (1)

Silent Death (2)

Sacrificial Weapon (3)

Head Hunter (4)